"My *husband* didn't do anything wrong!" Britt burst out. "You've got the wrong man!"

"Maybe *you've* got the wrong man, Britt."

"You definitely weren't the right one," she shot back. "Which is why it's over between us, McSween."

"Didn't feel over ten minutes ago," he commented dryly.

"We're divorced!"

Actually, they weren't. McSween might have corrected her, but Baby Romeo suddenly squealed. And Britt turned in shock, her chin lowering by degrees until she was staring at the floor.

A very long silence ensued.

Then Britt raised a manicured finger and pointed accusingly at the baby. "Who exactly is *that*?"

ABOUT THE AUTHOR

In 1993, Jule McBride's debut novel received the
Romantic Times Reviewer's Choice Award for
"best first series romance." Ever since, the author
has continued to pen heartwarming love stories
that have met with strong reviews and made
repeated appearances on romance bestseller lists.
This year, in 1996, she's been nominated once
again by *Romantic Times,* in both the categories
of "career achievement" and "best American
Romance." Says Jule, "Baby Romeo: P.I. was a
very special book to me, and of the men I've
written about, Sean McSween is my favorite.
I hope readers will love him!"

Books by Jule McBride

HARLEQUIN AMERICAN ROMANCE

JULE McBRIDE

BABY ROMEO: P.I.

Harlequin Books

TORONTO • NEW YORK • LONDON
AMSTERDAM • PARIS • SYDNEY • HAMBURG
STOCKHOLM • ATHENS • TOKYO • MILAN
MADRID • WARSAW • BUDAPEST • AUCKLAND

To Liz Simmons—
for her large heart and many small kindnesses

ISBN 0-373-16636-2

BABY ROMEO: P.I.

Prologue

"Some lady 'round the corner's gone crazy!" A wizened homeless man with a natty gray beard jerked his grocery cart to a halt, making the soda cans inside rattle and clank. The man pointed toward Gramercy Park. "Yes, sirree, she says she's gonna wash her man right outta her hair!"

Assistant Detective Sean McSween glanced away from the man, then through the windshield of his unmarked tan sedan. Seeing that the traffic light was still red, he gripped the steering wheel with one hand, swung his other through the open window, then groped across the roof.

Sure enough, he'd left the flashing dome light up there. No wonder the guy knew he was a cop. His siren whooped once as he brought the light back inside and tossed it onto the seat. Waving through the window as the traffic light turned green, he called, "Thanks for the tip."

But so much for heading home to Britt—and getting a jump start on celebrating our first anniversary, he thought.

All day McSween had imagined his wife's long, tanned fingers clasping tightly around his neck and her lightly glossed lips pressing gently against his mouth. He'd fantasized about how he would shut his eyes and glide his palm over her bare silken skin. And about how that one magic touch would make everything in the world—but her—disappear.

Not that he couldn't be wicked with the woman. And wild and hot and passionate. But mostly, in Britt he'd discovered peace. And a New York City cop rarely found much of that.

He and Britt lived on Gramercy Park, and the Thirteenth Precinct *was* right around the corner on Twenty-third Street, so McSween guessed it wouldn't kill him to do his civic duty and arrest just one more crazy lady on his way home.

If the traffic will just move. He lay on his horn. Then he raked his fingers through his short raven hair and rubbed his eyes, glancing at them in the rearview mirror. Same as always. Bottle green and bloodshot. He looked older than thirty-five, too. And with days like this, it was no wonder.

He'd nearly made it home hours ago, but then his old boss at the Sixth Precinct had called the Thirteenth—and him—into the Saint Vincent's case.

It was just McSween's luck. Four armed white males had entered Saint Vincent's Hospital, searching for pharmaceutical drugs. They'd switched off the power, leaving the hospital to run on auxiliary juice alone. It was only a matter of time until all operating rooms and the E.R. were disabled. McSween had spent the entire afternoon finding and arresting the four perpetrators. Then he'd stayed to help assist frightened patients back to their rooms.

A faint smile flickered over his lips. For some reason he'd had to tolerate more than the usual ribbing from the guys during the ordeal. But could he help it if his Irish good looks had turned a few nurses' heads? Or if today marked a full year since he'd eloped with Chief Charles Buchanan's only daughter? *As if family dinners with my cantankerous boss and father-in-law are some kind of picnic.*

McSween shook his head. He'd just driven Tony Barrakas—his latest in a long line of partners—home. All the way to Queens, Tony had talked about taking a safer, desk-type job, so he could marry his girlfriend, Donya, and start a family.

And, as always, starting a family was the last thing McSween wanted to discuss.

All he wanted was his rightful promotion to full detective. Which was why—wedding anniversary or not—he needed to investigate the current citizen complaint. Every solved case was bound to help. McSween rounded Gramercy Park West, squinting against the hot June sun and keeping his eyes peeled for signs of disturbance.

"It figures," he whispered distractedly. There wasn't a single parking space. He sighed, glanced in both directions, then drove right over the curb, ducking to offset the bounce of his bad shocks. He pulled onto the sidewalk nearest the park.

"She's going to kill somebody!" a man shouted.

McSween's eyes darted around, but he didn't see the crazy lady. Gawking onlookers huddled under the canopy of Gramercy Park's shady trees and peered curiously back at him through the foliage and tall wrought-iron fencing.

McSween got out of the car slowly, automatically pocketing the keys and buttoning his sports coat. Simultaneously, he straightened his dark tie and shoulders. Looking official always helped when it came to crowd control.

"No loitering," he called calmly to the pedestrians. Those inside the park began to drift away from the fence, but a group of teenagers remained on the sidewalk. They didn't appear to be dangerous, but they did seem to be eyeing his hubcaps.

McSween shot the kids a warning glance, thinking of his new radio and radar scanner. Then he took an assessing look around—and groaned.

He should have known.

Raising his voice, he called, ''There's really nothing to see here, kids. Move along. This is just a domestic dispute, a police matter.''

Trouble was, McSween was the policeman under fire, the domestic dispute was his own, and the crazy lady in question was apparently his own wife.

As if on cue, Britt's bloodcurdling shriek pierced the air.

From the corner of his eye, McSween saw a brown, oval-shaped object sail over the second-floor balcony rail. A rock maybe. *The area beneath the balcony's secure. No pedestrians in the way. No little kids.*

McSween sighed in relief—until the unidentified flying object hit his city vehicle hard enough to dent the hood. Only when the object bounced onto the pavement did McSween realize it was his old football. He'd carried it to a stunning victory in a Fordham University homecoming game.

And I wasn't a great running back for nothing. At the moment, he felt sorely tempted to run right out of town.

He remained on the curb, his disbelieving eyes starting to take inventory. What could he have done wrong? Why were all his personal effects on the sidewalk?

''And should I arrest my wife for littering?'' he murmured philosophically, just as his police-academy diploma landed on the sidewalk next to a Thirteenth Precinct bowling-league plaque.

Some of his belongings were on the narrow strip of brownish grass that he and Britt so generously called a yard. Others, such as the Hawaii-print shirt she'd bought him a year ago in Maui, had snagged on the black metal fence that fronted their apartment building. Everything else was on the sidewalk.

Except for Mr. Hornsby. Their usually dignified, uniformed doorman was crouched just inside the lobby door, his terror- stricken gaze trained heavenward. Even though he was safely on the interior side of the glass, Mr. Hornsby's neck remained all scrunched up, as if he were ducking a blow. Each time an object hit the pavement, the poor man jumped.

When their eyes met, McSween mouthed, "Sorry."

Mr. Hornsby threw up his hands in despair.

McSween could hardly blame the man. Somehow, the messy scene reminded him of the sort of obstacle courses one found in army boot camps or police academies—with mud pits to jump, tires to hop through, and walls to scale with knotted ropes.

"So, we might have a few obstacles to overcome in our married life," McSween muttered.

When he noticed his ancient Bachman Turner Overdrive eight-track tapes in the grass, he winced. There were some things a man wanted to forget he owned.

"And don't you dare leave your cute little critters behind, McSween!" Britt yelled.

A stuffed panda bear lurched over the balcony rail, making McSween feel inexplicably murderous. Long ago, most of Pandy's stuffing had escaped through an unrepaired tear where an eye used to be, so McSween was hard-pressed to say why he'd hauled the bear around with him all these years. As Pandy tumbled downward, McSween's eyebrows furrowed, and he tried to assure himself he wasn't really the sentimental type.

"My personal album with our wedding pictures?" he said levelly when Pandy belly-flopped on top of it.

Now that was low.

But McSween refused to react. He and Britt weren't going to have a knock-down-drag-out fight on their very first anniversary. Probably, it was nothing. The simplest things always started these spats. That Britt was sloppy and he was neat, for instance. Or that he read the *Post* and she read the *Times*. Or that her decorative taste ran to country geegaws and floral chintz while his was contemporary.

None of it mattered. The real issue was adjusting to marriage. Some days, Britt blew like a pressure cooker. On others, McSween fought not to run. But they belonged together. The second their eyes had met, they'd known. Twenty-four hours later they were making love. And within three months, they'd eloped.

They'd traveled the rocky road of their first year together, too. And now they'd reached the end—alive, intact, and still very much in love. Sure, they blew off their share of steam. But the fights always ended—in tears and kisses and heartfelt promises. And in lovemaking sweeter than any McSween had ever known.

He put his hands on his hips. "Britt?"

No answer.

He craned his neck, trying to glimpse her through the open door that led to the balcony—only to flinch when another football shot over the railing. He ducked in time, but heard the ball whiz right past his ear. His temper flared, and it was a strain to keep his voice even. "Seven of the New York Giants signed that football, Britt."

"You care more about football than you do about me!"

"Only during the Super Bowl," he retorted.

"That's not funny, you swine!"

"Look, I'm sorry I'm late."

"Late?" she shouted. "How can you be late when I never want to see you again?"

To the left of the balcony, McSween saw movement in an open window. He squinted at a plastic cup on the windowsill that probably contained iced coffee. Then Britt's hand appeared, the gems on her manicured fingers sparkling as she scooped up the drink and spirited it out of sight. The cup reappeared a moment later. She slammed it down so hard on the windowsill that liquid sloshed over the top.

McSween sighed. "I didn't forget our anniversary, if that's what you're thinking."

"This first anniversary will certainly be our last!" declared her disembodied voice.

He decided Britt thought he'd forgotten. Now she was pretending otherwise, to save face. "I made a reservation at The Gotham." It was supposed to be a surprise, but telling her might calm her down.

"I wouldn't be caught dead in there!"

"It's your favorite restaurant."

A suspicious silence fell.

He glanced around. It was too nice a day to fight. Inside the park, flowers were in full bloom and sunlight dappled the shady walkways. He considered going upstairs to talk some sense into Britt, but the instant he did, the kids might strip his car. And then Britt's father would be just as furious as his daughter.

Without warning, a paperback book shot through the air. When it narrowly missed his shoulder, McSween stepped off the curb and into the street. "Britt, you know I can't leave a city vehicle parked on the sidewalk. Please, why don't you come down, so we can—"

"If you don't quit using that syrupy tone, I'm going to shriek!"

"You're already shrieking."

"I'm not some suicide you're talking down from a rooftop, McSween!"

"No, but you might be the next victim in a homicide case."

"Ha, ha, ha."

McSween realized he was holding his breath and exhaled, just wishing he knew why she'd turned so rageful. "Britt," he shouted, "I care about our marriage." It was an understatement. The woman was his whole life. "If you'd just—"

Stopping in midsentence, he started dodging the rest of the books. He felt like an amateur tennis player accidentally set loose on the courts of the U.S. Open. Some of the books came from the balcony like professional serves, sure and fast. Others opened in the breeze, pages riffling.

When a hefty hardcover titled *Modern Crime Solving* missed his head by a fraction, McSween gave up and roared, "Damn it, Brittany, that's the one from the library!"

"And it's overdue."

"You said you were returning it!"

In response, an American flag that was neatly wrapped in a plastic carrier thudded squarely on a growing heap of his worldly possessions. It was the flag that had been draped over his father's coffin twenty-five years ago.

McSween shot a penetrating glare at the kids who were eyeing his car, then he headed across the street. Forget saving the hubcaps. He'd had it.

"Don't you dare break into my apartment!" Britt cried indignantly.

That was annoying. Technically, it *was* her apartment. "We've shared this apartment for a year. It's my apartment, too, Britt."

"Not anymore. I changed the locks."

Now, that was a first. Feeling suddenly helpless, McSween opened his arms wide. "Please, honey, what have I done wrong?"

Behind him one of the teenagers giggled.

McSween's jaw set.

And then Britt actually stormed onto the balcony.

McSween's heart lurched at the mere sight of her, and his anger vanished. How had he managed to marry a woman this perfect? Everybody loved her, not just him. She was always bustling around the precinct, organizing get-togethers with other officers and their wives.

Sure, she was mad now. But usually she was so friendly and outgoing. Such an inventive lover and so in touch with her feelings.

And those looks. She had fresh, clean-scrubbed-looking skin that gave her all the appeal of the girl next door. Not to mention sexy long legs that made her seem a little forbidden. Shoulder-length feathered honey hair swirled around her cheeks and framed her sultry, doe-like brown eyes. And her pouty mouth stayed puckered as if she was always ready to kiss him.

God, he was in love with her.

McSween did his best to ignore the black one-piece bathing suit she was wearing—because she was also hefting a fifteen-pound barbell. Suddenly his heart ached. All he wanted to do was make his wife happy—and some days it was simply impossible.

Warily, he called, "That barbell's heavy, hon. If you're not careful, you're liable to kill somebody."

"That's the general idea."

Even at this distance, McSween could see tears start to slide down her cheeks. "You don't really want me dead, do you?"

She stared down at him and sniffed. "Maybe."

At least she'd quit screaming. The Thirteenth Precinct was less than two blocks away. One more decibel and her father might have heard her and come running. With Mc-

Sween's luck, Chief Charles Buchanan would incarcerate him for spousal abuse, too.

But what had he done wrong? He glanced over his shoulder. Unfortunately, the kids hadn't budged. Before addressing the sensitive issue, McSween tried to lower his voice in such a way that it would still carry. "Is it your—"

"Time of the month?" Britt spat out venomously. She leaned over the balcony rail. "Yes, if you must know."

Relief flooded him. By the time he cleaned up the mess on the sidewalk, Britt would be her usual sunny self again. To cure the mood swings, the doctor had told her to avoid caffeine, granulated sugar, and salt.

"You know what this means, don't you, McSween?"

That you shouldn't be drinking that iced coffee. Knowing Britt, it was laced with chocolate sprinkles and three packaged sugars, too. "What?"

"That I'm not pregnant."

Feeling as though the wind had been knocked out of him, McSween fought the knee-jerk urge to completely double over. If she'd been trying, it was certainly news to him. *You merely heard her wrong.* "What?"

"I said I'm not pregnant!"

He stared slack-jawed up at the balcony. Over a year ago, on their second date, he'd made it crystal clear he was never having kids. He'd enumerated his reasons, too. "I sure hope not," he growled.

"McSween, I'm begging you." Britt's voice broke. She swiped at her tear-stained cheeks with the backs of her hands. "I'm thirty-three . . ."

Steeling himself against her pleading, McSween damned the chief for being a widower. If Anne Buchanan had lived, maybe the man wouldn't have spoiled his only daughter. "Britt, we've been through this a thousand times."

"Please..." Britt's voice rose. "Oh, please, let's make this the very last time we talk about it! All you have to do is give me a baby. Please, McSween, you're my *husband*...."

How could one woman make him feel so miserable? All the threads of McSween's tightly sewn-up temper unraveled at once. Only years of police training, where a man had to keep a cool head no matter what happened, prevented him from completely losing control. "Britt," he called out evenly. "My not wanting children has nothing to do with my love for you or the level of my commit—"

She groaned. "Oh, give it a rest, McSween!"

"Britt—" his tone carried a warning "—I said I was never having kids. I have my reasons, too. Reasons you accepted until we actually got married."

"Well, I don't believe any of them are the *real* reason!" She swiped at her cheeks and rubbed her tearing eyes again. "Why don't you just leave?"

Because tonight marks the end of our first year together. He'd made arrangements for the harpist at The Gotham to play "Happy Anniversary," and for a waiter to bring Britt roses. He'd even ordered her very favorite triple fudge cake, in spite of the fact that the sugar would aggravate her mood. *Please, tell me that by midnight my wife will be in love with me again.*

"Oh, Sean ..."

He grunted softly in astonishment. She had some nerve, using his first name. She always called him McSween—unless they were in bed. Well, maybe this meant she was about to apologize. "Yeah, Britt?"

"I'm sorry—" A fresh tear splashed down her cheeks. "But I—I just want ..."

To say I'm sorry. His chest constricted. "What do you want, honey?"

"A divorce!"

"A divorce?" he echoed softly.

"A divorce!" Britt shouted. Then she stomped inside, the balcony's screen door snapping shut behind her.

Just as McSween realized that maybe this wasn't exactly your standard, average, everyday kind of fight, the teenagers' pounding footsteps sounded—and the siren in his car started to wail.

Part 1
Hawaii

Chapter One

Where are we? you might wonder.

Elementary, my dear Mr. Scaly. We're at a police station. And see the guy behind the windowed wall? The one with the big hands and crinkly green winkers? The one who's sporting a dark suit and hunt-and-peck typing at lightning speed on a laptop? Well, they don't call me Baby Romeo, P.I., for nothin' and unless I've deduced incorrectly, he's our deadbeat dad.

'Course, I'm not gonna get the least little bit excited. Ever since the bad thing happened and left us homeless, we've been bumped around too much. The guy looks okay, but since we don't know any proper English yet, we can't exactly inquire about our fate. All we know is these thought-words, and so far, they don't seem to be translating.

Whoops! Nearly lost you there, Mr. Scaly! Now we've gotta crane all the way to the left to look at the guy. This woman who's hauling us around keeps twitching her hips like she's doing the cha-cha-cha. Just wish I knew what she means by "coochie- coo." It sure is a mystery. If she'd simply point to objects when she said stuff like that . . .

And if she'd just put us down for a sec! My knees are itchin' to crawl, and I'd sure feel grateful if I could slip out of these plastic pants. Not that I mind being crushed against

*this particular lady. My winkers never saw skin as dark as
hers and she smells real nice to my sniffer, like a big bouquet.*

But since we're in a police station, I bet I could find a few
grown-up-guy gadgets on the floor—maybe a magnifying
glass or binoculars. Then I could search for clues and get a
positive ID on the man in question.

What? Oh, you're sure right about that, Mr. Scaly. I'm
getting to be an ace detective. When you're my age, which
is one year old, you've gotta be. New stuff keeps comin' at
me every minute—and all I can do is my baby best to figure
it out. 'Course, the way this lady keeps glaring at the guy is
a dead giveaway. He's gotta be my dad.

And gosh, is he tidy! Personally, I take great pleasure in
slinging stuff around. 'Specially pacifiers and fistfuls of
mushed vegetables. So, this is a real disappointment. Where
does this guy keep his...well, his guy stuff? I don't even see
any smelly gym clothes. Or an office putt-putt green. And
look at the guy's—

Oh, I forgot. I promise I'll try to start thinking of him as
my dad. Ah...Dad. Has a nice ring, don't you think?

If only I knew some proper English, I could say it out
loud and impress him. Uh-oh. Maybe he won't even like me.
First, I don't know a single word. And second, my hair's
kind of funny— just a black tuft on top of my shiny head.
But you're right, Mr. Scaly, a lot of nice guys are nonver-
bal. Not to mention thin when it comes to the scalp.

At least the big guy's one of New York's finest. Maybe
he'll even give us some special sleuthing instructions, seeing as I'm his kid and all. Hey, I bet he even knows the solution to the "coochie-coo" mystery!

Ah, my dear Mr. Scaly, maybe there really is more ahead
of us in life than mere toilet training and first grade.

Well, here goes nothin'.

The lady is charging in his direction. Oh, boy, is he gonna be surprised to see us!

"McSween!"

The soft Jamaican accent that rolled through his open office door told McSween that the speaker—or yeller—was Donya Barrakas. No doubt, his ex-partner's wife had run into a snag at Child Placement.

"Don't let me keep you, Mr. McSween," said the dark-haired, dark-eyed, stubbly-jawed man who was seated across the desk.

The man's name was Sal Luccio and he owed eleven thousand dollars in back child support. "Just keep talking," McSween growled.

"Well, last month, I *swear* I sent her a check...."

McSween started typing his report again.

"McSween!"

This time he glanced through his windowed wall at the crowded squad room, then acknowledged Donya with a grim nod. Otherwise he kept typing. *Great.* Donya, who looked as classy as ever in her cream-colored maternity suit, was filling out papers at the front desk. And she had a kid with her.

Seeing how much her pregnancy showed, McSween grunted softly in surprise. Tony had taken a desk job and married her—and already they'd started a family. McSween's throat tightened.

Cut yourself a break. Don't think about Britt.

But it was impossible not to. Tomorrow it would be one year since the breakup. A hundred times a day McSween still caught himself staring across the squad room at the chief's office—as if Britt, who'd been so much a part of station life before, would actually visit.

She never did.

McSween sighed. The chief had bumped him down to deadbeat-dad detail, which was hardly helping his mood. Not that he could help Donya with today's crisis child. He had less than one hour to finish his paperwork, grab his garment bag, pick up the surveillance gear from his apartment in Queens and then get to LaGuardia Airport. He had a plane to catch to Hawaii.

"McSween!" Donya shouted again.

She sounded hopping mad. His fingers continued flying over the laptop keys, but he raised an eyebrow inquiringly.

"Please, if you've got other business..." Sal Luccio rubbed his jaw.

"Like I said—" McSween glared at the deadbeat dad "—just keep talking."

Luccio started telling his side of the story again. As McSween typed, a frown tugged at his lips. The kid on Donya's hip appeared to be traveling with all his earthly gear. Two tote bags—one blue, one yellow—were slung over Donya's shoulder, and she was pushing a stroller. Was the poor little guy homeless?

At least, McSween assumed the kid was a he.

He was real cute, too. In fact, he was so irresistible that McSween almost wished he'd given in and made Britt pregnant. Yeah, tomorrow would have been their second anniversary. And there was just no denying that McSween had started noticing kids after Britt threw him out. Even from here, he could see that the baby boy was wearing a Giants shirt and clutching a stuffed toy.

He forced himself to focus on Sal Luccio. When the man fell silent, McSween said, "Anything else you'd like to add to your— er—story?"

"I swear I paid that child support!"

The man's eyes said he hadn't, but McSween began dutifully typing again. It was the usual saga of rambling defenses—the court set the payments too high, the man didn't really believe the child was his, his ex had moved and he couldn't find her . . . blah, blah, blah.

McSween just wished Luccio would wrap it up, so he could catch his plane. Donya still looked livid. Not that McSween blamed her. As the newest staffer at Child Placement, she usually got stuck with the dirty work. Running the gauntlet between foster care, lawyers and adoption services wasn't easy. And when she got squeezed too hard, she would ask McSween to run interference.

He hated turning Donya down, too. Especially today, since the kid showed telltale signs of having no place else to go. But McSween had to make his flight. As it was, he wouldn't arrive in Hawaii until five in the morning, their time.

Not that he was actually taking his three-week vacation. Hell, he hadn't taken so much as a sick day since Britt threw him out. No, he was investigating a red-hot tip—the one that was going to get him off deadbeat-dad detail and back on the fast track where he belonged.

With any luck, he'd soon single-handedly capture Duke Perry, alias the Sutton Place Swindler. For ten years, the blond, blue-eyed Perry—using various names—had seduced and robbed New York's wealthiest unmarried women. Among the victims was the mayor's spinster sister, who'd lived on Sutton Place at the time. Now the mayor wanted the Swindler caught.

And McSween was going to make the collar. Chief Charles Buchanan and his petty vendetta be damned, McSween thought now. All year, his father-in-law—who clearly knew about McSween's unwillingness to have babies—had created a situation of maximum discomfort. Right before the brilliant deadbeat-dad assignment, McSween had been forced to spearhead a Cops for Kids program. Visiting various communities—on a newfangled department bicycle, no less—he'd lectured to gradeschoolers. While he was busy building goodwill, the kids had stayed just as busy—attacking him with paper planes and spitwads.

Before that, McSween's assignment had been to work every major parade in town. All last autumn, he'd directed traffic and kept curious tykes from being trampled by Big Birds. It was so humiliating that McSween couldn't even believe he still worked here.

Not that pointing mothers and their kids toward portable toilets was the worst job in the world. Someone had to do it. But McSween was the best detective in Buchanan's division. Just this spring, the chief inspector had sent McSween to the prestigious L.A. training course. He had experience with countless patrol details. Jail and SWAT work. Two years with the bomb squad, and they still called him in when cases turned tough. He appeared regularly in court as an expert witness on ballistics for Nate Simon, the internal affairs attorney.

McSween had paid his dues. And he craved his hard-won shot at the real puzzlers—the old unsolved cases, the knotty missing persons. He deserved it, whether he was still living with the chief's daughter or not.

Catching the elusive Duke Perry was the only option he had left. If McSween arrested the Swindler, the mayor would override Chief Buchanan, take him off this ridiculous deadbeat-dad detail, and then make him a full detective.

Suddenly, McSween's fingers stilled on the keys. He realized Sal Luccio was staring at him. "What?"

"Did you get everything?" Luccio said.

"Yeah. Are you sure that's all you have to say for yourself?"

Luccio scratched his jaw stubble thoughtfully. "Well, I told her I didn't want to have babies with her."

That was what they all said. It was so sad. Hearing tales of woe was part of McSween's job, but it was the worst when the cases involved kids. Why couldn't these guys just grow up and use protection? In this day and age, condoms were an absolute necessity.

"Are you finished?" McSween repeated gruffly.

"Yeah."

The second McSween nodded at his door, a bullish older man popped his head inside.

"Looks like Sarge O'Connell's come for you," McSween said to Luccio. "He'll let you make a call if you want."

As Sal Luccio was led from the office, Donya made a direct beeline for McSween, baby still in tow. McSween glanced at his watch and winced. It was nearly five o'clock. The closer the baby got, the cuter he looked, too. Donya had probably dressed the kid in the Giants shirt on purpose, since McSween was a fan. A navy baseball cap sat jauntily on the baby's head, with the bill in back, and green shorts peeked from beneath the football shirt. Sports socks completed the ensemble, and the stuffed toy turned out to be a green dragon with six pointy scales and a red cape.

McSween almost wished he'd gotten a refundable ticket. But he hadn't. Never taking his eyes from Donya, he smoothed his tie, then buttoned the Brioni jacket Britt had bought him the spring before last. He'd definitely grown more accustomed to the designer suits than he should have, he thought grimly.

It's just another difference between you two. Britt lived on money from her mother's considerable estate, while he was the son of a beat cop who'd been killed in the line of duty. Could he help it if the woman had been determined to outfit him in style?

Quickly traversing the office, McSween reached behind the door and lifted his garment bag from a hook. He draped it over the office chair Sal Luccio had just vacated, and then he waited. Donya was really showing. She'd started to walk in that way peculiar to pregnant women—as if all her weight were centered at the small of her spine. Somehow, it made McSween want to offer to carry her around for a while.

"Just five minutes," McSween said levelly to Donya when she reached his doorway. "It's all I've got. I'm sorry, but—"

"I'll bet you are," Donya said in a murderous tone.

McSween was completely taken aback. In their years-long acquaintance, this was the only time he'd ever cut Donya short. "Sorry, but I've got a plane to catch."

Donya shifted the baby from one hip to the other and gaped at him. "You're actually skipping town?"

"Hardly. I'm taking a vacation." He squinted at her. "I'm allowed."

"Not anymore, you're not."

"Excuse me?"

Donya merely gawked at him. As she stepped forward, he searched her face for clues. She wasn't the type to fly off the handle without just cause. When his eyes dropped to her swollen belly, he thought of Britt's hormonal mood swings. *Case solved,* he thought. He only had five minutes, but he'd do his level best to make Donya feel better.

"Donya?" he said gently when she stopped in front of him.

"Here," she said simply. And then she quickly thrust the kid on her hip right into his arms. In the next instant, pint-size, sock-clad feet were kicking at McSween's abdomen and a tiny palm was slapping at his chest. The kid's chubby legs wrapped around his midsection, and McSween's hand instinctively supported his back.

"Donya, what are you— Are you crazy?" McSween sputtered.

The kid giggled. Then he craned his neck so far upward that his back got wobbly. Staring at McSween with large, round, liquid brown eyes, he lost his balance—and dropped his dragon.

McSween caught it in midair. On closer examination, the green dragon was a little faded, with a pink, plastic-coated diaper pin stuck through a tear in the last of his six scales. The silky red avenger-style cape gave him an air of inflated importance. Realizing the toy was essentially football-shaped, McSween shoved it under his free arm.

With the other, he tried to hold on to the kid. "Couldn't we just put him in that stroller, Donya?" McSween pointed. "Or is there something wrong with it?"

"How could you?" Donya demanded.

"How could I what?" McSween continued staring hopefully at the stroller—until the kid caught his eye and shot him a disarming, lopsided grin. Fortunately, the baby was wearing plastic pants. This was McSween's best suit.

"You're a cop!" Donya cried indignantly, her rolling accent thickening with her rising anger.

McSween gave the stroller a final, wistful glance. "And?"

"And you're supposed to be solving murders—" Donya wagged an index finger in his face "—not getting away with them!"

McSween's lips parted slightly. "What do you mean by that?"

Donya stared back stoically, her hand dropping to her swollen belly and resting there. Suddenly she bent over, reached for the rack beneath the stroller and brought up a clipboard. "It's your job to track down guys who won't take responsibility for their own kids."

"Thank you for reminding me."

"Somebody has to!"

Just as McSween nodded toward the squad room, the baby reached up, grabbed a fistful of his hair and yanked. "Ouch," McSween muttered. To Donya, he said, "I just arrested Sal Luccio."

"You know what I'm talking about, McSween!"

He didn't. Even worse, he glanced down just in time to see the kid drool on his lapel. He quickly held the baby out and said, "Please, Donya, I'm begging you."

But she didn't budge. Shouldn't someone who was so obviously pregnant show signs of possessing maternal instincts? *Guess not.* McSween's heart sank. He winced and gingerly repositioned the kid on his hip.

"You've got the highest solved-case rate in this department," Donya finally continued, her eyes narrowing to obsidian dots. "You saved my husband's life when he was your partner. You've helped find homes for countless babies, just like this one. And remember that bust last year at Saint Vincent's Hospital?"

McSween nodded warily, wondering where she was heading.

"Well, when the primary source of power came back on, all the mothers in the hospital were so relieved...."

"So?"

"So I really thought you were a better man than this!"

McSween lifted his wrist from beneath the baby's behind, and tried to glimpse his watch. Donya's five minutes were definitely up. And he *had* to make that plane. Solving the Swindler case was the only thing that could save his floundering professional life.

"Donya, if you'd just tell me—"

She shoved the clipboard under his nose.

McSween peered over the top of the kid's blue baseball cap, at the paper attached to the clip. Everything on the standard form seemed to be in order—until he read the fine print and nearly lost his grip on the baby whose name was apparently Romeo.

In the space for Romeo's father's name, it said, "Sean Michael McSween."

There were vital stats, too. Sean McSween was six feet tall, black-haired, green-eyed, of Irish descent, and worked as an assistant detective with the NYPD. Even the social-security number was right.

But surely this was a mistake.

"They're saying I'm this kid's father?"

"I guess you've been out of touch with his mama." Donya's expression softened. "So far, all I know is that something happened to her, and you were just named the sole guardian in court."

Donya gently wiggled a pen between McSween's fingers. Not knowing what else to do, he signed on the dotted line she indicated.

Only then did Donya lower the clipboard and shoot him a fleeting smile. "I knew you'd never be a deadbeat dad yourself, McSween. I knew you'd do the right thing."

"Do the right thing?" McSween echoed numbly.

"Yes." Donya took the pen from McSween's hand and replaced it with a pacifier. "And now he's really yours—signed, sealed and delivered."

McSWEEN CLUTCHED the phone receiver, feeling dog-tired. It was eleven in the morning New York time, 6:00 a.m. here. And he hadn't slept. While he waited for Nate Simon to come on the line, McSween wedged the receiver between his ear and shoulder and stared down at the bed. Romeo was lying on his back and wriggling, clad only in his Giants shirt. Was this really his son? Hours of living with the information hadn't made it seem any more real. *I've got to track down the two possible mothers of my child,* McSween thought. Donya said something had happened—but that could mean anything. Had the mother merely abandoned Romeo? And was she Laurie McGrath or Kay Wilcox?

Either way, Romeo belonged to McSween. Tilting his head, McSween could see the resemblance. It was in the nose—straight but nothing special. And in the dark hair and strong jaw. Of course, the kid did have the roundest, brownest, most soulful eyes McSween had ever seen—discounting Britt's, anyway—and his own were green.

That meant the brown-haired, brown-eyed Laurie McGrath was probably Romeo's mother, rather than Kay Wilcox.

"Why don't we try that diaper again?" McSween said.

Romeo sniffled.

McSween held his breath. After the last try, Romeo had cried until he turned bright red all over. McSween was dialing the hotel doctor in panic when the baby finally settled down. Fat teardrops still clung to Romeo's thick black eyelashes, making them stick together, and his lower lip quivered pathetically. If the baby could talk, he'd surely demand to know why McSween was so hell-bent on torturing him.

Reduced to begging, McSween said, "Please quit staring at me like that."

Reaching over, he dipped a plastic spoon into an open jar of baby-food cherries on the nightstand, then dunked the red goop into Romeo's mouth. The kid made a sour expression, but licked his lips, looking marginally less unhappy.

McSween blew out a long sigh. "Now, if we could just get you changed."

He glanced at the diaper rejects. They'd refused to fasten, but McSween couldn't figure out why. Hell, they were disposables, and the sides fastened with a sticky material. Or they were supposed to. Every time McSween lifted the kid, it turned out that the leg holes were too big. One by one, the diapers had puddled around the kid's tiny feet.

Steeling himself against another failure, McSween slid a diaper under the kid's behind. This time he pulled the sticky sides supertight, wincing and feeling sure he'd just cut off the baby's circulation.

"Let's hope that does it," McSween muttered.

Romeo reached up and grabbed his hands. McSween pulled him to a sitting position, then the kid pulled himself to his feet. The pull-ups were the baby's main source of entertainment. That, and chewing on his hands until the teensy wet fingers were shriveled and prunelike.

The diaper remained snug. Romeo took a half step on the mattress—and plopped promptly on his rear. A long tense silence followed, during which McSween willed the kid not to cry again. How so much air could fit into such a pint-size set of lungs, he would never know. When Romeo suddenly giggled, McSween was so relieved that he actually cooed, "Now, aren't you the best little boy?"

"Uh . . . McSween?"

Caught in the act. McSween felt the first flush of embarrassment he'd felt in years. Still, he wasn't sure which made him happier—hearing Nate's voice or seeing Romeo's gummy grin.

"Look, I know you were busy," McSween began. He whisked Romeo onto the floor, so he could crawl around. Instead, the kid sat down next to McSween's feet and started squeezing the toes of his oxfords.

"You must be in big trouble to be calling me," Nate said.

Or little trouble. Staring down at the baby, McSween switched the receiver from one ear to the other. "Well, not the kind you're thinking about." The balding bespectacled Nate usually handled complaints against officers.

"Does this concern internal affairs?" Nate asked.

"Affairs, anyway."

"Uh-oh," Nate said.

Uh-oh was right. McSween had to determine whether Kay or Laurie was Romeo's mother—and soon. A baby belonged with his mother. He sighed and started filling Nate in, beginning with Donya's visit. "On the legal papers," he finally said, "the baby was identified as Romeo. No last name. The papers regarding the mother were missing. I have no idea why the kid wound up in Child Placement, either. All I know is that I'm the father."

"Birth certificate?"

For the umpteenth time, panic seized him. What if something horrible had happened to Kay or Laurie? How was he supposed to take care of a baby? *Stay calm, McSween. This is all just a mistake.* "Don't know where it is."

"Is the baby Britt's?"

McSween stared down at the tuft of black hair. The kid quit squeezing the toes of his shoes—and started trying to untie them with his wet, sticky fingers. As if sensing McSween's gaze, he looked up. Then he craned his neck so hard that he fell onto his side. McSween chuckled. "I doubt it," he said into the receiver. "All the stewardesses assumed he was at least a year old or more, so he can't be Britt's."

Nate made a choking sound. "Stewardesses?"

McSween nodded absently. Strange, he thought. He had a kid, but not by the woman he loved. And Britt had wanted a baby so badly. Suddenly, a knife twisted in his heart. How he could have denied his wife something so simple—the baby a woman he didn't even love had gotten from him? Then the feeling passed.

"What stewardesses?" Nate said again.

"On the plane."

"If they were stewardesses," Nate stated tightly, "I assume they were on a plane. But where exactly did you *take* the plane?"

"Hawaii."

"Donya gave you this kid at five o'clock Eastern standard time—and you've already taken him to Hawaii?" Nate groaned. "I knew this was another one of your *Die Hard*, rogue-cop stunts."

"I'm after the Swindler," McSween admitted. "But don't tell Buchanan."

"With a baby in tow?"

"Makes me look trustworthy," McSween tried to joke, thinking that babies did make decent partners. When they'd arrived at the front desk of the Aloha Oahu Hotel, Romeo had created such a diversion that McSween had gotten Duke Perry's registration information. Now, Romeo and McSween occupied the bridal suite right next door.

"I think—" McSween began.

"Hold it." Nate sighed. "I'm taking notes."

McSween glanced around. This bridal suite was exactly identical to the Swindler's—with two connecting rooms, all-white decor, watercolor seascapes above the beds, and complimentary fruit and flower baskets. According to the desk clerk, Duke Perry was getting married—surely to his latest victim, McSween had realized—right outside on Waikiki Beach at ten tomorrow morning.

McSween had already unloaded the baby food from Romeo's yellow tote into a small refrigerator. Next door, in Perry's suite, surveillance equipment was in place, so

McSween could monitor both the Swindler's movements and his calls.

To install the bugs, McSween had simply called housekeeping and pretended he was locked out. The room was opened, no questions asked. Who wouldn't trust a guy with a baby? That the Swindler had been out was just dumb luck. *He's probably seducing his bride-to-be before he robs her.*

McSween snapped to attention. "Hmm?"

"I said, who else could the mother be?"

"It's Kay Wilcox or Laurie McGrath." McSween sighed. Before today, only Britt and the Swindler had occupied his mind. Now he had to identify and find the mother of his baby. In the background, McSween could hear Nate scribbling.

"So, you were sleeping with two women, McSween?"

"Not at the same time." McSween frowned, wishing he knew Romeo's exact age. No doubt, the baby was conceived right before he met Britt. Probably, Romeo was closer to fifteen months old than a year.

"Look," he continued with a start, "I don't even have Kay's or Laurie's phone numbers. They were in my proverbial little black book, but Britt tossed it into the fireplace when we got married." He gave Nate a rundown of everything he remembered about the women. "I don't have the resources here to try to track them down."

"I'll take care of it," Nate said. "But it may be a few days. We'll start with Donya and the judge who presided over the case. The judge should have the paperwork on...on your son."

Hearing the words, McSween felt uneasy. He'd never wanted a kid, but this wasn't exactly planned. *I told her I didn't want to have babies with her.* That was what Sal Luccio had said today. And what McSween had once said to

Britt. It was enough to make him cringe. "I really appreciate your help, Nate."

"For my best expert witness?" Nate chuckled. "No problem. And congratulations on being a dad. Kids are the best."

Nate should know, McSween thought dryly. He and his wife, Alyssa, had seven. After he hung up, McSween glanced at his watch. He ought to sleep before the Swindler's wedding.

He crossed to the window. A spectacular sunrise was giving way to a beautiful day, and his hand stilled on the curtain cord. He'd barely had time to process his arrival in paradise—the salty smell, the ocean breeze, the gently swaying palm fronds. And it was just as well. This whole damn place reminded him of Britt.

At least it's Oahu, not Maui. With a quick jerk of the cord, McSween snapped the drapes shut, as if closing the curtain on his marriage a final time. Somehow, he would forget Britt—and their elopement two years ago in Maui. He stripped down to his boxers, lifted Romeo onto the bed and lay down. Just as he reached for the light, the kid started crawling toward the edge of the mattress. *Why didn't I ask housekeeping for a crib?*

Well, he was too tired to call now. He got up, put Romeo on the carpet, then stripped the covers and made a bed on the floor. Enthralled, Romeo crawled onto the bedspread.

When McSween turned out the light, Romeo wailed.

When he snapped it on again, Romeo stopped.

"Fine," McSween muttered. He dimmed the light in compromise, then lay on his back in the floor, covering his eyes with a pillow. Romeo crawled onto his chest.

And then everything hit McSween at once—the sleeplessness and the jet lag. The fact that he was a father. That the identity of his child's mother wasn't known—and that she'd vanished. McSween was back in Hawaii, too—where he'd spent the happiest moments of his life with Britt.

A sudden, wrenching sadness twisted inside him. And then he felt a rush of vertigo, as if everything was spinning out of control. Reflexively, his arm curled around Romeo's back and he whispered, "C'mere, kid."

"BRRRR-RING."

McSween groaned, wondering why he'd fallen asleep on the floor. As he raked his fingers through his chest hairs, something didn't seem quite right. Ah... The uncomfortable weight that had been pressing down on his chest all night had been removed. *Probably anxiety.*

He drifted to sleep again.

And then he bolted upright. How could he have forgotten to request a wake-up call? Next to his phone, the red button on the recording device was flashing. The ringing had been Duke Perry, making a call. McSween half crawled to the machine and punched the Replay button.

"And it's after ten," he muttered. Rubbing his eyes, he rose to his feet and found his suit slacks. For the first time in his life, he hadn't hung up his clothes before going to bed. The pants were so rumpled, they could have been linen.

From the recorder, a female voice said, "Hello?"

"I'm marrying the woman this morning," Duke Perry whispered.

As McSween reached into his garment bag for a fresh white T-shirt, he cocked his head toward the recorder.

"Even though she wouldn't give you the money from her bank accounts?" the woman purred. "Duke, are you sure you're not losing your touch?"

A sockless McSween grunted in surprise as he slipped quickly into his oxfords. So, the Swindler had a female accomplice.

"If nothing else, I'll get her credit cards and jewelry," Perry said. "Then I'll take off."

Just listening to the man made McSween furious, and vanquished any guilt he might have felt at resorting to the illegal wiretap. How could the swine prey on women? he wondered as he shrugged into his sports coat. Even worse, Perry's victims were usually so lonely, so vulnerable, so ready to find love.

The woman said, "Duke, I can't wait to see you."

"Where?" McSween murmured in exasperation. "Please, just give me a location. Tell me where you're going to meet."

Instead, the woman whispered, "I love you."

"Love you, too."

"I'll bet," McSween muttered.

That was the entire extent of the conversation. McSween opened the drapes, then grabbed his binoculars and police badge from the windowsill. He was halfway through the door when he stopped in his tracks.

The weight on his chest hadn't been anxiety, he realized. It had been the kid. He whirled around. Romeo had disappeared.

"Where are you?" McSween whispered in panic.

Not knowing what else to do, he hiked up his pants, got down on his hands and knees and started to crawl. Sure enough, the kid was way under the bed, curled up with the dragon. McSween flung his arm beneath the bed and swept Romeo out.

He was wet.

McSween sighed. "Here goes another five minutes."

He changed the diaper, fixed Romeo a bottle of juice and then bolted out the door, with the kid on his hip. Just as he punched the elevator's Down button, Romeo sniffled.

McSween shut his eyes. *I forgot the damn dragon.*

He ran back to the room, binoculars banging against his arm, Romeo bouncing on his hip. "Here," he said. He thrust the toy into Romeo's hands and shoved the bottle into his own trouser pocket.

Once inside the glassed-in elevator, McSween sighed in relief. Then he saw himself and Romeo in the mirrored interior doors. He looked more like a kidnapper than a father. His suit was rumpled, his hair disheveled. Romeo's shirt was spotted with cherry stains and juice. And now, McSween realized he'd forgotten to bring his camera. Shots of the Swindler's wedding might be useful in court. Well, it was too late now.

You need a woman, McSween. Yesterday, it had made perfect sense to bring the baby. What had he been thinking?

When the elevator doors whooshed open, he jogged through the atrium-style lobby of the modern glass-and-steel hotel—and right into the June heat. "There they are," he whispered.

In the distance, past the hotel's landscaped shrubbery and near the water, were Duke Perry and a veiled woman in a short yellow dress. A man in vestments stood in front of the couple, and it looked as if the ceremony was well underway.

We'll stick out like sore thumbs if we go onto the beach. Especially if Romeo starts crying.

At the edge of the shrubbery, McSween seated himself in the sand, plopped Romeo into the cradle of his crossed legs, and lifted the binoculars. As the wedding couple came into focus, something—a sense of familiarity, maybe—tugged at McSween's consciousness. Was it a forgotten clue? A memory?

He shrugged off the feeling. Well, he had to give Perry credit. The man looked great in a tux. The woman didn't look bad, either. Her face was veiled, but she had great legs. Nice hips. A tush to die for.

And she was marrying a criminal. She was probably in love, too—all the victims had been—and hadn't a clue that Perry was just using her. At least she hadn't given him access to her bank accounts, which was what the mayor's sister had done.

But maybe this was worse. Instead of white, the poor woman was wearing yellow. McSween hoped she was a divorcée, rather than a widow. But then Perry wouldn't think twice about swindling a woman in mourning.

"C'mon," McSween whispered. "Lift the veil for me."

He felt Romeo crawl off his lap, and started to lower the binoculars, but then Perry and the bride turned toward each other. Ever so gently, Perry caught the edges of her veil.

McSween remained motionless, staring through the binoculars and holding his breath. "Finally," he murmured as Perry lifted the sheer fabric. "Let's see your face."

The next thing he knew, he was choking. He lowered the binoculars in disbelief, then brought them to his eyes again—so quickly that they slammed the bridge of his nose.

It couldn't be.

But it was.

"Oh, Britt," he said softly.

He lowered the binoculars in shock. Sure enough, his own wife had just married the Sutton Place Swindler.

Chapter Two

"We're about to make a baby, Brittany, darling," Duke singsonged through the bathroom door.

"We sure are." Britt's raspy whisper caught with hope. As she stepped from her scented bubble bath, she slipped a fluffy white towel from a rack and glanced over her rings— until her eyes rested on the new band of gold.

I can't believe it. I'm really married again.

Smiling wistfully, Britt listened to the sweet, sweet silence. A baby next door had stopped crying. As she began gently patting her skin dry, she imagined a loving parent scooping up the infant and smothering it with kisses.

Soon, I'll have one of my own. That's what tonight's all about. Sucking in a quavering breath, she began powdering herself with an oversize puff. Tonight, everything had to be perfect.

But it can't be, Britt. Not without McSween.

It took all her willpower, but she shoved aside the thought. Suddenly her manicured hand stilled. Loose powder sifted toward the tile floor, dusting her tanned feet and pearl-painted toenails. She knew she'd already asked countless times, but irrational terror gripped her heart. "Duke," she called, "I remembered the pills, didn't I?"

"The bottle's right here, darling. You need two?"

"Yes, two," she called on a sigh, pressing a palm to her chest. She'd made her doctor swear on his life that the pills would help her conceive. Setting aside the powder puff and reaching for her perfume, she dabbed her wrists and behind her ears. After a moment's hesitation, she flushed. Then she pressed dots of the subtle scent against her inner thighs.

"This time, please make it happen," she begged as she lifted a white nightgown from a hook on the back of the door. It and the matching robe were of sheer illusion lace and silk, both as delicate as a butterfly's gossamer wings. Ever so gently, Britt lifted the nightie over her head.

Now, if I could only forget Sean...

Except she couldn't. And oh, God, somehow she had to. Their marriage was over. The man was never coming back. And even if he did, she wouldn't have him. She had to move on with her life.

But how could she when the sun-kissed Oahu beaches, so like those on Maui where they'd spent their first married days together, kept reminding her of him? Every time her eyes strayed toward the reefs, where the ocean turned sparkling jade, she thought of Sean McSween's Irish eyes—and of how their very first lucky glance had won her heart forever.

"Oh, Britt, don't torture yourself," she murmured.

But no matter how hard she tried, she couldn't stop tasting his skin in the salty island air that was all around her. Or remembering how, after long nights of love, that taste used to linger on her lips like a song she couldn't stop singing.

She wanted him more than she ever had. Maybe she was even obsessed. Surely, she loved him. Her waking mind centered on him, while her sleeping mind conjured dreams of him that left her restless, her heart hurting and her body aching. Everywhere she went, she still inadvertently referred to him as her husband.

Damn you.

As she began brushing her hair, she wondered who she was really cursing—McSween or herself. She'd been so naive, so foolish, so sure their love could conquer all.

Two years ago, the sands on these Hawaiian beaches had signified eternity. Just looking at them, she'd known the sands of time would never run out for her and McSween.

From their very first night together, the man had sealed their fate. He'd given her a kiss at the door that, quite simply, had never ended.

As they'd entered her apartment, he'd stripped off her stockings—ripping them and hiking her dress, parting her legs and lifting her. And he'd taken her against her front door, her own raw need matching the tenacity of his assault.

"I'll be back tomorrow night and every night after," he'd whispered.

"I just bet you will," she'd whispered back.

But of course that had all been a lie.

And oh, had she found out the hard way that, sometimes, even love couldn't make a marriage work.

But that first night, she'd known they had a future. What kind, she wasn't exactly sure.

Once alone, she'd turned on the TV—and found herself staring at the screen in shock. News footage showed Sean McSween standing precariously on the ledge of a high-rise building, coaxing down a young man who'd clearly been intent on jumping.

McSween hadn't even mentioned the incident—or the life he'd saved that day. Most men would have. But the man the anchorwoman dubbed "the finest of New York's finest" simply didn't know how special he was.

Right then, Britt had decided what kind of future she would have with Sean McSween. She was going to marry him. And she was going to convince him he was a hero.

Let the past go, Britt. Don't think about McSween and don't think about Daddy.

Her widowed father had driven her to drastic measures by insisting that no man was good enough for her. No doubt, he'd be as furious about her second elopement as he'd been about her first.

Britt swallowed hard, lifted her jaw determinedly and slipped into her robe. Very carefully, she donned a pair of diamond drop earrings. They'd belonged to her mother, as had the other jewelry she wore—a black opal, an emerald-and-ruby ring, a diamond watch. Now she removed everything but Duke's simple gold band, placing the rest in a jewelry box. Her eyes lighted on the rings from her first marriage—a simple diamond and band—and she quickly closed the box. *Why did I bring McSween's rings?*

"At least Duke understands you," she said softly to her reflection. She might not love him the way she had Mc-Sween, but their mental connection was uncanny. It was almost as if Duke had read her mind and told her everything she wanted to hear. They'd spent a quiet day together, and he'd saved lovemaking for tonight, their wedding night. He was helping her make sure they got pregnant their very first time, too.

And yet the whole thing just didn't feel right.

In fact, Britt felt so guilty about marrying Duke Perry that McSween could have been right next door.

Although her mom had died when she was seven, Britt often imagined her nearby. And right now the ghost of Anne Buchanan laughed softly and whispered, "Honey, things have a way of working themselves out."

But how could they?

Duke called, "Are you almost ready, Brittany?"

Nowhere near. But she desperately wanted a baby to love. The urge was deep and primal, too. Overpowering and undeniable. She needed to nurture and nourish. To provide for and protect. Heaven help her, but she was a natural-born mother.

"Brittany, are you nervous, darling?"

Extremely. "Here goes nothing," she whispered. She took a deep breath and exited the bathroom in a trail of lace and scent. "I'm ready," she lied.

"To make you a fertility goddess." Duke held out his palm, offering her the prescribed pills and a champagne flute.

Britt swallowed the pills, then looked into Duke's blue eyes. So, this was it. Her insides started shaking, and she tried to assure herself it wasn't in protest. Her eyes darted around anxiously—taking in the entrance to the adjoining room, then the furniture in this one—the two deep, white leather armchairs. A round table with ladder-back chairs. Seascapes above the headboard. A wall unit with a TV that faced the bed.

Her gaze landed on an untouched fruit basket. It was of white wicker and tied on top with a huge, white satin bow. In bold script, the heavy vellum card said: "The Aloha Oahu Hotel congratulates you on your marriage!"

Britt, you can still walk away.

Instead, she walked toward the bed and turned gracefully, the white robe's hem swirling around her bronzed calves. Then she lay across the white spread that covered the mattress.

Duke smiled. "This baby is going to be beautiful. All our kids'll be beautiful, Britt."

It was exactly what she needed to hear. "I know they will, Duke," she whispered as her new husband strode toward the bed.

"OH, YES, MY LOVE," Duke Perry continued gently. "We're going to have a wonderful family."

Romeo giggled. McSween's eyes trailed murderously past the accumulating room-service trays, then over the surveillance equipment he'd just switched on.

No wonder the bride's backside had seemed familiar.

As he leaned back in a white leather armchair, he shifted Romeo from one knee to the other and whispered, "I can't believe I'm listening to my own wife's wedding night."

What were the odds against it? A zillion to one, maybe. But then Duke Perry had been swindling New York women for ten long years. Given his modus operandi, Britt was the perfect victim. Unmarried, wealthy and under forty.

Vulnerable, lonely and needy, he added with guilt, wondering if she really was. Had their separation taken its toll on her, too?

"McSween," he said levelly, "don't forget you're the one being tortured here." Surely, having to listen to the love of your life carry on with another man was right up there with being drawn and quartered. Or fitted with thumb screws. He glared at the spinning wheels of his tape recorder, willing Perry to say something more.

He didn't. McSween wished he'd planted the bug on the headboard, rather than under the bedside table. Maybe that would have improved the sound quality. He wished he'd started listening hours ago, too. But he simply couldn't bear it.

Now, he heard the soft creak of steps made by bare feet, the near-silent sigh of well-oiled mattress springs. His mouth went bone-dry. Perry had crossed the room and sunk onto the bed with Britt. McSween was sure of it.

He felt all the blood drain from his body, drop by agonizing drop. Anger, he decided dispassionately, wasn't even the word for what he felt. Anger was hot and temperamental, as full of boiling lava and flashing fire as Hawaii's volcanoes.

But McSween felt as cold as ice. And as hollowed out as an empty Arctic cave. No matter what happened, he meant to stay that way, too. Britt Buchanan had married another man. Never would he allow her to know it affected him.

"Don't worry," Perry crooned. "I want you to relax, Britt."

McSween's eyes narrowed to slashes of cool green. "I'll just bet you do," he murmured venomously.

The newlyweds' voices dropped to whispers, the words too low for McSween to make out. After a moment, Britt chuckled softly—and McSween's lips stretched into a thin, bloodless line.

When the kid dropped his little green dragon, McSween sighed, swept it from the beige carpet and stuffed it into his own lap. "It's a good thing you're here," he said quietly to Romeo. "Otherwise, I would have found her this morning. And I would have killed her."

Just as McSween had been about to approach Britt and Duke Perry, Romeo had vanished. McSween had crawled through the hotel's landscaped shrubs for a full, panicked half hour before he'd finally found the baby in a thicket of ferns. He'd been relieved—until he realized the kid had seemed to ingest a healthy amount of peat moss. By the time the hotel doctor had pronounced Romeo fit, the Sutton Place Swindler had left the beach—with McSween's wife.

"What are they doing in there?" he muttered impatiently.

Tilting his head slightly, he shut his eyes and strained his ears, but he heard only vague murmurings. At least that meant they weren't kissing.

Realizing he was holding his breath, he slowly exhaled. Before he did anything, he needed to make the kid sleep. Housekeeping was fresh out of cribs, but they'd brought a serviceable, old-fashioned playpen. It was set up in the adjoining room, but every time McSween left Romeo in it, the baby wailed.

Not that McSween had decided what to do yet—short of murdering Britt, anyway. He kept expecting himself to simply lose control, charge next door and bodily wrench her from Duke Perry's arms.

Calling Chief Charles Buchanan was nearly as tempting, though. McSween might get hell for going outside his jurisdiction, but boy, would the payoff be sweet. Especially after a year on the deadbeat-dad and parade details. He kept imagining himself saying, oh-so-casually, "Gee, Chief, while I was on vacation, I just *happened* to find the Swindler. And yes, well...he *is* with a woman."

Yeah, McSween could spend all night planning that call. What could possibly be more satisfying than informing the chief that his very own daughter was the Swindler's latest victim?

Making Britt love you again.

"Love you as what, McSween?" His voice was laced with bitterness. "Her stud?"

Lord, what's that woman done to me to make me turn so evil? Suddenly, he wondered why he was even hesitating in making Perry's arrest. He didn't need more evidence, and what he was collecting was inadmissible in court. Besides,

the mayor's sister's testimony alone would get the man ten
to fifteen.

Maybe he was eavesdropping out of sheer perversity.
Feeding his anger at Britt. Wanting to strike at the exact
moment that would mortify her most. Over and over, he
found himself wondering how she could do this to him. And
yet he also knew he had no real claim to her.

He shook his head. He could arrest Perry, or he could call
the chief. The final option was to let Britt make a fool of
herself by actually sleeping with the Sutton Place Swindler.

He was definitely angry enough, he decided.

Later, maybe he would even tell Britt he'd listened.

We're going to make beautiful babies. The words replayed in his mind. Couldn't she hear the insincerity dripping from Duke Perry's cheating voice? McSween tried to
ignore the guilt that washed over him. Duke Perry had read
Britt like a book—and he was probably playing her for all
she was worth.

He groaned. "Why am I torturing myself?"

Suddenly Romeo sneezed. Then he made a gurgling
sound, pulled a wet, pruny finger from his mouth and stuck
it into McSween's ear.

McSween leaned away. "Gross."

"Ah, Britt." Perry sighed, his sugary voice dripping with
phony emotion.

"Serves her right," McSween whispered gruffly. All
morning, while he'd tried to track down Britt and Perry,
he'd been miserable. Finally he'd given up and taken Romeo shopping. Suddenly his lethal expression softened.
He'd bought the kid a brightly colored Hawaii-print shirt.
And clad in only that and a diaper, the kid looked pretty
cute.

Should he charge next door and tell Britt that if she had
to have a baby, she could have this one? he thought with

irony. Nate had called, but neither Kay nor Laurie had surfaced. The second the gavel came down on Romeo's case, the judge, a man named Elliot, had left town for vacation, and Nate was now looking for the judge's assistant. So, maybe McSween should deliver the baby to Britt, just as Donya had. He would thrust it into her arms, say a quick "Here," and then vanish.

"What the hell's happening in there?" McSween whispered.

And what am I doing?

Had he really stooped to eavesdropping on his wife and another man? He reached past Romeo for the recorder. Just as his finger touched the Stop button, Britt sighed. McSween's hand stilled. Against all his better judgment, he leaned back in the white leather armchair again.

"I've wanted a baby for so long," Britt said.

McSween shifted uneasily in his seat. She sounded so drowsy and dreamy, so undeniably seductive. He might not love her anymore but he had once. And that deep, throaty voice reminded him of where he'd heard it before—when they were alone in the dark, in bed, her breath whispering against his ear. God, how that voice made his heart ache.

Britt cleared her throat. "McSween...he...he never wanted babies with me, you know."

McSween's temper flared. "Oh, please."

"Well, he's out of the picture now," Duke Perry assured.

McSween strained to keep his voice level, even though no one besides Romeo could hear him. "I'm right next door."

Perry said, "I'm your husband now, Brittany."

McSween gasped. "Like hell you are."

There was a long silence, during which McSween simply refused to contemplate what they might be doing. He knew he should turn off the recorder, but he was powerless to move. Every word stoked the rage that was starting to melt his icy reserve. He felt positively compelled to hear whatever else Britt might say about him. It sounded as though Perry had rolled closer on the mattress.

"Don't worry, darling," the man said. "We'll have a huge family. I want it all with you, lover."

McSween merely shook his head in disgust. "'Lover'?"

"I knew I'd find a man who wanted what I did," Britt said breathlessly.

The first man you found who wanted what you did now wants to strangle you, McSween thought.

Britt made a low, contented humming sound. "McSween, he..."

There was another pause that sounded suspiciously like a kiss.

"He what?" McSween demanded.

"I just knew it would never work with him..." Britt began. "He never loved me. I mean, he *said* he loved me. But emotionally..."

McSween couldn't wait to hear this one.

"Emotionally," she said, "he was such a liar."

McSween's jaw dropped open in astonishment. She was ten times the liar he was. Abruptly, he leaned forward and lowered the volume on the machine. He would continue taping, just in case Perry dropped a hint as to the identity of his female accomplice, of course. But McSween sure wasn't going to listen. At least not now.

Let her sleep with the guy. All he wanted was to see the look of mortification on her well-loved face in the morning—when he brought in the Honolulu cavalry and arrested Duke Perry.

I'm a liar. McSween shook his head as he rose with Romeo and headed toward the playpen. Now, that was rich. The woman had married him under false pretenses. She'd said she accepted his decision never to have children. And then she'd gone back on her word—and broken his heart.

"Well, I've got a real hard truth for you, honey," he said softly as he and Romeo crossed the threshold of the adjoining room. "I never did get around to signing our divorce papers."

Now, Brittany Buchanan McSween was illegally married to two men. And her cop husband wasn't going to arrest her robber husband—until he'd made her pay dearly.

WHEE! OH, MY DEAR Mr. Scaly, I just love it when Dad tosses us into the air and lets go-o-o-o-o! But maybe we'd better put on our invisible, good-little-boy hat and give the poor old guy some rest. He's looking tuckered out. And I'm yawning, myself.

Here we go again! Vroom. Down into our new bed, with its race-car sheets. Ah. Doesn't Dad know he's got to raise the side bars, though? A wily guy like me could get curious and escape.

Not that I will. He needs peace and quiet.

And it's all because of that woman. From the second we saw her on the beach, he got edgy. All day he paced, carrying me on his hip. To and fro. To and fro.

Then when he heard her on that machine, he just started staring at everything in the room real mean. Until his winkers landed on us, of course. Then he tried to smile.

Not that the poor guy could. Mostly, he just talks to himself. At least I got to crawl around in the sand this morning. And after we went to see the doc about the peat moss, I even got a teensy sip of soda pop.

"Good night, Romeo."

That's me! That's me! Next thing ya know, the big guy'll be kissing me with his smoochers! How come I can't let him know I realize he's talking to me?

"Goo-ga."

So much for my attempts to communicate.

"Coochie-coo," the big guy says.

What do you think that means, my dear Mr. Scaly? Oh, well. Good night, Daddy. Good night, Mr. Scaly.

"McSween?" Britt croaked.

Something was wrong. Her throat was parched. Her head felt woozy. Even though she was lying down, her whole body was spinning, turning horizontal cartwheels.

She buried her face in the pillowcase, still half dreaming of McSween—that he was sliding kisses down her neck and whispering words as hot as his breath. And then she remembered McSween wasn't even her husband. Lord, had she really married Duke Perry?

And had they made a baby?

Why couldn't she remember? Surely, any self-respecting woman would remember such a thing! Her hand groped over the bedspread. But she was lying on top of the mattress, the bed was made—and she was fully dressed!

A door slammed.

Was it her door? When she fumbled for the light cord, she missed and a heavy lamp toppled to the floor. Funny, the loud crash did absolutely nothing to further waken her.

She forced herself to stand. For a moment, she merely teetered uncertainly on her feet. Then her hands skated quickly over her white robe, checking nooks and crannies. Realizing her panties were snugly in place, her heart sank. There wasn't one single sign that she'd been tampered with.

We didn't make love, so I'm not pregnant.

Her eyes darted around the darkness. She felt so strange, almost drunk. *The pills,* she thought. The doctor had warned her there might be side effects. But how was a woman supposed to get pregnant when her fertility pills knocked her out like a light? Well, at least she knew that they were working.

Now, all she had to do was find Duke. And this time she was going to get aggressive. She blinked in the dark, hoping to reorient herself.

The door was open a crack! She staggered toward it. *Take it easy, Britt. It's the side effects of the pills, but you need to be careful.* When she stepped across the threshold and into the hallway, she felt like Alice stepping through the looking glass.

Everything seemed slightly off-kilter. Brass doorknobs seemed to recede rather than protrude from all the identical mauve doors. Her toes, with their pearl-painted nails, seemed miles away. So did the gray mauve speckled carpet.

The sheer quiet suggested it was the wee hours of the morning. Or was she in some timeless time? Had she really stepped through a looking glass? "Or looking door, as it were," she whispered giddily.

There! The light from the vending-machine alcove beckoned her. Remembering she had to find Duke, she staggered down the hallway a few paces. Duke had probably left the room for a soda or some ice.

She paused. But why was Duke awake? With a sudden start, she realized she'd come to a complete standstill again. She glanced up and down the hallway. How long had she been standing here like a zombie? All at once, her body tipped to one side, as if it were a glass someone had lifted and tilted. She flung out her hand for balance. It hit the door, which swung inward.

She squinted into the interior darkness. "Duke?"

Sure enough, she could make out his shape beneath the covers. He was lying on his side, an enticing silhouette in the dark, with his face turned away from her and the sheet bunched around his waist. How had he slipped past her, gotten into bed and fallen asleep again? Britt frowned. He must have been in the bathroom, she decided.

She shut the door quietly, groped across the room, then fell thankfully onto the bed and slipped beneath the sheet next to him. "Oh, Duke," she whispered in relief.

"Hmm?"

His absent hum told her he was asleep. And she'd hoped he would still be awake. She wanted to make a baby. They had to. He'd promised and she'd taken the pills tonight. She wiggled closer, still feeling woozy, her smile curling against his naked back. Licking her dry lips, she pressed them to the silken skin between Duke's shoulder blades. Tentatively, her hands slid upward, cupping his round, powerful shoulders.

Maybe this wouldn't be so difficult, after all, she thought dreamily. She would just pretend he was McSween. She shut her eyes, conjuring his image—the taut body, the tight muscles, the raven hair and green Irish eyes.

For what felt like an eternity, she merely lay there in the darkness—her front pressed to his back, her breasts crushed against his hard sleek nakedness, with only the white lace of her gown between them. Against her stomach, she could feel the waistband of his boxers.

It had been so long since she'd been with a man.

But the longer she lay there, the more this man seemed like McSween. It was in the honied-salt flavor that lingered on her lips. And in the way he smelled. Dreams of desire blended with reality as her tongue darted outward again, feathering butterfly kisses across his back.

All our kids'll be beautiful, Britt. Duke had said that earlier and now she heard the words in her soul. Her hands slid down his body slowly—feeling his steady heartbeat, studying each rippled rib, slipping beneath the sheet. When he tensed against her, she drew in a sharp breath. He was awake now.

After a moment, he relaxed, made a soft humming sound, and snuggled. No man other than McSween had ever fit so perfectly against her curves. She drew a deep breath for courage and slid off his boxers. Then her trembling hand stilled on his upper thigh, the hairs of his legs brushing her fingertips.

Everything seemed so hushed, so very quiet.

Then he moaned softly in the darkness.

The deep sound rippled through her languid limbs, then eddied against her core. She felt as if helium suddenly filled her body, making her float toward heaven. Even without the side effects of the pills, she would have been dizzy.

I'm going to get pregnant tonight. She was so scared it would happen. And so scared it wouldn't.

She waited with anticipation—breathless, dry-mouthed, her heart pounding—until he reached behind himself and began to caress her hip with his splayed hand. He found her hand and covered it, forcing her fingers wide apart. His long, tapered fingers fell between hers, then curled, holding her hand tightly. Slowly, he inched her hand across his thigh until she was touching him, feeling his hard heat.

Even though her eyes were shut, they seemed to shut again—taking her to a place that was darker still. A place of such intense desire that there were no words. Heat poured through her veins like lava, and the gossamer fabric of her gown became cloying, as heavy as velvet in summer. She leaned away, lifted her nightie over her head and tossed her panties aside. Then she pressed her naked body against him—perspiration beading her skin, the tips of her breasts pebbling against the smoothness of his bare back.

She had to remember this sweet, quiet moment forever. Because this was the prelude to the conception of her baby. She arched against him, willing him to turn around and face her. But he didn't. Instead, he rubbed silken circles over her thighs and between them, claiming her as his wife with each intimate touch.

He found her fingers and drew them deep between his lips, sucking them one by one. And when he let her hand drop, she touched his nipples and felt them harden in response to the wetness of her fingertips. He moaned deeply then, and in one fluid motion turned toward her, claiming her lips as she rolled onto her back.

The dark was like a cloak, hiding her, keeping the depth of her passion a secret. Never opening her eyes, she let him take her—crushing her with his weight, grinding against her in torturous rhythmic circles. He made her body turned pliable. And so hot, he was twisting her into melting knots.

Time and time again, she arched toward him. She drank in his lips; felt the spear of his tongue touch where his hands had once been, felt his lips scald her skin until her soft cries and whimpers rent the air.

It was like nothing she had ever felt. Not even with Sean. *Sean. Had she accidentally said his name aloud?*

She wasn't sure. She thought she had. But all she really knew was that when she opened her eyes, the room seemed even darker. It was a deep black delicate glass that was about to shatter.

"Come," she finally begged in wrenching sobs, in words McSween had taught her to say without shame. "Come with me this time."

And then the night did shatter. It broke apart, came back together, then broke up again. He exploded and Britt's heart filled. The whole world was about to become a different place because they were making a baby. Right now. At this moment.

Deep inside her, she could feel him pulsing like a heartbeat. And she felt whole and complete.

They lay there, skin to skin—his heart pounding against her right breast. Her heart pounding, crushed against his left. They had one heart. One body. One skin.

He'd made a baby with her. The emotion of it overwhelmed her and she whispered the only thing that seemed right. "I love you."

"And who's that?" he said.

Britt's strange giddiness returned full force. Everything seemed to tilt and slide sideways. Whose voice was that?

"Duke?" she croaked.

"Guess again."

This time, she didn't have to. She planted her hands on the man's shoulders and shoved with all her might. Because the man definitely was not Duke Perry.

Chapter Three

As McSween rolled away, his hand caressed her lovingly from hip to calf. He tugged the lamp cord, then glanced warily over his shoulder.

Britt's eyes darted around the dim room. "Duke?"

McSween's heart was still thundering against his rib cage, but he felt strangely at peace, too—as if all the tension had left his body...as if he'd just come home after a long day. Somehow, he managed to look his wife right in the eyes.

"Duke?" she ventured again.

"If you're so in love with Duke," McSween said with calculated calm, "then why don't you sleep with him?" *And why did you call out my name in the darkness?*

She gaped at him, no doubt wondering how he came to be here, how long he'd been awake, and why he'd been making love to her. Since he knew Britt well enough to know what would happen next, he prepared to duck. But she just kept staring at him through dark, haunted eyes.

"Would you quit looking at me like you've seen a ghost?"

She sat up very slowly, as if she was afraid of moving too fast, and drew the sheet against her chest. "I think I have."

So had he. And he could still feel the way she'd clung to him, believing he was another man. When those sweet kisses had whispered between his shoulder blades, McSween had thought he was dreaming. By the time he realized it was Britt, he was either too far gone to stop himself—or simply not enough of a gentleman.

Most likely, it was the latter. Beneath the sheet, which was now clutched to her chest in fistfuls, she was all curves and long legs—shadows and outlines. Her honey hair was shorter now. Cut to the jaw, it feathered across her cheeks. He could see deep lines where his fingers had raked through the strands.

She was beautiful. But she thought of him as a ghost. Dead. Finished. Out of her life. Snippets of conversation replayed in McSween's mind. *We're going to have beautiful babies, Britt.... A big family... I love you.* "Happy Anniversary," he said dryly as he flung back the sheet and got out of bed.

"It was..."

Her quavering voice trailed off, sounding dry and parched. He considered offering her some water. Instead, his eyes roamed the room for his boxers. "It was what?"

She cleared her throat. "Over at midnight."

His eyes strayed to her again. Dim lamplight spilled onto the side of the bed he'd just vacated. "So, you remembered."

She looked mortified. "Only now that you mention it."

There was a long silence.

Britt finally whispered, "Oh, my God. I can't believe this."

It wasn't exactly encouraging. Nor was the fact that his boxers seemed to have disappeared.

"Could you please get dressed?" she asked in a shocked tone.

His temper flared, but he kept his voice deceptively steady. "You've seen me naked hundreds of times. Isn't it a little late in the game to act surprised?"

"I suppose this *is* some sort of game to you."

He shot her a mock jolly grin.

Her eyes narrowed. "What are you doing in my room, McSween?"

"You mean, besides making love to you?" His gaze landed on his shorts. He snatched them from the floor and slipped into them. He considered tossing her panties onto the bed, but didn't.

She made another strangled sound. "My... my God."

"He's everywhere," McSween said. "So, He probably heard you the first time."

With feigned çasualness, he seated himself in the shadows, sinking into one of the white leather armchairs. All year, he'd fantasized about taking her the way he just had—with slow, deliberate stealth under the cover of night. He knew her body, and he'd touched it in ways certain to make her remember him. But now, her panic-stricken expression kept reminding him her response was for another man.

She called out my name, though. I could swear I heard it. McSween assured himself he didn't care one way or the other.

"I said, what are you doing here, McSween?"

That Duke Perry wasn't here apparently hadn't crossed her mind. "I hate to tell you this, Britt, but you're in *my* room."

She craned her neck and peered at the seascape hanging above the headboard. Then she took in the two white leather chairs. "This *is* my room!"

McSween squinted. She was awfully slow on the uptake... and was swaying from side to side as if balance eluded her. Her words were slurred, too. *She drank too much champagne with Perry.* "It's my room," he repeated.

She gulped audibly, her expression one of disbelief. "You're staying in this hotel?"

"Obviously." He continued scrutinizing her. She looked like a deer caught on a lonely road in car headlights. Her dark eyes were vulnerable, confused. His chest got tight and he decided he liked her better when she was throwing things. She fumbled next to her for her gown.

"But . . . but . . ."

The aftershocks of their lovemaking still buffeted his body. He shot her a long, penetrating glance. "But?"

"Quit looking at me like that," she said.

"Like what?"

"Like I did something wrong."

He chuckled in warning. "Didn't you?"

When she didn't respond, he watched her don her nightie and robe. With his every breath, he was taking in air that smelled of her—of powder and perfume, flowers and musk. The scent ate his oxygen, making his mouth dry. He licked his lips, still tasting her annoyingly waxy lip gloss. He'd kissed off most of it, but hints of her eye shadow and blusher remained. He shook his head in disgust. She'd even worn makeup to bed for the man.

"So, didn't you?" McSween repeated.

Her gaze dipped to his naked chest. As if she suddenly realized what had happened between them, spots of color rose on her cheeks. "Didn't I what?" she asked weakly.

"Do something wrong."

Even in the dim light, he could see she was flushing crimson. Dawning awareness crossed her features. "McSween, what are you doing—"

"In bed with you?"

"No." She inched toward the edge of the mattress. "In Hawaii."

"What are you doing with Duke Perry?" he countered.

She gasped. "What do you know about Duke? How do you even know his name?"

"You called me Duke when you came in the room." *But she hadn't said the name Perry.*

Her mouth dropped open in shock. "You were awake and you didn't..."

Stop making love to me?

Seeing her eyes widen in horror, he felt a twinge of perverse satisfaction. "Of course I didn't stop. You know me better than that."

Her eyes gained a steely expression. She was waking up fast. "What do you know—or *think* you know—about me and Duke?"

It probably wasn't the best time to tell her she'd married a crook. Or to announce that he'd never properly divorced her—and that she was still legally Mrs. Sean McSween. Not to mention a bigamist. "I'm in Hawaii on a case."

Her eyes trailed ever-so-slowly over the rumpled bedcovers, as if to say that working was the last thing he'd been doing. "Oh, is that right?"

He nodded. She shot him a look that could kill. By the second, she was becoming more like the Britt he knew and loved. Or used to love.

Suddenly, she grimaced. One of her slender tanned feet peeked from beneath the covers and dipped outside the bed. She looked like a swimmer at pool's edge, testing the waters with a toe and expecting a rush of bone-chilling cold. Her voice still sounded oddly unsteady. "And this—er— *case* just happened to place you next door to me?"

The way she was acting was making him feel testy. "Have your powers of comprehension always been this slow?"

"Last I heard, NYPD personnel don't chase deadbeat dads beyond the state line."

Her words may have slurred, but the line sure had punch. So, Britt had heard. He should have known. A daddy's girl from the word *go,* she and her father still dined together at least once a week. Probably, McSween's lowered status gave the two a good chuckle. Call it ego, but all along, he had hoped Britt thought he was advancing at work and dating countless interesting women.

Britt's rapid succession of blinks was clearly calculated to rouse her. "Did my father send you here?" she suddenly demanded, her tone turning murderous.

He ignored the question. "How long have you been sleeping with—er—Duke?"

Her eyes widened. "None of your business, McSween."

He shrugged. If she had done so tonight, the whole wretched business would be duly recorded on the surveillance equipment—if he could bear to listen to it.

The surveillance equipment.

McSween lowered his eyelids, surreptitiously scanning the room. His binoculars, badge, and a 35-mm camera with a telephoto lens were resting on the windowsill. In the corner was a telescope mounted on a tripod. The recorders were on the bedside table just inches from Britt's hands. As both the daughter and wife of a cop, she would know what they were, too. McSween took a deep breath and slowly exhaled.

And then he saw Romeo.

Great. How did he get out of the playpen? The baby was sitting on the threshold between the suite's two adjoining rooms. Tiny airplanes were printed on the cotton fabric of his pajama top and although the top was clean, it had ridden up, exposing a large stripe of roly-poly tummy. His diaper looked dangerously loose, and the dark hairs in the center of his scalp were sticking straight in the air, as if fashioned in a Mohawk. Even worse, the kid was staring at Britt curiously, with a mischievous expression in his sparkling brown eyes.

McSween's gaze captured Britt's, willing her to look at him—and nowhere else. He felt torn. He desperately wanted to get back in bed with her. Making love to her had stirred his senses, making him feel alive and vital. Yeah, Britt had definitely roused the slumbering, hibernating beast in him. But he had to get her out of here. If she saw the kid, he was in real trouble. "Look, Britt..." He smiled, trying to look friendly. "I must have left my door unlocked. You probably headed for the vending machines, then accidentally wandered in here. This is just a..." *What?* He racked his brain. "An unfortunate accident."

What an understatement. He could still feel her hands cupping his shoulders and hear her cries. What he'd done hadn't been the least bit accidental. He wasn't sorry for it, either. He realized his gaze had landed on the fruit basket with the hotel's card congratulating him on his marriage. *Some marriage.* He glanced away.

Britt's foot was still hovering over the floor. She swung her other next to it. "I refuse to discuss what's just happened."

The longer McSween watched her, the more his warring emotions were tugging him apart. He loved her. He hated her. And now he was sure there was something wrong with her. Concern won out. "Are you all right, Britt?" She seemed barely cognizant of her surroundings. She hadn't noticed the surveillance equipment. Much less Romeo.

She scowled at him. "I'm fine."

But she wasn't. Britt should be furious—shrieking at him, throwing things, losing control. He watched her carefully. He tried to fight it, but found himself remembering her legs wrapping around him. A warm shiver tingled down his spine. She'd been so responsive. . . .

And all for Duke Perry. McSween's voice hardened. "C'mon," he said. In a swift, lithe motion he rose from the chair and crossed the room. Placing his arm beneath her elbow, he manhandled her out of his bed.

She attempted to shrug off his grasp and failed. "What are you doing to me?"

"Taking you back to Duke," he said decisively.

She stumbled along next to him. "What? Now that you've had your way with me?"

McSween forced himself not to roll his eyes. "Don't pretend you didn't enjoy yourself."

She stopped dead in her tracks and stared at him. "I will return to my *husband* by myself," she declared haughtily.

McSween shrugged. "Since you bring all your husbands to Hawaii . . ." He pinned her with his gaze, then stared pointedly toward the rumpled bed. "It's no wonder you get so confused."

She said nothing, which was strange. Why wasn't she reacting? Asking questions? He'd shown no surprise at the fact that she'd called Duke Perry her husband. That should set off alarm bells in her head. "I'll escort you next door," he said coolly.

"You're going to deliver me to my husband—" She had the audacity to stop in midsentence and yawn. "And you're going to deliver me bodily. He'll just love that, McSween."

A smile ghosted over McSween's thinning lips. "I just want to make sure you arrive without wandering into yet another man's bed."

"You left your door unlocked," she said airily.

His jaw set in a grim expression. "So, it's all my fault?"

He didn't exactly want to leave her with Perry. But he had to get her out of here before she saw Romeo and the surveillance equipment. McSween reached for the knob, swung open the door, then pointed. "Let's go. He's probably worried."

"You've sure gotten considerate since I divorced you."

He'd had it. Without warning, he leaned close and backed her up against the wall. Realizing that if she stared past him, she would see Romeo, he whirled with her in his arms, so that his own back was against the wall. He drew her against his chest.

"What are you doing here?" she repeated.

"Like I said, I came here on a case."

"I don't believe you. You wouldn't take a bridal suite." Suddenly, she tried to wrench around. For the very briefest instant, it seemed as if Britt was still in love with him and trying to search the room for signs of female habitation.

Not that she could. He held her in an iron grip. "Don't worry, *I* didn't marry someone else."

"I'm hardly worried," she retorted.

On the floor, Romeo rolled onto his chubby little belly. McSween watched in terror as the kid crawled toward him and Britt at breakneck pace. When Romeo stopped and started picking at the carpet, McSween blew out a hidden sigh of relief.

The feeling didn't last. He was holding Britt, with only the whisper-thin fabric of her gown between them. Her breasts brushed him, and the tips constricted against his bare chest. Something inside him almost gave in. He wanted to forget their odd circumstances—and simply beg her to let him come home. He wanted their lives back. Her nearness was so unspeakably erotic that he drew her just an inch closer.

"Let go of me."

"Why?" The sheer fury in her tone almost made him want to hold her tighter. "Because I'm not Duke Perry?"

"Yes."

He yanked her against his chest until their lips were so close he was nearly kissing her again. Their warm breaths mingled, softly stirring the air. "I hate to tell you this—"

"You keep saying that," she whispered. "But I get the distinct impression you're enjoying yourself."

Maybe he was. Very softly, he said, "It wasn't you I followed down here, Britt. It was Perry."

He tried to catch her, but it was too late. She wrenched away—and got a good look at the room. His gaze followed hers—from the equipment on the windowsill to the bedside table.

She pivoted and glared at him. "You were spying on me!" she accused hotly.

And then she slapped him. Or tried. He caught her hand in midair. She may have been about to do him bodily injury, but his fingers wound up twined through hers.

"Honey, I didn't know it was you," he said in a near whisper. It was hard to stay mad when he was so close to her. The room turned so silent he could hear her heartbeat. Or maybe it was his. The surface of her dark eyes turned ever harder by degrees, but deep inside they were liquid and soft.

"I know this is a weird turn of events," he said, wincing at his own understatement. Glancing over her shoulder, he was sure he didn't quite believe what was happening, either. The room, for all its palatial splendor, suddenly seemed airless and confining. The light was too dim. Was a child—his child—really playing silently on the floor, unnoticed by Britt?

"You were spying on me," she repeated.

"Britt," he said softly. "I don't want to hurt you any more than I already have—"

"You have never once hurt me!"

It was a lie of course. They'd hurt each other deeply, but he forced himself to nod. "I mean, if I did."

"You didn't," she said emphatically.

He nodded again. "The thing is, this guy you're with... Perry. He's also known as the Sutton Place Swindler."

Her eyes widened, and she clapped her hand over her mouth. Probably her father had mentioned the case to her during one of their dinners.

"He uses a number of aliases," McSween continued.

Her hand dropped to her side. Color flooded her face. "Duke Perry is *not* the Sutton Place Swindler."

McSween winced. Romeo was crawling toward him and Britt again. When the kid stopped, McSween relaxed—until the baby wrapped a tiny, wet fist around Britt's underwear. Smiling, Romeo rubbed the silky fabric against his knee. McSween could only hope that Britt wouldn't decide to look for her missing clothes.

"I'm not making this up," McSween insisted.

"You're serious?"

Never taking his eyes from Romeo, McSween edged Britt toward the door again. "You know, your dad's given me a lot of lousy jobs lately...."

She came to a standstill. "That's hardly my fault!"

But it was. If McSween had given Britt a baby, his professional life would be on an even keel. His eyes darted between Britt and Romeo. "I thought maybe I could get off deadbeat-dad detail if I found the Swindler, Britt. But the lead brought me right here... to you."

"That's why you're here?" All at once, she sounded groggy again. "You're chasing the Swindler?"

"What else could I be doing?"

She stomped her foot and nearly lost her balance. "You know what I think?"

He shook his head. "No clue."

She wagged her finger in his face. "I think Daddy heard I was getting married and sent you down here to stop me! Either that, or you decided to stop me yourself."

So, she thought he was pining after her, did she? And while she was happily marrying another man. "Who you marry is up to you," he returned icily.

"Duke wouldn't do anything wrong!"

"I'm arresting him." He shot her a quick smile. "So, I guess you can kiss the rest of your honeymoon goodbye."

Pure panic flashed in her eyes. Was it because her father was going to find out she'd been played for a fool? Or was it because she'd fallen for the man? A trembling hand shot to her ear, and she worried her unadorned earlobe between her thumb and index finger.

Then her eyes turned guarded and unreadable. "Were you really listening to our room?"

Suddenly he felt sorry for her again. "I turned off the equipment. I didn't hear...."

His stomach turned.

She looked embarrassed. He wouldn't have thought it possible but her flush deepened.

"Duke can't be the Swindler," she said tightly. "You've got the wrong man."

A sudden ache went through his body. Reflexively, he pulled her against him again. How could she have let another man hold her this way? "Maybe *you* got the wrong man, Britt."

She wiggled against him, as if his proximity was making her uncomfortable. "You definitely weren't the right one."

"Maybe I was."

"It's over, McSween."

"Sure didn't feel over, ten minutes ago."

Britt wrenched away. This time he let her take a step back. "You aren't my husband," she said passionately. "We're divorced!"

He didn't correct her. In a flash, he imagined signing the papers and sending them in. He didn't want her to know he hadn't yet. Since he wasn't the type to procrastinate, she might suspect the truth: that for a whole year he'd wanted her back.

Not that he did now, he assured himself. She was getting on with her life—even if she'd made a false start by walking into Duke Perry's clutches. McSween stared deeply into her stormy eyes and jerked his head toward the door. "Surely the love of your life has started missing you by now."

She lifted her head and started imperiously for the door.

And then, the worst imaginable thing happened. Romeo squealed.

Very slowly, Britt turned around. Her chin lowered by barely perceptible degrees, until she was staring at the floor.

McSween found himself wishing he really was a ghost. Especially when Romeo shot Britt a disarming grin. The kid raised his hand excitedly and waved, so that the silk panties flapped like a flag.

Britt whirled toward McSween so fast that she really did lose her balance. He grasped her elbow firmly to steady her, but she jerked away as if she'd been burned.

"I don't know how this—this disgusting mix-up happened," she snarled. "I won't even have it discussed. But, I do want the answer to just one question."

McSween sighed. "Which is?"

"Who in the hell—" Britt raised a manicured index finger and pointed accusingly at Romeo "—is that?"

More than life, McSween wanted to lie.

"McSween?" Her voice was a near growl. "Who is it?"

"My son."

Even as he said the words, he reached out instinctively to catch Britt. But she was already wrestling against him and slipping from his embrace.

"Your *son?*"

"It's a long story," he said softly.

She looked him up and down. "Well, pardon me if I don't stick around to hear it."

As she ran for the door, he grabbed her hand, making her swing around. "Please, Britt..."

"Lay so much as one finger on me again and I'll kill you."

"Just let me explain."

"We are divorced," she returned succinctly. "And I never want to see your face again."

With that, she strode through the door. This time she didn't even stagger. And she didn't look back.

McSween glanced at Romeo—just in time to see the corners of the kid's mouth turn downward. A split second later, a wail rent the air, sounding so dangerously loud that it could have been a five-star alarm.

Chapter Four

"His *son?*"

Britt hit the overhead lights in her room, and then she slammed the door. Seeing the toppled lamp on the floor, she realized that this really was her room. *Get ahold of yourself, Britt. You've got to think.*

But her mind was reeling. And her body was still burning from McSween's lovemaking. She remembered how he'd casually strolled toward his boxers. No matter how hard she'd tried, she couldn't divert her gaze. The man had a cop's body—lean and hard. Dark hair covered his chest and gleaming skin stretched over sharply defined muscles.

Another year of character lines had made his face look craggier. His short dark hair was slicked back, less for style than because he hated it in his eyes. It accentuated his high forehead, stubbled no-nonsense jaw and intense expression. Not to mention those damnably green eyes.

But what was her ex-husband doing with a son?

Britt made it to the bed, sank onto it, and covered her mouth with her hand. No, hallucinations weren't listed as a possible side effect of the fertility pills she'd taken. There really was a baby. She could still hear it crying next door.

But she sure felt odd. Should she call a doctor?

The whole world seemed to have gone crazy. Surely, McSween wasn't really here. How could she have wound up in his room, making love to him? And had he really said the baby was his? "As in it came from his loins, his flesh and blood?" she murmured. *Impossible.*

Britt gasped. "Who's the mother?"

She'd been so shocked, she'd barely noticed the baby. Now, she decided it was a boy. He looked about one year old. Whom had McSween dated before they met? Kay? Wasn't that the woman's name?

Icy fury curled through her veins, then plain hurt ached in her heart. McSween had had a baby with that Kay woman.

And something else was wrong. Her mind kept racing, as if it was searching for something. Whatever was missing seemed terribly important. What could it be?

Duke!

He was gone. She could sense it without even looking. Pure hurt roiled through her again. Her eyes ventured around the room. Sure enough, the closet was open and Duke's expensive leather luggage was gone. Their whirl-wind romance replayed in her mind—how he'd seemed to want everything out of life that she did.

"I slept with McSween!" she suddenly whispered in hor-ror.

She was supposed to sleep with Duke—but she'd slept with McSween!

And the doctor had given her those fertility pills.

Even though she'd just had her nails done, she started to gnaw on them. "I simply can't believe this!"

She could be pregnant with McSween's baby now! She jumped to her feet. Then she sat down again. Oh, Lord, af-ter all those fights they'd had about her wanting to get pregnant, she could never tell him.

"Besides," she whispered murderously, "he has a son."
*Did Kay tell him she was pregnant? Did he know he had a
baby when he wouldn't have one with me?* Probably not,
she decided. The man simply wasn't capable of that kind of
closeness, even if his lovemaking said otherwise.

"It doesn't matter," she murmured. "If I'm pregnant I'm
not telling him."

But how was she going to keep him from finding out? All
the police functions she attended with her father shot
through her mind. She'd avoided McSween all year, but
could she avoid him for a lifetime? No, he would find out
about the pregnancy.

For the moment, there was only one solution. She had to
get out of here.

She leapt into action, tossing her suitcase and carry-on
onto the bed. She grabbed clothes by the handful, then
threw them in the general direction of the bags.

"What have I done?" she moaned.

But she wasn't going to think of McSween, or that baby
in the other room...or whatever woman had borne it. Duke
Perry was apparently long gone. So that little problem was
already taken care of. Suddenly, her hand stilled on her
suitcase.

Everything was in it now—and she was still wearing her
wedding nightie! The sexy gown hadn't even made Mc-
Sween jealous. Or it was hard to tell. He was so calculating
and hard to read.

Whatever the case, his son suddenly quit crying. Since
yesterday, she'd heard that baby. How could Sean Mc-
Sween be the doting parent she'd imagined soothing the
child? She shook her head, tugged off the delicate gown and
robe, and tossed them on top of her other clothes. Rummaging inside her suitcase, she pulled out a sundress and
slipped it on. In the closet, she found her sandals.

Then she called the airport, mentally coaching herself. *I married the Sutton Place Swindler, accidentally slept with him—and am probably pregnant by my ex-husband.*

It might not be the end of the world, but she was starting to feel awfully hysterical. Somehow, the ticket agent's voice calmed her.

"This is Jack at Oahu Air. Where would you like to go?"

"To another planet," Britt muttered.

Jack chuckled dutifully.

"When's the next flight, to—" Britt slammed down the phone.

"Sorry," she murmured, as if in apology to the clerk she'd just cut off. The news about McSween's fatherhood had shocked her so much that she'd forgotten he was monitoring her calls.

"Well, I'll just—" *Quit talking to yourself, Britt. He's probably bugged the whole suite.* She would simply head for the airport and get on the first flight to New York.

That decided, she zipped her suitcase. *The bathroom. I'm forgetting my toiletries and pocketbook.* She glanced around the room. Lord, it *was* exactly like McSween's—even the pictures were identical.

In the bathroom, she felt tears suddenly sting her eyes. The floor was dusted with her powder, the air smelled of musk. Just a few hours ago, she'd been ready to make love to her new husband. *I wanted a baby so badly, I think I would have married anyone.*

She took a deep breath, then started cramming her toiletries into a small zippered bag. She reached inside her pocketbook and opened her wallet, intending to put her stray hairpins inside the change compartment. Her hands stilled. She brought the wallet out of her bag, opened it fully and stared inside. Had she moved her credit cards?

"And my cash?" she whispered. Dropping the toiletries bag, her fingers groped at her ears. When she'd touched her ear in McSween's room, she'd known something was wrong. Her mother's earrings were gone. *Duke really is the Sutton Place Swindler!*

Her hands shot to her jewelry box.

Sure enough, everything had been stolen. For the umpteenth time that night, her hand covered her mouth. Most of the pieces had belonged to her mother. *Except the rings McSween gave me.* That his diamond and band were gone hurt far more than she wanted to admit. Impulsively she tore Duke Perry's wedding band from her finger and threw it onto the floor. It pinged against the tile, then rolled behind the toilet.

If McSween knew Perry was the Sutton Place Swindler, then why hadn't he offered to help her? Feeling a surge of pure, angry adrenaline, she stormed back into the hallway and then pounded on McSween's door.

He didn't answer, so she pushed—and the door swung inward. When she saw McSween, her heart really did break. He was seated in the white leather armchair, still wearing his boxers and cradling the baby against his naked chest. Tears sprang to her eyes, but she fought them.

How many times had she imagined McSween lovingly comforting a crying baby? She sniffed and swallowed hard. *Yeah, but in all those fantasies, the baby was ours.*

When he glanced up, her throat closed, feeling raw and achy. He looked like such a perfect father. She wouldn't have imagined she'd be capable of it, but she found herself despising the baby. The little boy was supposed to be hers— hers and McSween's.

But the man she'd loved hadn't wanted her baby.

The baby I'm probably carrying now, she thought with rising panic. The unwavering steadiness of McSween's eyes wasn't something she'd exactly forgotten but right now that gaze was making her edgy.

McSween sighed. "Yeah, Britt?"

She tried to tell herself she had no choice but to ask for his help. "Duke's disappeared and he took all my money, credit cards and jewelry."

McSween stared at her. His stoical expression reminded her that minutes ago she'd said she never wanted to see him again.

"The jewelry was my mother's. And you know how Daddy..."

McSween lifted his chin a barely perceptible notch, as if daring her to continue. Ever so gently, he bounced the little baby boy on his knee. He arched an eyebrow. "What exactly do you want me to do about it?"

"You're a cop," she retorted. "And you came here to solve this case."

"So?"

"So, go after him!"

"GO AFTER DUKE PERRY?" Forty-eight hours ago, that was all McSween wanted to do. But now... His eyes roved over Britt's short sundress. Its cut was as strappy and summery as her high-heeled sandals. And even though the swirling olive-and-rust leaf print made him think of autumn, revealing crisscross ties in the front and back were a sore reminder that his wife knew how to dress for a man.

And undress. That virginal, whisper-thin white peignoir was still making McSween ache. Damn. He'd known better than to make love with her again. Just when he'd begun to rearrange his priorities—having decided to find the mother of his child instead of the Swindler—he'd been mysteriously reunited with his wife.

At least the kid had dozed off. He drew Romeo closer. "You really expect me to track down Perry?" he repeated.

"You said that's why you came to Hawaii."

McSween sighed, his patience wearing thin. Whatever Britt had done next door had apparently awakened her. The dreamy, groggy quality had left her voice. "Maybe finding you in bed with the man ruined my appetite for the case."

Britt's expression softened. "Don't tell me you're jealous."

He shot her a look that said such emotions were beneath him. "Hardly."

"C'mon, McSween, you know Daddy's going to kill me."

If I don't first. And for no other reason than that her brown eyes did him in. Looking into those velvet depths, he'd never been able to deny her anything. Well, one thing . . .

"And you know what Mama's rings mean to Daddy."

Daddy. In a flash, McSween imagined Romeo talking in that tone—worried about what his dad thought, wanting him to be proud. "I'm supposed to retrieve your mother's jewelry, so your father won't get upset?"

Britt leaned against the doorjamb and folded her hands primly in front of her, her eyes skating toward the baby's belongings in the corner—the stroller and the totes.

"And quit looking at the kid's things like that," McSween said.

"Like what?"

"Like I owe you, Britt. I gave another woman a child, so now, feeling guilty and duty-bound, I have to chase down Duke Perry for you."

Britt's facial expression remained calm, but she clasped her hands more tightly, until the knuckles turned white. "I didn't say that. Besides, Duke's probably long gone by now," she accused, her voice rising. "And you *should* feel guilty for—"

McSween's quick scowl cut her off. "For what?"

"For not chasing Duke immediately! And for not wanting a family with me...when I was *supposed* to be your wife."

"You *were* my wife." *You still are.*

She drew in an audible breath. "Look. I've got to find Duke. Daddy..."

Romeo let out a soft baby cry, and McSween's heart softened. He had no intention of keeping the kid, but he felt a fierce need to protect him. He guessed that was how Charles Buchanan felt about Britt. "Your dear old Dad hasn't exactly been looking out for my feelings over the last year."

"Why don't you leave Daddy out of this and just help me, McSween?"

"Answer me one thing first."

She unclasped her hands, then crossed her arms. The defensive gesture only served to accentuate the gentle swells of her breasts. "Sure."

"What were you doing with Duke Perry?"

When her teeth clenched together, her jawline hardened as if she never intended to speak another word. But McSween had her where he wanted her—between a rock and a hard place.

"While you're so intent on interrogating me, my—er—husband's getting away," she argued in a strangled tone.

McSween shrugged. "Let him."

Exhaling a long-suffering sigh, she drew herself up to her full stature, nearly six feet with the heels. "We met a month ago and...and he just sort of swept me off my feet."

"You're lying."

Light deep inside her dark eyes flared. "I wanted a baby, McSween," she said with sudden venom. "And you know it. This particular man happened to be willing—'' Britt gave him a swift once-over ''—and able.''

A wry smile curved a corner of McSween's mouth. "An hour ago, I'm sure you would have said *I* was still able."

"Of having sex," she retorted. "But not of being a father."

Maybe he'd asked for that one. But he was a father now. And when Britt's gaze landed on Romeo, McSween could see the blood drain from her face. Her tanned cheeks turned a full shade paler and guilt washed over him.

"Don't worry," he found himself saying. "I'll find your—er—husband."

"Good," she said curtly.

With Romeo in tow, McSween stood and crossed the room. He reached past the recording equipment, trying not to draw too much attention to it, and called the front desk. No one had seen Duke Perry leave. McSween hung up and dialed the local police, then the Honolulu Airport Security office, alerting everyone to the criminal's presence and leaving his hotel number, so people could call him if there was a lead.

The entire time he was talking, he could feel Britt's eyes boring holes in his back. Or maybe she was glaring at Romeo, who was asleep on his shoulder. McSween started for the door. "Well, c'mon."

"Where are we going?"

"Your room."

She stared straight at him as if his near-nakedness didn't bother her in the least. "Aren't you going to get dressed?"

Glancing down at his boxers, he wanted to say that she'd gotten dressed, but it hadn't made her look any less desirable. Instead, he laid Romeo on the bed, found a pair of jeans and dutifully tugged them on. All at once, he became aware of the room's silence. The casual intimacy felt awkward, and his fingers fumbled on his zipper.

"Little trouble there, McSween?" Britt asked swiftly.

He glanced up—and caught her staring at his chest. "No."

Her taunting chuckle filled the air. "I mean, we've seen each other naked thousands of times, so..."

Why the sudden awkwardness? "Hundreds," he corrected.

"You mean you counted?"

He pinned her with his eyes, smiled, and said, "You bet." Glancing down, he pointedly tugged up the difficult zipper, which sounded unusually loud. Lifting his eyes again, he saw the pulse madly ticking in Britt's throat. He lifted a lazy eyebrow. "Do I pass muster?"

"You'll do."

McSween picked up Romeo and a bottle. "Thanks."

Then Britt whirled in a graceful circle. When her leaf-printed dress skirt swirled, the falling leaves looked as if they'd been caught in a spiraling wind. She preceded him through the door, as if to intentionally make him peruse her luscious legs. The long, never-ending legs that had been wrapped tightly around his waist not an hour ago, he reflected. The legs that he no longer had any claim to touch.

Her hand was on her doorknob before she bothered to shoot him another peeved glance. "That may be your son—"

"This *is* my son." McSween leaned against the wall in the hallway. "And I'm getting tired of your attitude."

"Attitude?" she returned innocently.

He merely stared at her. His eyes said, *I want you to show some interest, to ask about the baby—about his age or who his mother is or where he lives.* Britt's eyes said she would rather walk across hot coals.

McSween shrugged as if they'd been having an audible conversation.

"Okay," she said. "It *is* your son—but do you really have to carry him like he's a football?"

McSween squinted down. Sure enough, Romeo was wedged under his arm. The kid seemed to like being carried that way.

Britt heaved an exaggerated sigh. "Oh, darn it, Mc-Sween." In three quick, long-legged strides, she was at his side. Her gestures were so mechanical that she could have been readjusting the cogs and wheels of a machine instead of the arms and legs of a baby. Nevertheless, she resituated Romeo in his arms, and he shifted the bottle from one hand to the other.

Drawing in a deep breath of her musk and powder, he found himself saying, "I thought you liked babies."

"Not yours." She shook her head adamantly. "I don't want that child near me."

How could she be so hard? he wondered. Had he hurt her that much? Feeling Romeo's warm, shallow breath against his cheek, McSween tried not to think about all the nice touches she'd brought to his Spartan existence. Tailored designer suits and fluffy down bedding, Sunday mornings spent listening to opera. Hell, he'd missed Britt's specialty coffees so much that he'd bought himself a cappuccino maker. He still couldn't get the steamer to work right.

"McSween—"

Her clipped tone brought him back to earth. "Yeah?"

"One year ago, we divorced because you wouldn't have a baby with me. And *voilà,* here you are—" She nodded at Romeo.

"This wasn't exactly planned parenthood, Britt."

"Please—" She shrugged and pushed open the door to her room. "The less I hear about your messy personal life, the better."

"At least *I* didn't marry the Sutton Place Swindler," McSween couldn't help but say.

"Just do your job and look for clues."

As he followed her across the threshold, he leaned so that his chest pressed against her back. Bringing his lips to her ear, he said, "If you want my help, fine. But if you keep ordering me around in that imperious tone, you're not going to get it."

She tossed her head. "Would you kindly remove the bugs you so illegally installed in my room so that you could eavesdrop on my honeymoon?"

Beneath the false sweetness, her words sounded as brittle as snapping twigs. As she marched toward the other side of the room, he watched her back, her stiff shoulders. No, he definitely wasn't the only one who had felt bitter after he moved out.

McSween laid Romeo on the bed and then glanced around. Without being told, he would have known his wife occupied this room. Her scent was everywhere; so was her trademark messiness. Sexy wisps of lace peeked from corners of her open suitcase. Forcing himself not to touch the delicate lingerie, he shook his head. How could such a slobbish woman step outside looking so darn good?

The rumpled bedcovers gave him pause. He made his mind go blank, refusing to imagine Duke Perry lying next to Britt. Trouble was, he saw himself tumbling into the bed with her. He shot her a surreptitious glance. Lord knew, he'd cheated tonight—making love to her when she thought he was Duke Perry. But was it really over between them? Was tonight the last night he would ever hold her—naked, hot, trembling against him?

She stalked to the bed and pretended to tidy the clothes in her suitcase. Clearly, she'd packed after waking in his room. That her first impulse had been to leave town annoyed him more than it should have.

So did the fact that the invisible barrier she'd erected covered her like a glass bubble. Not that it could shield her from the electricity they generated when they were in the same room. They'd made love tonight, and the air was still alive—crackling with tension, pulsing with unseen currents.

She looked at him pointedly. "Are you going to stand there staring at me all night?"

I could so easily. McSween forced himself to glance away. "If my son wakes and crawls toward the edge of the bed, would you mind stopping him?"

Britt looked offended. "I may be trying to ignore him, but I wouldn't let bodily harm come to your precious little child."

McSween nodded curtly. "Call and cancel your credit cards."

"Okay," she said, sounding marginally contrite.

He started dismantling the bugs. Feeling sure that Perry must have forgotten something of interest, McSween searched the room—between the mattresses, under the bed, behind the pictures.

Finding nothing, he shut his eyes and cleared his mind. He'd been trained to mentally recreate crime scenes, but then no textbook had covered this. The scene had never included a bed where his own wife had intended to seduce another man. *Even if Britt wasn't the victim, you'd have to find the Swindler. If she's going to let you search her room for clues, then so be it.*

McSween opened his eyes. This time, as he walked through the room, a story started to unfold. *She's readying herself in the bathroom,* he thought. Dried suds made a ring around the interior of the tub, indicating that she had taken a bubble bath. As she stepped from the water...

McSween's mouth turned dry. He could see Britt, dripping wet and stepping from the bathtub. He shook his head and tried to concentrate.

"She powdered herself," he murmured. The powder spatter on the tile floor left a very clear outline of her bare feet, indicating that she'd been alone. Later, Duke had stepped inside the room, wearing his street shoes.

McSween wouldn't have thought it possible, but his professional side took over. Britt might be his wife, but she was also Duke Perry's latest victim. And McSween was a good cop. So, when he realized she'd taken off her new wedding band and tossed it onto the bathroom floor, he barely even cracked a smile.

"She exited," he muttered as he left the room himself. "Perry met her outside the door. He handed her one of these champagne flutes." McSween made a mental note to bag the two glasses. Then his eyes trailed over the dresser and he cautiously picked up one of two pill bottles.

Nothing much surprised McSween. But as he read the label, his eyes widened. The bottle contained a powerful painkiller. Was Britt taking drugs? It would explain her groggy behavior earlier. But would a drug this potent wear off so soon? He set the bottle down, then reached for the second. With lightning speed, Britt's hand appeared. Before he could protest, she'd whisked away both bottles.

"Stay out of my personal belongings," she snapped.

"You told me to look for clues."

"These are bottles, not clues."

"Are you into pills now, Britt?"

"Oh, right! I was so brokenhearted after I threw you out that I started popping pills!"

Put that way, it did sound ludicrous. Had Duke Perry slipped her a Mickey?

"These pills aren't even mine, McSween."

He frowned, hoping she was telling the truth. She headed toward her suitcase and shoved both bottles into a zippered side pocket. He would look at them again later.

"I'm sorry, but I need to ask you a few questions." He winced. *She's my wife, and I sound so professional.* He seated himself at the round table, and Britt sat down across from him. He reached behind himself and grabbed a pencil and some hotel stationery. "Did you give Perry any money?"

She looked at him strangely. "So, we're going to be all business now?"

He shrugged. "I'm just trying to help you find your jewelry."

She sniffed. "Well, I can see you're still married—"

His eyes narrowed. Did she know he hadn't signed their divorce papers?

"To your job," she finished.

Not this old argument again. "You grew up with a cop," he said calmly. "You knew the hours were long and hard when we got married." He glanced toward Romeo who was sleeping peacefully. "Now, please, we're wasting time."

She shrugged, looking unconcerned. "What's a few minutes, when we wasted a whole year of our lives?"

They were staring straight at each other, their eyes never wavering. *Damn it, Britt. Our marriage wasn't wasted time. Tonight proves you still want me, still call my name in the darkness.*

"I never gave him any money," Britt said. "He took off with my credit cards and jewelry. That's it."

"Do you know where he might be headed?"

She shook her head. "No."

"Did you... have real feelings for him, Britt?"

"Is that a necessary question?"

McSween's voice broke. "No."

She glanced downward, as if not wanting to meet his eyes. "I just wanted a baby," she said miserably.

"Then...I guess that's all I need to ask." McSween stood. He walked to the bed and gently eased Romeo into his arms, being careful to carry the baby the way Britt had shown him.

"Where are you going?"

He shrugged. "Downstairs. But the trail looks pretty cold."

"I'm coming with you."

For a long moment, he merely looked at her. Warmth flooded his limbs and he was tempted to put his arms around her, wrapping her in a tight embrace. *What you should do is put her on the very next plane to New York.*

He mustered his most matter-of-fact tone. "Good, you'll need to make a statement to the local authorities."

"ALL WE CAN DO NOW is wait," McSween said when they were in his suite again.

Britt nodded. Police work was ninety-nine-percent waiting, and one-percent pure high-octane action. She'd learned that long ago from her father. "Mind if I open the curtains?"

McSween shook his head. Romeo started wiggling in his arms, and she watched as her ex-husband headed for the refrigerator, fixed a bottle, then returned and sat down in an armchair.

Outside, the sun was peeking over the horizon. Downstairs, the case had ground to a standstill. No one had seen Duke leave. The desk clerk had been in the ladies' room. Britt had described each piece of her missing jewelry to hotel security. Over the phone, she'd relayed the same information to the local police and to airport security.

Now, she wondered how McSween had reacted when she described the engagement and wedding rings he'd given her. Had he been surprised that she was traveling with them? She hadn't had the nerve to glance at him and gauge his response.

And what did he think of her marriage? Downstairs, he'd helped make arrangements for her to annul it in the morning, but his expression had remained professional, a mask of calculated competence. Nothing seemed to get a rise out of the man.

Maybe he thought she felt used. What she really felt was relief. A year ago, after their last fight, she'd fled to a Connecticut spa. She'd told herself she would meet a new man—one who believed in lasting commitments and families. She had, too. There had been men everywhere—reclining in mud baths with cucumber slices resting on their closed eyelids. And not a one of them could hold a candle to McSween.

Then recently, she'd met Duke. Oh, she'd known he was too aggressive, too quick to wine and dine her. But he'd seemed to want a baby.

What he wanted was my jewelry. And face it, Britt, you want McSween to help you find it. Like a knight in shining armor, Sean McSween had magically appeared at her side again—literally so close, she could feel the heat emanating from his skin.

Not that he was supporting her emotionally. McSween would find Duke, but only because he wanted his promotion to full detective. *So, be careful. He doesn't love you. Maybe he never did—or at least, not the way you loved him.*

He could sure drive her to distraction, though. When he entered a room, the air got heavy and close. So thick that she was sure she could swim through it. His proximity made her breathless and antsy. Tight-chested and light-headed. Every time she looked at him, she came awfully close to saying what she had said before they married—that she didn't want a family; that a husband alone would be enough for her.

But could she ever say that and honestly mean it?

She turned slowly away from the landscape and surveyed McSween. As her eyes drifted to the baby in his arms, countless questions circled in her tired mind. She shook her head. Rhetorically, she whispered, "What's wrong with you?"

McSween raised an inquiring eyebrow. "Me?"

"Men," she clarified.

McSween shrugged. "Duke Perry's a thief."

Duke had been the last thing on her mind. Britt said nothing, only stared at the baby. That sleepy, wiggling little mass was sure pulling at her heartstrings. McSween was still holding him all wrong, too. The poor child hadn't gotten any proper rest, and heaven only knew what was in that bottle.

She told herself to flee to the relative safety of her own room, which was where she should have gone in the first place. Instead, she crossed the room and leaned over Mc-Sween. "He'll eat better if you tilt him back a bit."

Worry crossed her ex-husband's features. Will the baby suffer long-term effects because of my negligence? his sparkling green eyes seemed to ask.

"It's not that big a deal—" Britt knelt beside the chair and resituated Romeo. As she gingerly moved McSween's elbow and tilted the bottle at a more appropriate angle, a tingle of wariness skated up her arm.

"Thanks," he said gruffly.

Britt bit back a smile. McSween was now seated very stiffly in the chair. It was as if moving even one of his hard, well-honed muscles would destroy the baby's future.

"You can relax a little," Britt said, her voice soft. She stood. "But feeding is really important, you know...."

McSween glanced up, clearly trying hard not to look too interested. "Oh?"

She nodded as she seated herself in the other armchair. "Right now, you're really bonding with the baby." That McSween didn't know that, suddenly tweaked her temper. He had a baby and wasn't even bothering to find out how to raise him.

"Makes sense—" McSween chuckled softly. "He can't talk, but he sure understands food and juice."

Once again, all her questions teased the tip of her tongue. She had to get out of here—away from McSween and his son. They looked so appealing together. The large, strong man and the tiny baby with his half-shut eyes, sucking so contentedly on his bottle. "How old is—er—Romeo?"

McSween shook his head. "I'm not real sure."

Her eyes widened. "What?"

"Yesterday..." McSween glanced through the window and sighed. "Well, day before yesterday, I guess..."

"Yeah?" Britt prompted, feeling sure she wasn't going to like this.

"Romeo was delivered to me by Child Placement." McSween glanced up and his green eyes settled on hers. "I didn't even know he existed, Britt."

She tried not to react, but she must have because McSween quickly said, "Just hear me out."

She gaped at him, listening in horror as he told her how Donya had brought the baby. "What?" she finally said. "Romeo simply came with a note saying, 'I'm your son'?"

"More or less."

McSween continued with the tale and when he was finished, she said, "So, who is the baby's mother?"

McSween sighed. "Britt, I've had very little sleep. And I really don't want to arg—"

Blood started rushing in her ears. *He's not your husband. You have no right to feel jealous.* "Who?"

"I don't know that, either."

Surely he was lying. "Excuse me?"

McSween stared at the floor. Then his gaze fixed on hers again—sharp and steady.

"I thought it might be Kay what's-her-name," Britt managed.

"Before I met you, I went out with a woman named Laurie, too."

Now the blood was zipping through her veins, and her pulse was pounding dangerously fast. The last thing she wanted was for McSween to know she was jealous. She managed a shrug. "Laurie?"

"Laurie McGrath."

Britt realized she was slumping and somehow straightened her shoulders. But no matter how hard she tried, her lips wouldn't quite close. She didn't know which was worse—marrying the Sutton Place Swindler or marrying Sean McSween. "You were sleeping with two women?" she said in a hushed voice.

"Like I told Nate—"

Britt shot out of her chair as if from a cannon. "Nate!"

"He's helping me track down Kay and Laurie."

She'd never felt so humiliated in her life. "Nate knows about this?" Alyssa was one of her best friends. The Simons' seven kids all called her Aunt Britt.

"Don't worry." McSween's voice took on a hard edge. "Nate won't tell your father."

She put her hands on her hips and swallowed hard. "Right now, Daddy's the least of our worries." At the words, she wanted to kick herself. Had she really said "*our worries*"?

Well, she rationalized, marriage did strange things to a person. After she and McSween eloped, they'd taken vows a second time in New York. That day she'd stood at the altar and said "I do" in front of God, her father, the mayor and all the guys at the Thirteenth Precinct. Two times over, Sean McSween had become hers. *Until death us do part.*

He was watching her carefully, not saying a word.

"I hate you," she suddenly whispered, her emotions getting the best of her.

"I used protection," he offered defensively.

"Should I applaud?" she volleyed back.

His jaw set. "I tried my best to be responsible."

"Well, I guess your best wasn't good enough."

McSween glanced down. "But I am being responsible, Britt. Donya handed Romeo to me—and I took him. Now, didn't I?"

Her feelings were so mixed up she wanted to scream. Things were supposed to have been so different—with her and McSween married and having their own kids. And yet she was touched. Once he had a child, McSween had accepted his fatherhood.

She tried to hide her emotions, but her heart was suddenly breaking. *Oh, why couldn't he have been this way a year ago—before it was too late for us? Before our marriage was over?*

Or maybe McSween hadn't really changed. Looking for Duke Perry—a case her father hadn't assigned him—had taken precedence over the baby. "So—" Britt cleared her throat "—when Donya gave you the baby, you just brought him to Hawaii?"

McSween surveyed her, with no apology in his expression. In fact, Britt was fairly sure she saw the hint of a challenge. She hoped not. The man was unnervingly logical. He had reasons for everything he did—and most of them were good.

He shrugged. "I had a plane to catch."

"And what are you going to do with Romeo when Kay or Laurie or whoever shows up?"

McSween lips were thinning. "There's no 'whoever.'"

"What are you going to do with that baby?"

"None of your business, Britt."

She gaped at him. The mother of the child was clearly negligent, and McSween was going to take full custody. Britt was suddenly sure of it. Of course, he didn't want to admit it, least of all to the very woman he'd married—but with whom he'd refused to have a child.

And how could she have doubted it? Britt wondered now. Her husband—ex-husband, she quickly amended—was holding the baby with such sweet tenderness. Yes, McSween's rough exterior hid gentler emotions. Britt had always believed that. The trouble was making McSween believe it.

"Maybe you ought to go get some rest," McSween said levelly.

"You're probably right." But she didn't move. Britt's gaze strayed to the baby's belongings. Strange, but she was feeling wide-awake now. The queasiness and grogginess had passed. Obviously, those had been side effects of the fertility pills. All at once, she felt a strong urge to tell McSween she'd taken them. If he'd accepted another woman's baby after the fact, surely he would accept theirs.

But just thinking about their past fights infuriated Britt all over again. Not two days ago McSween hadn't even known he was a father. What was she supposed to do now? Announce that Romeo probably had a little half brother or sister on the way? Besides, McSween's lack of reaction to her second marriage indicated he no longer had any feelings toward her. "Have you taken him to a doctor or anything?"

"He got into some peat moss this morning, but the doctor said he looked fine." McSween very gingerly removed the bottle and laid the sleeping Romeo across his lap. "He hasn't had a general checkup, if that's what you mean."

But he could have allergies, she thought, or reactions to medications they knew nothing about. "Have you gone through his things?"

McSween sighed. "Britt, basically we just got here." He glanced toward the door. "And I've been . . . pretty busy."

It was nice of him not to remind her that she'd married Duke Perry, so she decided not to mention that the baby should have been more important than bugging her room.

McSween stood. "I'd better put him in the playpen."

Britt suddenly squinted and rose from her armchair.

"What?" McSween asked.

Gently, she pried open Romeo's mouth and touched his gums. "He looked too old for a bottle," she murmured. "He's teething. He shouldn't be on the—"

"The bottles came with him," McSween protested, his eyebrows knitting with concern.

She sighed. "Well, tomorrow we'd better see if he can drink from a cup. This is just terrible for his mouth development." Seeing McSween grimace, she almost wanted to take back the words.

McSween headed toward the adjoining room. "I guess that's why he's been chewing on his fingers."

"You helped raise your four sisters—" Britt followed him toward the playpen. "I'd think you would have known—"

"They were already in grade school when Dad died." He glanced over his shoulder. "Following me?"

"Just because you're beneath contempt," she retorted, as she picked up the first of the totes, "is no reason to penalize a baby." She paused. "While you're in there, you'd better put the side bars up as high as they'll go. I'll start going through his things."

She could feel McSween pause in the doorway between the two rooms of the suite. Ignoring him, she began rummaging through the baby clothes. Strange, but the prints on all the fabrics seemed to suggest motion, as if Baby Romeo were headed somewhere else. There were tops with planes, trains, bicycles, and tiny cars.

"Britt?"

She glanced up. He was empty-handed, so apparently Romeo was down for the night. "Hmm?"

"You don't need . . ."

To help me, she finished.

She surveyed him. In spite of what he'd just said, the relief in his gaze was obvious. Sean McSween didn't know the first thing about babies. She would wager the last day or so of his life had been nothing less than pure hell.

"For all you know," she said, "the missing papers that Donya didn't have might be in these bags."

But they weren't. "If you want, I'll pick up some outfits for him tomorrow," Britt finally said. "He's only got eight or so and most are dirty. He needs a teething ring, too. More diapers."

"I thought you didn't want anything to do with him."

"I didn't say I was going to like it," Britt returned quickly. "But he needs things. . . ."

"I could go with you," McSween said softly.

Could she bear to shop for baby things with her ex-husband? Or was it just too close to the core of the problems that lay between them?

Already, she was entertaining dangerous fantasies. She would get to know Romeo—and she and McSween would get back together. Then she'd tell him she was probably pregnant. This time, he would want the baby.

Who am I kidding? She shook her head, completely lost in thought. "I can't believe I married him," she murmured.

"I can't believe it, either," McSween agreed.

"Oh, McSween," she said on a sigh. "I was talking about you."

Chapter Five

"I found Laurie."

For an instant, McSween didn't even register the name. Then he clutched the receiver more tightly, his heart pounding. Romeo's mother had surfaced. "Nate?"

"Shoot," Nate said in a hushed tone. "The D.A.'s coming."

McSween's lips parted in protest, but it was too late. Nate put him on hold. Listening to the Muzak, McSween stepped over a rattle on the floor, then sat on the edge of the bed and waited.

A week had passed with no news. Duke Perry had vanished without a trace and Judge Elliot, who'd given Romeo to Donya, was still vacationing at an undisclosed location. The judge's assistant was trying to find him, and there had been no leads on Kay and Laurie until now. McSween glanced at the clock. He wasn't meeting Britt and Romeo on the beach for another twenty minutes, so he still had time.

"Nate found Laurie," he murmured. That meant he might be relinquishing Romeo to his mother today—if Laurie *was* the baby's mother. "So why don't I feel relieved?"

Because you're getting attached to the kid. And even worse, you're getting reattached to your wife. Besides, what kind of parenting had Romeo received until now? Didn't McSween owe it to the kid to make sure he was well taken care of?

He glanced around again. Evidence of Britt was everywhere. New toys she'd bought were messily strewn around the room. Plastic cups depicting various Disney characters were stacked on a counter, and brightly colored removable plastic bumpers had been snapped onto the sharp-edged corners of the hotel furniture.

When McSween caught his reflection in the dresser mirror, he could only shake his head. He was barefoot, barechested, and wearing new olive swim trunks. His city pallor had been replaced by a bronze South Pacific tan that rivaled Britt's.

All week, he should have been tracking down Laurie, Kay and the Swindler—making phone calls and establishing relationships with the local authorities. Instead, he'd let Britt and Romeo drag him to island hot spots, including a touristy hula show that he'd enjoyed far more than he would ever admit.

McSween sighed, thinking that no matter where they'd gone, the excursions all led straight to hell. Britt's surreptitious touches and glances put him in agony. Once or twice he'd nearly kissed her. The old fights kept flaring up, too. He worked too hard. She was too much of a Daddy's girl. And there were new battles, mostly about Romeo and his mother.

"I've got to get out of here," McSween muttered. But he also had to bide his time until a lead on the Swindler turned up. Another search of Britt's room had rendered no clues as to where the man was headed. The pill bottles were no longer in the zippered pocket of her suitcase, either.

Well, as soon as he got a lead, he was out of here. Since Britt had a vested interest in getting her jewelry back, she'd said she would help him find Duke Perry by watching Romeo. But why was it that the kid could make her happy in a way McSween himself never could?

Not that he would ever forgive her. She'd sworn she didn't want children—only to change her tune after they'd tied the knot. Romeo might be a factor in McSween's life now, but that hardly meant he was any closer to planning a family with Britt. Not after the way she'd manipulated him during their marriage. No, as soon as he got back to New York, he was going to quietly finalize the divorce.

McSween shifted uneasily on the bed. If Laurie was Romeo's mother, how was he going to tell Britt that the baby was being returned to her? Obviously, Britt realized he was angry about the kid winding up in Child Placement. Now, she thought he wanted to take full responsibility for the baby. Her estimation of him had risen because of it and he hadn't bothered to correct her.

The phone clicked back on.

"McSween, you still there?"

"Yeah."

"Sorry," Nate said, "but the D.A. stormed in here. Then the chief buzzed the other line. He's looking for Britt. I don't know what to tell him."

McSween winced. "Just don't tell him she's here with me. Or that she married Duke Perry."

"He knows you're both in Hawaii," Nate said. "He called the airlines."

I can't worry about the chief now. In his mind's eye, McSween saw himself hand Romeo and his little dragon to Laurie—for the last time. "Laurie," he reminded. "You found her?"

"She says she's not Romeo's mother. Her benefits package offers maternity leave, which she's never taken, and her co-workers swear she was never pregnant. We found her at

Mercy Hospital. If you want to call her, here's the number."

"Not his . . ." *Laurie's not his mother.* The thought came with a bone-deep relief McSween wasn't about to examine. "She's in a hospital?"

"That's why her apartment's vacant. She had a sailing accident off Martha's Vineyard."

McSween hadn't even known she sailed. "Is she all right?"

"Broken leg."

The news sank in while McSween rummaged in the bedside-table drawer. He found a sheet of hotel stationery with palm trees gracing the border. The paper was far brighter than his mood.

"I know Laurie wouldn't lie," McSween said as he situated the paper on his knee, then took down the phone number Nate dictated. "So, Kay's his mother," he mused. But Kay was fair, whereas Laurie, with her brown hair and eyes, looked more like the baby.

"We'll find Kay," Nate said. "According to what we've got, she's between places—moving up by Columbia."

"The country," McSween said, "or the university?"

"The university. She's just moving uptown."

"Well, I owe you."

Since co-workers had corroborated Laurie's story, McSween decided not to call her. Instead, he found himself staring at the blinking recording device next to the phone. All week, he'd been ignoring the tapes he'd made of Britt and the Swindler.

What kind of detective are you? he wondered now. For all he knew, the tapes contained Duke Perry's home address. Was he merely going to sit here, hoping the Swindler would make a mistake and reveal himself? And all because the latest victim happened to be his own wife?

McSween rewound the tapes—both the one that had monitored Britt's room and the one that had monitored her phone. Then, simultaneously, he hit Play on both machines.

Oh, yes, my love, we're going to have a wonderful family.

Oh, Duke...

God only knew what the two had said to each other before McSween turned on the recorders. He crossed his arms, glared at the whirring tapes, and reminded himself that he'd visited shocking crime scenes without flinching. Disassociating himself from his own emotions was something he had down to a science. Still, listening to the replay was making him feel vaguely queasy.

McSween—he—he never wanted babies with me, you know.... I just knew it would never work with him.... He never loved me. I mean, he said he loved me, but emotionally... Emotionally, he was such a liar.

"Here it comes," he muttered when the annoying dialogue ended. He gritted his teeth, waiting to hear Britt's sweet whispers and ragged cries.

Snoring?

McSween leaned forward and stared at the winding tapes. Sure enough, Britt was softly sawing a log.

The only whispers he heard were of fabric. Duke Perry dressed quietly and stepped into his street shoes. On the tape connected to the telephone, Perry punched in a number. McSween strained, but he couldn't discern what number had been dialed from the touch-tone sounds.

"She's out like a light," Perry said when a woman picked up. "I'll just take whatever's of value and then bolt."

"I'll see you at the cape, then?"

"Soon, darling."

When Perry replaced the receiver, McSween felt a weight lift from his shoulders. Quickly, he assured himself it had nothing to do with the fact that Britt hadn't made love to the man. He was simply glad he'd found a clue.

"The cape." Surely, Perry was referring to Cape Halawa on Molokai Island. McSween could leave in the morning.

He just wished Kay was as easy to find—and that Britt wasn't so hard to forget.

BRITT GLANCED FROM beneath the shade of a huge beach umbrella where she and Romeo had been building a sandcastle, and she waved at McSween. "Hey, there!"

Hearing the telltale leap in her own voice, Britt felt color flood her cheeks. No matter how hard she tried, she couldn't control her body's traitorous responses to her ex-husband. As his discerning eyes drifted over her bikini, her heart fluttered and she inadvertently sucked in her tummy.

"Hey, there, yourself."

Even the gruff, manly rumble of McSween's voice still got to her. She imagined nestling her cheek against his bare chest, just the way she used to, so she could feel the vibrations when he talked.

"I've got to go to Molokai in the morning." He squinted against the sun, his eyes two intriguing slits of green. "I got a lead on Perry."

Don't leave me now—not when we're getting to know each other again. Not when I want to tell you I'm almost certainly pregnant. Britt cleared her throat. "Well, that's just great."

Romeo started rooting around in the oversize straw bag Britt had brought outside, so she turned him around and sent him crawling in the opposite direction. The baby really was adorable, she thought. Tiny sailboats were printed all over his powder-blue trunks, and they twitched as he headed toward the sandcastle. When she glanced up again, Mc-Sween flashed her a quick smile.

"Aren't you going to miss me?" he asked.

More than I'd ever admit. Britt managed to roll her eyes. "My heart's breaking into a thousand teensy pieces."

For a moment, McSween merely stood there watching her. The sun was in his eyes. Sand had blown against his bronzed skin, making it sparkle. He was barefoot, wearing only swim trunks, and a rolled towel was wedged under his arm. His body looked harder than granite. Each inch of him said he was in a hair-trigger profession where one less muscle could make a life-and-death difference.

Suddenly, Britt's eyes narrowed. Was there more to why he was leaving? His stance made him seem guarded, like he was hiding something from her. Or was that because *she* was keeping secrets? Should she mention her possible pregnancy before he left for Molokai? To do so would be strange. What were they to each other now—ex-lovers... sort-of friends? Feeling self-conscious, Britt leaned over Romeo, filled his red plastic bucket with damp sand and placed a tiny shovel in his hand.

McSween's towel made a snapping sound as he unrolled it next to her. "Figured I'd leave on the first flight tomorrow. It's at six in the morning."

Just as she nodded, Romeo dropped his shovel, grabbed a fistful of her bikini top and tugged. She quickly disengaged the baby's hand and covered herself, but she could feel McSween's eyes flitting over the space Romeo's hand had vacated. "Romeo and I will be fine here," she managed to say.

McSween lay on his towel and rolled toward her, propping himself up on an elbow. "You really think you can get along without me?"

She shrugged, wishing it wasn't so easy to fall back into their old, flirtatious patterns. "Hard to tell. You know how I thrive when there's someone aggravating around."

McSween wiggled his eyebrows. "So, I aggravate you, do I?"

He might as well have said *arouse*. "You don't bother me in the least," she assured.

But he did. Miles of sandy beach and infinite ocean lay in front of them. And yet, beneath the giant umbrella, Britt felt positively cramped. That McSween wasn't really the talkative type hardly helped matters.

She drew in a sharp breath. "Look," she found herself saying. "Just because we used to be married and we've now found ourselves kind of flung together..."

McSween's lazy gaze drifted over her again.

Her mouth went dry and she swallowed hard. "Oh, never mind."

He merely shrugged. Lying in the sun today had left her feeling warm and languid, but the way McSween gazed out to sea through those dreamy green eyes sent a searing heat to the farthest reaches of her extremities. Why hadn't their year together made his physical presence more familiar and easier to ignore?

Instead, her body had sprouted special memory tentacles during their marriage. Now, when McSween so much as sat next to her, all those tentacles started waving like crazy. He wasn't touching her now...but she could still feel his silken hand on her thigh, his wet mouth covering hers, and the slight quiver of his taut belly as she arched against him.

Everything seemed to have come to a standstill, she realized. The air had stopped circulating. Romeo's baby gurgles had ceased. McSween's body was utterly still. Her eyes trailed from his pectorals, over the unruly dark hairs that arrowed toward his trunks.

Well, she definitely didn't want a life with McSween. She'd been over it a thousand times in her mind. It was just too bad her body wouldn't listen. A week ago, his lovemaking had made her feel like Snow White being kissed awake by the Prince, but there was more to love than physical passion. *Kids, a family, real lifelong commitments.*

Suddenly, everything started moving again. McSween casually raked his fingers through his hair, his biceps bulging as if he'd picked up a barbell. Romeo giggled and crawled toward him. Britt reached for her soda to quench her thirst.

When Romeo grabbed McSween's calves and pulled himself to a standing position, she said, "He'll be walking soon."

"You think so?"

"That's why he's doing those pull-ups." Even as she mentioned it, Romeo took a tiny, shaky step. His chubby thighs quivered as he inched along McSween's leg. As soon as the baby let go, he plopped onto his behind, then grinned right at McSween.

McSween chuckled. "Good going, kid."

Britt tried to fight it, but her insides turned as warm and runny as syrup over hotcakes. *I knew he'd like kids. Now that he's got Romeo, maybe he'll be glad I'm pregnant.*

McSween nodded toward the sandcastle. "Looks like Romeo's one hell of an architect."

"I've done most of the work," she admitted. The castle covered a four-foot-square area. A wide moat surrounded it and four bridges led across the moat. Attached to the castle were two round, crenellated towers. Britt chuckled softly. "Actually, Romeo keeps knocking down my towers."

McSween grinned. "Destruction can be a creative force."

Britt thought of all the dishes she'd broken during their fights. "Maybe when it comes to sandcastles."

Not when it comes to marriage. The words hung in the air as if she'd spoken them aloud.

McSween sat up abruptly. "Can I borrow your bucket, kid?" Romeo chortled, then picked up two fistfuls of wet sand and dumped them into his pint-size bucket.

"And Britt said you weren't much help," McSween chided as he packed sand tightly inside, then dumped the bucket upside down, creating a new outbuilding. Britt leaned over, took the bucket and began her own additional structure.

For some time, they worked in silence, passing the bucket between them, while Romeo helpfully dusted them both with handfuls of sand. Britt missed moments like this. The silent rhythm of shared tasks. As she sculpted fluted edges on her new tower, her gaze kept returning to McSween.

When he caught her looking, the corners of his mouth curled. He glanced at the tower, then into her eyes again. "What do the castle dwellers do there? Sacrifice the virgins?"

Britt glanced at Romeo. "Please," she teased in a hushed tone. "Not in front of the children."

"Child," McSween corrected.

Britt shrugged and glanced at the tower again. "Maybe I'll live up there, myself."

"So lovesick knights can joust for you below?"

"No men allowed," Britt declared.

"Not even me?"

"Especially not you."

At that, McSween actually belly-laughed. Lord, but she'd almost forgotten the sound. His laugh was as true as a bell. Genuine and resonant, it started in the deepest part of him and warmed her more than the Hawaii sunshine.

Get it through your head, Britt. Nothing's ever going to work between you two. Your marriage was as rocky as a mountain during an avalanche. She shook her head, as if to bring herself back from fantasyland. "Maybe I'll just lock all my ex-husbands in there."

"Please—" McSween laughed even harder "You can't hate me so much that you'd lock me in a room with Duke Perry for eternity."

Her voice caught. "I don't hate you, McSween."

He glanced up sharply.

"I—I just don't love you anymore."

A silence fell. Britt reached for the bucket and shovel and started yet another outbuilding. McSween produced a culvert that rerouted water from the moat to the castle. At one point, Romeo knocked down one of the two crenellated towers.

"You made a boo-boo," Britt said.

Romeo giggled.

And then silence fell again.

"Well . . ." McSween finally said.

She glanced up—and wished with all her heart the man hadn't been born with those eyes. They were as arresting and penetrating as he was compact and controlled. She couldn't force herself to look away.

"Well, what?" she asked.

"What do you think of my latest addition?"

Feeling relieved, she glanced down a walkway between her tower and one of his outbuildings. "Is that so you can visit the damsels in distress?"

"Damsels?" McSween frowned in mock distaste. "You know I can't stand people who don't take care of themselves."

She quirked an eyebrow. "But you save people for a living."

He shrugged as if to say it was no big deal. "Actually, I'm putting my master bedroom over here."

Suddenly it all seemed to be too much. McSween's son was crawling onto her lap again, and McSween himself was building a bedroom in her castle. Even worse, she kept catching a certain evasive expression in his eyes that said he was keeping a secret from her. What could it be? Her gaze darted toward the shoreline, as if seeking something—an answer or an escape. "Nice view of the ocean," she managed. "Still, you'd have more space . . ."

Her voice trailed off. She and McSween had had this same conversation before. But last time space versus view was an issue, they'd been talking about their apartment. And they'd been in bed.

"I'm more of a view man."

When McSween's eyes landed on her bikini, there was no doubt that the double entendre was intentional.

Britt gulped. "That's exactly what you said two years ago."

He whistled. "Now that was a fight."

She sighed. "It sure was." And yet two years seemed as long ago as the era of knights and damsels and castles. Britt started to say it was a shame they'd wound up sharing her co-op, but she managed to refrain. McSween had wanted to buy their own place, but given Manhattan prices, sharing her apartment had been the logical thing to do.

"Well—" Britt nodded toward the sandcastle "—I think your view's very nice."

McSween was watching her, an odd expression on his face. "It's just a sandcastle, Britt."

Not a real place where we're living together.

Why did everything seem to lead right back to the problems of their marriage? Lord knew, neither she nor McSween wanted to rehash or solve them. Their failed life together was behind them. A phantom, a castle in the air.

Britt reached for Romeo and her hand slid around his back. "I know it's just a sandcastle, McSween."

This time, she didn't even care that her voice sounded wistful.

McSWEEN SQUINTED AT Britt. "Sure we got everything?"

Glancing at the tote he was carrying, Britt tugged the tails of her white, shirt-style cover-up around herself. She nodded as she lifted her oversize straw bag. "Yep."

Leaving the beach, McSween peered toward the hotel in the distance, then settled Romeo on his hip and draped his arm casually around Britt. He'd forgotten how perfectly his palm cupped her shoulder. "You mind?"

After a long moment, Britt shook her head. "No."

He nodded, knowing he had to tell her that Nate had found Laurie, and that Kay was definitely Romeo's mother. He wasn't even sure why he was hesitating. *Because it will ruin the illusion you've been fostering all week—that the three of you are a family, just the way Britt wants.*

Inadvertently, his grip tightened on her shoulder. By rights, he should tell her they were still married, too. Not that he would.

"The McSweens?" someone shouted.

He frowned. He and Britt weren't really the McSweens anymore and he knew no one in the islands. He stared in the direction of the voice, thinking the accent sounded faintly Asian. When his gaze landed on a row of artist's stalls in the distance, he realized a woman was waving. "Lina Itami," he suddenly said. "Don't you remember her from—"

"Of course!" Britt interjected quickly, before he could say *our honeymoon*. "She must have moved from Maui."

"I wonder if she's still painting," McSween said.

"I hope so."

He did, too. Lina supported herself by drawing portraits of tourists, but she was also a watercolorist. In Maui, McSween had bought a large painting from her. He started to ask Britt if it was still hanging above the mantel in the living room, but then he thought better of it.

Lina hadn't changed, he decided as they neared. She was an elderly Japanese-American woman, with a petite, compact body and dark, razor-sharp eyes. Silver threaded through the strands of her once-black hair, and she wore a no-nonsense bob, cut right to the line of her firm jaw.

"Lina!" Britt called.

Lina waved. "Hello!"

As soon as they reached her, Britt shook her hand, and the two women began to talk as if they were the oldest of friends. Britt really was amazing with people. Where he'd always been described as the strong silent type, Britt could sidle up to complete strangers and chat all day long.

"Girl talk," McSween explained to Romeo.

Romeo's eyes widened. He reached up and grabbed a fistful of McSween's cheek. Tilting his head, McSween shot Romeo a quick smile, then stuck out his tongue and licked the kid's nose. That sent Romeo into gales of laughter. *What is it about having a kid around that makes me feel like a kid again, myself?*

"Of course we'll have a portrait!" Britt said.

"We'll what?" McSween glanced up, wondering how long he'd been amusing himself with the baby.

"Have a seat," Lina urged.

The next thing McSween knew, he was posing on a bench next to Britt. As Lina positioned Romeo between them, seating the baby on both their laps, McSween tried to ignore the soft, warm pressure of Britt's thigh against his. Physically, he'd never found a woman who was anywhere near so compatible.

McSween's mouth quirked when Lina handed him the little red plastic bucket. "You really expect me to hold this?"

Lina's lips twitched. "I most certainly do." She handed Britt the toy shovel.

"See, Romeo and I don't complain," Britt teased as Lina headed toward her easel and began to work.

McSween shot her a droll glance.

Beachgoers began to pause, glancing back and forth between the arranged group and Lina's portrait. Some were clearly considering having their pictures done next.

"So, you've moved to Oahu?" Britt asked.

"My son's a concierge here now—" Lina wiped her hands on a rag as she looked over a box of pastels. Choosing a piece of chalk, she glanced up and smiled. "At the Aloha Oahu Hotel."

"That's where we're staying!" Britt exclaimed.

McSween shook his head as he listened to the ensuing conversation. He could remember the inventories of crime scenes down to the very last synthetic fiber. But that was about it. After two years, and what had been a relatively casual encounter, Britt still remembered the names of Lina's grandchildren. Not to mention their ages.

"I'll be happy to watch your baby." Lina's dexterous hand rapidly sketched. "If you need a sitter, just call. You two should go out, have some fun."

Beside McSween, Britt made a small choking sound. He shifted uncomfortably. Of course, Lina had misunderstood. She was busy drawing what he knew would be a perfect portrait. *A family portrait.* Self-consciously, McSween glanced toward the gathering crowd. It wasn't exactly the best time to explain their unusual situation to Lina.

Britt, began, "Well, we're not—"

"When a baby comes, new parents never get out," Lina interjected helpfully.

If he wanted to set the record straight, where would he even begin? McSween wondered. He and Britt were still married, but she didn't know it. In fact, she'd married a second man who was a criminal. Meantime, McSween had found out he was a father, but the mother of his child was missing.

Lina frowned. "Could you two please move closer together?"

No. As it was, he and Britt were on top of each other.

"Sure." Britt dutifully squirmed against him on the bench.

Lina smiled as she drew. "So, you've come back for a second honeymoon now that you've had your first baby?"

Britt murmured in a way that could have meant just about anything. When McSween managed to catch her gaze over the top of Romeo's head, she even smiled apologetically. It left McSween wondering how he'd managed to bear precinct parties without her over the past year. Smoothing over socially awkward moments had always come so easily to Britt.

"Please, don't move," Lina reminded.

McSween righted his posture. But his eyes trailed from Britt's face to her sexy cover-up. Beneath it, her bikini top didn't leave much to the imagination. Especially now that he was seated next to her and looking down. It was depressing. That body used to belong to him—it had been his to touch, to undress....

Lina sighed with satisfaction. "You two look so good together," she said moments later, as she disengaged the heavy drawing paper from the easel. She turned to Britt. "Your husband's got the dark hair and light eyes. You've got the light hair and dark eyes. Complementary opposites. Romeo's got a bit of you both. It's a sure sign you'll stay married forever."

"Well, actually we're . . ." Britt's voice trailed off.

"Done!" Lina pronounced and held out the picture.

Britt rose, brushing McSween's entire side as she moved. He hoisted Romeo onto his shoulder and followed Britt.

When he reached Lina, she told them, "Seriously, you two call me. I'm on the tenth floor of the hotel, and I'd be happy to watch the baby."

"We will," McSween lied as she handed him the picture.

All at once, he realized tourists were looking over his shoulder. So was Britt.

"What a lovely family memento!" a woman said.

Was it ever. One glance seemed to tell it all—the happy couple's long hot day at the beach with their firstborn son. An adorably chubby Romeo grinned at Mom and Dad, as he reached between them, touching the bucket and shovel. Britt's chin was tilted downward, and she smiled lovingly at Romeo. McSween's gaze seemed to encompass both mother and child, and no man had ever looked more paternal or more proud.

"A lovely family memento." Britt's effort to sound snide failed utterly.

And staring down at their family—at the family that could have been, but that never was—McSween suddenly, inexplicably, felt his heart break.

Chapter Six

Why are you staring at me like that, my dear Mr. Scaly? Oh, I bet you're scared inside this big glassed-in, high-rise elevator. Or maybe that fancy pine-scented water the big guy slapped on his cheeks is still tickling your sniffer. It sure gave me a case of the a-choo's.

What?

Ah, so that's why you're staring!

Well, let me tell you, this outfit did not exactly get my vote. If Dad had just quit primping and put me down on my crawlers, I would've scouted around and found some clues as to the whereabouts of my race-car pj's. But the big guy shimmied me into this stiff white shirt and fancy new gray shorts suit before I could say "no way, José." Then he skewered me with the clip-on, polka-dot bow tie.

Do you think the outfit means he wants me to be a banker when I grow up? You know, so I can support him during his latter-day infirmities? Well, I hate to be a disappointment so early on, but I've got plenty of problems to solve before we talk long-term career planning. Besides, I think I'd make a great detective. Especially if I got to wear a trench coat and a fedora.

'Course, the ladies do seem impressed by my more formal attire. Britt keeps straightening my bow tie. And when

*we saw the nice old dark-haired woman who drew our pic-
ture today, she smooched me right on my head. You woulda
thought we'd known each other for years.*

*Hmm. Well, maybe you're right. Romeo's the kind of
name a little guy's got to live up to, and I do fancy myself
something of a ladies' man. Still, just thinking about this
silly bow tie makes me want to cry. And speaking as a baby,
I can only say I'm powerless to stop myself.*

*Hey, maybe I can just... Hang ten, Mr. Scaly! By the day,
my finger feelers are getting easier to control, and I just
managed to tug off the bow tie! Now, Dad's accidentally
stepping on it, and Britt doesn't notice a thing!*

*No, they're too busy gazing into each other's winkers.
And now that I'm rid of the bow tie, I feel a hundred per-
cent like my old self. I'm ready to move on to our dinner
investigations—distinguishing yummy foods from yucky
ones.*

*Hey, maybe I'll even give the big guy a boost. You know,
do a little matchmaking. C'mon, Mr. Scaly. I'll lean away
away from Dad, then grab a fistful of Britt's dress and pull
her next to him! See, she's walking right into my open
arms—and snuggling up to the big guy in the process.*

*Boy, look at the way he's smiling down at us, Mr. Scaly.
I bet he's wondering how he ever managed before we came
along.*

"Romeo, Romeo! wherefore art thou Romeo?" Britt
chuckled, took a sip of her after-dinner coffee, then leaned
close to the high chair and playfully pinched Romeo's belly.
"So much for his clean suit."

McSween glanced around the hotel's ground-floor restaurant, then looked at Romeo and shook his head. Fistfuls of food had eluded his son's bib and landed on the new

white shirt. "The more I get to know the kid, the more I think he really might be mine."

Britt's eyes drifted slowly over McSween's chest. "I don't recall your shirtfronts ever getting quite this messy."

"I'm still as neat as a pin," McSween admitted.

Britt nodded, as if to say some things never changed. "Well, the papers Donya showed you proved you're his father. Right?"

"Yeah . . ." Should he tell her about Nate's call now? He didn't want to break the mood of the romantic evening. Besides, he wasn't sure how to read her occasional guilty flushes. If he didn't know better, he would think *she* was hiding something from *him.* "A piece of paper never makes anything really feel real," he finally said.

Britt flashed him a quick smile. "I guess not."

Unbidden, he thought of the divorce papers he'd never signed.

"You know," she said, her voice gentling. "You should quit calling Romeo 'the kid.' When he's older, he might think it's your way of putting a distance between the two of you."

That's exactly what I'm doing. If McSween wasn't careful, he was going to wind up with a playpen in his apartment in Queens. He sighed. Sometimes he thought that when men got in line for their Y chromosomes, they missed getting some significant strand of commitment DNA. At least, he had. A wife was one thing—but a family?

Feeling more uncomfortable than he had in a year, he casually sipped his coffee and glanced around the restaurant again. It was called the Palm Room. Candlelit tables were arranged in a peripheral circle and revolved slowly around a stationary central dance floor where couples danced to spicy island tunes. Most were honeymooners, he decided.

They were completely captivated by their partners. *The way you and Britt used to be.*

"You're so much like Daddy."

The last person McSween wanted to discuss was his cantankerous father-in-law. "I doubt it," he said dryly.

Britt smirked knowingly. "You both always sit so you're facing the door, and your eyes constantly scan the room."

At that, McSween had to chuckle. Sure enough, he'd angled his body so he faced both the doors—the one to the lobby and the one that led onto the beach. He unbuttoned the jacket of his tan summer suit, leaned back in his chair and ran a contemplative thumb beneath a chocolate-colored suspender.

"Great sunset," Britt observed.

I'd almost forgotten how easy you are to be with. McSween wanted to say the words aloud, but he nodded instead. Outside, the colors of the sky were vivid and ragged, like strips of torn construction paper. Surfers caught the high evening waves, their brightly colored boards flipping wildly in the air when they capsized. McSween's gaze landed on his son again.

"Isn't he about the cutest kid you've ever seen?" he couldn't help but ask.

Britt's coffee cup clinked pleasantly against the saucer as she replaced it. "Don't you think you might be a little biased?"

McSween raised an eyebrow. "Because I'm his dad?" Even as he said it, the words felt strange in his mouth. *I'm really this kid's father.*

She nodded.

"I'm completely objective," he assured with a teasing smile. "A cop's got to learn to disassociate himself." At the words, Britt tensed and glanced toward the window—and McSween could have kicked himself.

Britt had once said that he was like a faucet—running hot, then cold; turning on his feelings, and just as surely turning them off. She'd said he didn't want to make a baby because loving it might interfere with his tidy emotional world.

Hell, maybe she was right. After only a week, it was hard to imagine not having Romeo to cuddle with. And for McSween, it was even harder to fight the fear of loss that always came with loving. A quick scene flashed through his mind where he was handing Romeo over to the blond-haired, blue-eyed Kay Wilcox. He watched as Britt lifted the kid's toy dragon from an empty chair. She sang a few off-key bars of "Puff The Magic Dragon." Romeo stared back at her, utterly entranced.

Britt chuckled. "Well, he liked our fruit salads."

McSween glanced over the messy table. The bartender had personally delivered Romeo's juice, which had been fixed like Britt's mai tai, with a decorative umbrella and floating pineapple.

Catching his eye, Britt said, "And he loved his drink."

Romeo had accepted it as if it were the keys to his first car, and he'd drunk from the cup without spilling a drop. Of course, the vegetables hadn't gone over quite as well, and the kid had been in such a rush to taste the chocolate mousse that his new clothes had been destroyed. McSween's gaze drifted from Romeo to Britt. She'd pulled her short honey hair upward and soft tendrils curled around her face.

Her eyes narrowed. "What?"

I married the most beautiful woman in the world. "Nothing."

"McSween," she warned. She leaned farther forward, with her head tilted and eyes narrowed, as if he were a cryptogram she meant to decode.

He shrugged. "There's always some part of what you're wearing that I just can't figure out."

"Such as?" Britt lifted Romeo from the high chair and into her lap, and the baby curled sleepily against her shoulder.

"How do you get your hair to twist around like that?"

Britt arched one of her delicately shaped eyebrows. "Pins?"

He shot her a droll look.

"And I thought you were a detective," she chided.

"Assistant detective," he retorted.

Damn. He wished he hadn't said that, too. They'd had such a good time tonight—flirting, playing with the baby. It wasn't really her fault her father hadn't promoted him. "Sorry," he murmured.

She busied herself rocking the baby. "No big deal."

But marrying the boss's daughter hadn't been easy. McSween had offered to transfer back to the Sixth Precinct, of course. Instead of giving the go-ahead, Chief Buchanan had thrown a tantrum. He'd said that if a man wasn't good enough for the Thirteenth Precinct, then he certainly wasn't good enough for Britt.

McSween forced himself to smile. "I don't know how you make that dress stay on, either." It was strapless and nearly backless. By rights, the black confection should have fallen off when she'd leaned forward.

Britt gave Romeo a quick kiss on the forehead, then she glanced at McSween. "Gravity?"

"Well, what comes up—" he tilted his head and grinned "—must come down."

She shot him a long, penetrating look. "Not on your life."

His shoulders started to shake with laughter. "But it's a natural law," he protested.

"Not when it comes to my dresses, McSween."

I miss this, he thought. *Light banter. Relaxing after dinner. She's my wife. And I want her back in my life where she belongs.*

Britt frowned. "I just wonder what happened to Romie's little bow tie."

Romie? Uneasiness swept over McSween. They were talking about Romeo so easily that he could have been theirs. "I know he had it on when we left my room."

The waiter appeared and cleared their dessert dishes. When he whisked a crumber over the table, McSween glanced sympathetically over the cloth, which was strewn with bread crumbs, fruit chunks and cracker wrappers. "Sorry," he murmured. "Maybe we should've brought our own shovel."

The waiter glanced at Romeo, then smiled in merriment. He shrugged. "Kids."

"Kids," McSween echoed, as if that said it all.

The waiter moved on. Outside, night was falling. In the soft twilight, McSween, Romeo and Britt were perfectly reflected in the window glass. For the second time that day, McSween noticed the familial scene they created. *Isn't this how it should be? Man...woman...and child?* "There's Lina and her son," he said, when he caught their reflection.

Supporting Romeo with one hand, Britt craned around. She waved just as Lina's son headed for the restaurant's kitchen.

"So we meet again!" Lina arrived at their table, placed her hand on the back of the high chair, then glanced from Britt to McSween. When her gaze settled on Romeo, she smiled. Cradled in Britt's arms, the baby's heavy-lidded eyes were closing. "He looks so much like you, Britt," Lina mused.

Without looking, McSween knew Britt was composing her features into a blank expression. If he did look, he knew he would still see the hurt in her warm, brown eyes. "Mind watching Romeo while Britt and I dance?" he asked quickly.

"I'd love to." Lina shook her head. "Oh, Britt, he really does have your eyes."

"Lina," Britt began in a strangled, barely audible tone. "Romeo's not really—"

"And the nose!" Lina exclaimed. "Well, you two go dance."

"I'm fine right here," Britt said levelly.

"One dance probably won't kill you," McSween said.

"Probably not," she returned. "But then it might."

All night he'd imagined touching her. He'd patiently waited, wanting to caress her bare shoulders, draw her close and dance cheek-to-cheek. Why hadn't he had the common sense to pull Lina aside today and tell her Romeo was his baby by another woman? *Because it seems odd to divulge the information to a casual acquaintance.*

"What about a little walk on the beach, then?" Lina seated herself next to Britt and expertly lifted the baby into her own arms. "Know how to play patty-cake?" she whispered to Romeo.

Romeo squirmed and giggled sleepily. Then he screwed up his face, the dark eyes narrowing as he yawned.

"He's so cute," Lina said.

Too cute. McSween's heart sank. How badly Britt had wanted a baby came back to him all at once—the tearful nights, the screaming fights, the times Britt had come close to begging. Hell, the times she *had* begged. The woman had wanted the whole ball of wax with him. Marriage, babies, the getting-old-together.

And he'd walked away.

He stood abruptly. "Britt—" His voice sounded rusty. "C'mon, let's walk off some dinner."

Her eyes met his in a challenge. Rest assured, he wasn't the only one remembering their fights. "I guess I could use some air," she replied.

"I'm not sure that sounds as promising as a moonlight stroll."

"It's not," she said simply.

As they headed outside and went across the sand toward a boardwalk, McSween inhaled deeply, just feeling the light, salty sea breeze dance across his cheeks. Nearer the shore, blowing palm fronds rippled in silhouette against the night sky. Beside him, Britt slipped off her sandals, let the straps dangle from her fingers and walked barefoot through the sand. Glancing down, he remembered how he used to cup those sleek, slender feet in his hands, his palms curving perfectly to her high-arched insteps, his fingers grasping her delicate ankles.

All at once, his chest constricted. He was merely climbing the steps to the boardwalk, but it could have been a mountain. He felt breathless and the air seemed too thin. Everything seemed so darn quiet. His lips parted—so he could say something, anything.

But he was tired of starting safe conversations—about how cute Romeo was, about where they should eat, about the weather. A knock-down-drag-out fight would be better. At least it might put the past to rest.

She stopped on the boardwalk, leaned casually against the rail and stared out to sea. McSween leaned next to her. He surveyed her profile—the straight nose, the light sandy eyebrows and eyelashes, the dark eyes. *Okay, Britt,* he thought. *I've changed my mind. Let's get back together, and this time, let's start a family.* He wished he could say the words aloud, try them on for size, and then just take them back if they didn't fit.

But he couldn't, of course.

"It's still hot out," he commented gruffly.

"Sure is."

The beach crowd had thinned—there was a lone man with a dog, a woman jogging barefoot along the shoreline. The surfers seemed to have moved on.

"Nate called this afternoon," he finally said.

Britt's head snapped in his direction. "What did he want?"

"He found Laurie." McSween could see the warring emotions in her face. Over the past week, she'd tried to keep herself from becoming attached to Romeo, but she'd failed. Just as he had. He kept his gaze riveted on her face when he said, "She's not his mother."

Britt's dark eyes flashed with emotion, but she shrugged as if the news was of no importance to her. *Which it isn't,* McSween reminded himself. He blew out a sigh, hardly wanting to contemplate reestablishing some kind of relationship with Kay.

"So, Kay gets the mommy prize," Britt said, her tone falsely bright.

McSween stared at her. Before he thought it through, he moved closer, praying his sheer physical strength would convince her to stay reasonable. "It wasn't a contest, Britt."

The challenge in her eyes was as unmistakable as her acid tone. "Oh, wasn't it?"

His eyes roved over the soft feathering of honey hair on her cheeks. "No."

Britt whirled on him so unexpectedly that he merely reacted. Swiftly turning, he clamped his hands on the rail on either side of her. As he backed her against it, one of his legs settled naturally between hers. And when their chests brushed, the summer night became instantly more sultry. He could feel her breath and smell the heady scent of her skin. He imagined steam rising between them in wisps.

"This is the last time I'll say it." He leaned still closer and his hands skimmed the rail until they grazed her slender waist. "I didn't know I'd gotten the woman pregnant."

Britt craned her neck away from him and tossed her head. "So, you call the mother of your child 'the woman,' just like you call Romeo 'the kid.'"

The coolness of her voice didn't mask the aching hurt, but McSween reacted to the temper in her flashing dark eyes. He pinned her with his gaze. "I'll call him whatever I want. He's my son."

Her voice cut the air like a knife. "He's sure not mine."

McSween had about had it. "The way things worked out wasn't intentional."

With utter disdain, Britt glanced down at the hands that pinned her. "You never cared about me."

"I loved you, Britt." *I still love you.* But Britt didn't believe it. To her, love meant ties that truly could never be torn asunder. Love meant a family.

All at once, he became conscious of how she felt against him. How he'd made love to her a week ago came back to him in all its detail—her damp skin making the air thick, her silken hair falling between his fingers, her velvety lips searing his bare back. Now, she was so close he could smell coffee and chocolate, and he could feel the sudden quiver of her thigh against his.

He couldn't live with her.

But he couldn't live without her.

She was staring at him murderously. "I really thought you were considering being a father to that baby."

"Who says I'm not?" Only after the words were out did he realize what he'd said. And that there was no going back. "You've never even bothered to ask what I'm going to do."

"Are you keeping him?"

He threw up his hands, then resettled them on the rail. "I don't even know why Kay left him. Or how he got from her hands into Child Placement."

Britt's knowing smile was so biting that it pierced McSween's skin.

"Maybe I *am* keeping him," McSween found himself saying.

She merely shrugged. "And Nate called this afternoon *before* you came down to meet me on the beach?"

Not once during the past week had he mentioned her relationship with Duke Perry. As far as McSween was concerned, she had some nerve to question his motives. "I don't have to report my incoming calls. And I've hardly asked you to divulge the details of your life."

"The details of my life are an open book!" Britt jabbed his chest with an index finger. "You bugged my room. Remember?"

"I bugged the room of a criminal," he returned coolly.

She merely stared at him as if he were the most contemptible person on the face of the earth. "Is that why you had sex with me, then? To protect me from the clutches—" her eyes grew wide with mock show "—of evil?" She said the word "evil" as if it were the suffix appended to a town's name; as in Amityville or Jacksonville, she pronounced it, *E*-ville.

He hoped there was no trace of relief in his voice. "You didn't sleep with him."

"No, I never did," she said icily. "It was even worse. I slept with you. Or was it the other way around? I mean, I didn't exactly know who you were."

His chuckle carried a warning. "Didn't you, though? I could have sworn I heard you whisper my name."

Even in the darkness, he could see her face coloring. Had she known it was him? He doubted it; she'd been too befuddled afterward. He brought his face so close that their lips nearly touched. "Or were you fantasizing about me?"

She stared stoically at him. "I want to go back inside."

He would move when he was good and ready. On either side of her, his hands tightened around the railing. "In some deep, subconscious part of yourself, you knew who I was." He knew he was right, and his voice became a soft taunt. "I heard you say, 'Sean.'"

Everything in her eyes said it was true.

Not that it mattered. Their physical relationship had always been as right as it was undeniable. With one look, secret channels opened—and desire flowed. But it would never be enough. It wouldn't bring them together, make them want the same things.

"I didn't have a clue as to who you were." Britt's low voice was now trembling with anger. "And the only place you heard me say your name was in your dreams."

Liar. He shrugged, suddenly feeling glad he had to leave tomorrow and yet still wishing he could stay. "Who you sleep with on your own time is your business."

A strangled sound escaped from between her lips. "Oh, Officer McSween . . . was I sleeping with the bad guy on the Thirteenth Precinct's time clock? Should I have punched out?" Britt's choked voice twisted in the air. "Or maybe I should just punch *you* out, McSween."

He just wished they could get along. And that she wasn't quite so close, with nothing between his and her skin but a strapless, backless wisp of a dinner dress. He forced himself to keep his composure. But it was hard. It wasn't so much the way she was taunting him; it would take more than words to unman him. But he was standing so close to her—knowing he should step back, feeling powerless to do so. He tilted his head and angled closer, his lips just a fraction away from her cheek.

"I may not have given you a baby," he said softly, "but I don't deserve to have you goad me."

"You deserve that and worse."

"What about this week—" He damned his voice for catching with hope.

"What about it?"

They'd been spending time together. Getting to know each other again. She knew it. And he knew it. "I don't believe you're only spending time with me because I'll find Duke Perry for you...or because you think I'm incapable of caring for Romeo alone."

Britt's eyes darted toward the shoreline, as if seeking escape. "You think I want us to get back together?"

"Yeah," he whispered.

She said nothing. There was no sound except the surf. After a moment, someone called out to a friend. Closer still, Britt took a sharp breath that might have indicated desire.

It was all McSween wanted to hear. Swiftly, forcefully, urgently, he covered her mouth in a kiss that was like a dangerously spreading wildfire. Combustible, explosive, it burned hard and fast. Again and again, his wet tongue dove between her lips as if to douse the flames...or else further fan the fire.

His large hands encircled her slender waist, then his strong forearms wrapped around her back. Holding her tightly, he forced her close—so close that her back bent over his arm and she arched against him with a soft moan. Waves of white heat rippled through his body, forcing an arousal as swift and uncontrollable as the kiss itself.

And, oh, how she responded. He hadn't known if she would. Maybe he hadn't even cared. But the way she kissed him back was so raw and real that it almost hurt. Her sandals dropped to the walkway and her hands grasped his shoulders. When her fingers clutched at his muscles, springs of heat uncoiled inside his veins.

A moment could have passed...or an hour. "Let's make love," he urged raggedly against her mouth, still drinking her in, still kissing her. When she said nothing, he leaned far enough away to look at her. Her eyes were dreamy and bleary, her lips wet and glistening. Lower, her nipples beaded visibly against her flimsy summer dress. "Please," he whispered.

"No way," she whispered back.

Somehow, he forced himself to lean over and retrieve her sandals. As she took her shoes, their fingers touched, and he could have sworn he actually saw the red-blue static spark that flared in the air between them. "Just a thought," he said huskily.

Her voice was raspy. "Well, you keep thinking."

"I will."

As she turned toward the restaurant, he grasped her hand. Then he crooked his elbow, linked her arm with his, and smoothed her long, slender fingers over his forearm.

He turned toward her. "Britt?"

"Yeah?"

The fight hadn't gone out of her entirely. It was still in her eyes—deep down, past the desire. Maybe it would always be there. Maybe he had really hurt her to the depths of her soul. He'd never meant to do that.

"Right now—" *Right now, you look so lovely.* She seemed to shine in the dark. Distant lights in the night were like fire on her bare shoulders, flickering flames that danced on her skin. "I almost wish we'd never fallen in love—" his voice was gravelly, still rough with desire "—because . . . because then I never would have hurt you, Britt."

"It's okay, McSween."

"No, it's not."

Her voice caught. "I'm not sorry."

Maybe not, but her voice sounded bittersweet, sad. He sighed. "Don't you think we should try again?"

Britt swallowed hard, then a smile flickered over her lips. "Why? Because you just kissed me like gangbusters?"

He chuckled softly. "Well, it's a start."

She smiled again, a faint lopsided smile. Maybe she was thinking what he'd been thinking when he'd kissed her— that the physical aspect of their relationship had never posed a problem. She was watching him carefully. A lock of hair blew across her face with the breeze and he gently brushed it away.

"Between us, there are some truly irreconcilable differences," she said. "So, why would you want to try again?"

Because of moments like this. He sighed. "Well, maybe there's no future in it."

"There's a future, all right." Britt tilted her head and gazed wistfully into his eyes. "The trouble is it's full of us trading barbs and throwing household objects at each other."

"I never threw anything."

"I did," she said without apology.

He smiled ruefully. "You sure did."

She shrugged. "I have a temper."

He shook his head. Their marriage was like a huge onion that could make a man cry if he just looked at it. The hurt was in every layer of skin and went all the way through to the core. It felt as if it would take forever to peel back the thin coverings one by one and get at the truth.

"When did all those crazy fights begin?" he murmured. He'd thought they were merely first-year adjustment spats, but hadn't they really begun after Britt had said she wanted a baby—and he'd refused? Before she could answer, he said, "Britt, do you really think it would have been different if..." His throat tightened. Far in the distance, through the restaurant window, he could see Romeo, a tiny dot in Lina Itami's arms. "If I'd wanted a baby?"

Anger had left Britt's brown eyes by slow degrees, and now they were taking on that velvet, liquid quality. When her eyes looked like that, he could stare into them forever.

She cleared her throat and ran a hand through the silken strands of her hair, pushing them from her face. "Do I think we'd still be married if you'd wanted to make a baby with me? Do I think our commitment to each other could have grown...gone deeper?"

Strange, he thought. As he listened to her rephrase his question, he realized it was the one thing he had never asked her. He nodded. "Yeah."

"The answer is yes, McSween," she said softly. "Yes, I really do."

Chapter Seven

As McSween pushed open the door to her room, Britt cradled Romeo against her chest and murmured, "He's sleeping so soundly."

"Lina said he conked out the second we left."

Britt chuckled softly. "The chocolate mousse must have worn the poor little fellow out."

McSween nodded, then unbuttoned his sports coat so that it draped loosely over his fashionably high-waisted slacks, accentuating his flat abdomen and long legs. Gesturing her across the threshold, he shrugged out of the jacket. When he turned to hang it on the doorknob, Britt took in his broad back—how the chocolate-colored suspenders brightened the crisp whiteness of his shirt and outlined his powerfully rounded shoulders. She knew she never should have let him kiss her on the boardwalk. And then again, she wished he'd never stopped.

McSween caught her gaze. "Well, he's definitely an all-or-nothing kind of guy."

Britt pressed a kiss to Romeo's forehead, thinking he looked like a sleeping cherub. "You'd expect him to be more the cautious type."

McSween leaned casually in the open doorway and shoved his hands deep into his slacks pockets. "Because I am?"

Britt nodded.

"I get shot at for a living, Britt." McSween sent her an amused smile. "How could you possibly call me cautious?"

Emotionally cautious. "Oh, I don't know." She hugged Romeo closer and drew in a quick, quavering breath. She still felt weak-kneed from the way McSween had kissed her.

He reached up and loosened his dark, narrow tie. "It's getting late. I ought to finish moving my things."

But he didn't budge. He continued leaning in the doorway, his deceptively lazy-looking green eyes drifting over her. Britt reminded herself they were doing the practical thing. It was pointless to pay resort prices for McSween's room while he was in Molokai, or for him to take clothes he wasn't going to wear. Besides, if they settled Romeo here tonight, McSween wouldn't need to wake him in the morning. Suddenly feeling uneasy, Brit imagined her and McSween's belongings mingling together—suits and dresses, socks and stockings, suspenders and hair ribbons.

"Let me put Romeo on the bed," she said with a start. "Then I'll give you a hand."

"Don't worry. I'll take care of everything."

As McSween vanished from the doorway, his words remained, tugging at Britt's heart. *I'll take care of everything.* It was the kind of thing the man always said. He was so annoyingly self-contained. He didn't need anyone or anything—including her. But would he ever need Romeo— or the baby she was probably carrying? She seated herself on the edge of the bed and rocked Romeo in her arms.

McSween returned and slid the folded playpen across the threshold. "Do you want it here or in the next room?"

She glanced toward the adjacent room of the suite. "Here, near the bed." *I want the baby right next to me.*

Within moments, he'd set up the playpen and transferred most of his other belongings to her room, including the portrait Lina had drawn, which he propped against the dresser near his camera. When he returned a final time, a garment bag was draped over his arm. He strode toward Britt, laid his bag across the bedspread and unzipped it.

He glanced over his shoulder, toward the dresser. "Mind if I make some room?"

"Not at all." Her eyes slid toward her drawers. One was open and a pair of panties peeked out. Shoes tumbled from the carry-on in the closet floor. "Sorry everything's not neater."

McSween chuckled. "I don't mind."

"Really?"

He shot her a wry glance. "Actually, it's kind of sexy."

She gulped. Her fingers skated across the bedcovers, found the remote and flicked on the television. Trying to look interested in the news, she surreptitiously watched McSween tidily stack his and Romeo's clothes inside an empty drawer. Then he headed for the closet. The hangers grated on the rail as he shoved them back. A moment later, Britt's eyes stung. Seeing his impeccably pressed suits hanging in a neat row next to her rumpled sundresses made the year of their separation seem to drop away.

But it hadn't, she quickly reminded herself. On the boardwalk, he'd kissed her deeply—not just the way a man kissed a woman, but the way a husband kissed a wife. His lips bespoke ownership—a claiming. But they were divorced. And that was just as final.

As if reading her mind, McSween said, "Sure you don't mind my stuff being here?"

"Why should I mind?" she managed to say airily. "And feel free to leave more than just those suits."

"I guess I could leave a couple more shirts."

McSween's voice sounded as rusty as an old nail. He must be feeling as awkward as she. He reached into his bag, then stacked some shirts in the drawer. They were freshly laundered, perfectly starched and still in cardboard.

Britt glanced away. Unfortunately, her gaze landed on the portrait Lina had drawn. The pastel image was so soft and inviting. Romeo's hands stretched between the plastic shovel and pail, and Britt and McSween smiled downward like proud loving parents.

Now, Romeo squirmed lazily in her arms, emitting a soft, contented-baby sigh, and Britt's heart pounded in sudden panic. What were this baby's things doing in her drawers? And why was Sean McSween sliding a pair of his shoes across the floor of her closet? Emotionally, she decided, this was akin to suicide. She cleared her throat. "So, when do you think you'll be back?"

McSween shrugged. "I wish I knew. I'll call you in the evenings."

Was he going to call her every night? It was only natural, she thought. He would want to check on Romeo. Besides, McSween's calls were to be forwarded to her. Nate might find the missing witch. Kay Wilcox, Britt mentally corrected. Romeo's mother. Guiltily, she reminded herself that something bad might have happened to the woman. That was more plausible than thinking Kay had merely abandoned her baby.

McSween tucked fresh sheets into the bottom of the playpen. "What would be the best time to call, Britt?"

Never? "Six, maybe?" Just looking at him, she could still feel those strong forearms holding her tight, and the warm length of his hard body pressing against hers. She should have had better sense than to let him kiss her. This time, she'd been wide-awake. Cognizant enough to stop herself—and yet she hadn't.

He suddenly glanced over his shoulder. Realizing she'd been staring intently at his back, hot color flooded into her cheeks.

He raised an eyebrow in question. "Hmm?"

She shrugged. "Nothing."

But rather than let his kisses tempt her to distraction, she should have let his lips remind her of what he'd said during their marriage. Yes, those lips could have told one sad story, she thought now. The story of how he held the key to everything she had ever wanted—and everything she would never have.

He raised the side bars of the old-fashioned pen. When he checked their sturdiness, the small bars were dwarfed by his hands. She didn't dare think it—but had McSween really meant what he'd said about trying again? Well, she would never have the nerve to ask. If McSween said yes, it would mean making herself vulnerable to him again. And if he said no, then she would have to forget him once and for all.

Maybe if she told him about the fertility pills she'd taken before they'd made love, she could gauge his reaction to her possible pregnancy. "McSween . . ."

"Really, just hang on to him."

You're merely baby-sitting until McSween catches Duke and recovers your jewelry, so don't get involved, Britt. This isn't your baby, and if McSween wants a family now, he'll say so. She watched him stock her small refrigerator, then methodically circle the room, crouching down to fasten childproofing bumpers to the sharp corners of her furniture.

Finally he stood. "Well, that's about it."

Britt rose, crossed the room and held up Romeo, whose eyes opened in sleepy slits. "You'd better kiss him goodbye."

"Oh . . . right."

Why did he hesitate? Was it her imagination or did a frown cross McSween's features?

He gently lifted Romeo from her arms into his own. Tilting his head and leaning close, he whispered, "You gonna miss me, kid?"

Romeo stretched his tiny arms and yawned.

"I know he will," Britt whispered.

"I really appreciate your taking care of him for me."

The words shouldn't have stung, but they did. *See, you really are just a baby-sitter.* But for the past week she'd felt so much like a mother. So many people had assumed Romeo was hers, and she hadn't corrected any of them. Lina included, she thought guiltily. "Watching him's no trouble at all," she managed to say.

"I'd better put him down," McSween said.

But they merely stood there—him cradling Romeo, her standing close. Then McSween leaned and brushed his lips across Romeo's forehead. "Night, baby," he whispered.

Britt swallowed hard as McSween gingerly laid his son in the playpen and nestled the dragon next to him. Abruptly, she turned away and headed for the door. Behind her, she heard him lift his garment bag from the bed. Just as she opened the door, McSween retrieved his jacket from the knob and slipped past her.

He turned in the doorway. "See you when I get back."

"McSween . . ."

His eyes fixed on hers. "Yeah?"

He looked so open and receptive now. Was she really so spineless that she couldn't tell him about the fertility pills? "It . . . it wasn't really your fault." *The way our marriage turned out.*

He lifted his shoulders in what was barely a shrug. "How could you have known what you wanted?"

Britt shook her head. "I always knew I wanted a baby."
I lied to you and I lied to myself.

"But you thought things would be different," he reminded gently. "That you'd quit wanting kids when we got
married."

That was a mere fiction she'd invented. She'd never once
stopped wanting a child. She'd never once made the compromise he thought she had. "I—I thought you'd love me
so much...so much that you'd—"

"Change my mind?"

Why was she saying this? she wondered in panic. Why
couldn't she let their relationship die a graceful death? But
the words came in a sudden rush. "I said I wouldn't want
kids if we got married because I knew I'd lose you if I didn't
say it. I—I thought maybe I'd just get pregnant...and then
you'd have a change of heart and feel ready. I know how
awful it is to lie like that. But I thought if you loved me, really loved—"

His finger touched her lips, silencing her.

"I'm sorry, McSween," she whispered against his finger.
"On my part, it wasn't right."

His touch turned to a caress, then his finger drifted from
her mouth and traced the line of her jaw. "Not on mine, either."

Her voice turned raspy. "What?"

"Oh, Britt," he whispered, the words catching, "I always knew you were lying. I knew we wanted different
things, but I thought I'd get my way. And you know what?"

"What?"

"We have to forgive ourselves."

With that, McSween leaned through the crack in the door
and pressed his lips to hers with a slow, gentle pressure. It
was such a quiet kiss that when he drew away, she almost
wondered if he'd really kissed her at all.

It was hard to tell.

Because then he was gone.

"WAAA! WAAA!"

Where's my daddy? I want my daddy! This isn't even my daddy's room! Me 'n Mr. Scaly just woke up and Daddy's gone! Sure, this place has got the same color walls and carpet, the king-size bed and seaside pictures—but nobody can fool me! It's not the same room. It's a big old trick.

"Waaa! Waaa!"

Come back, Mr. Scaly! Oh, please, oh, please, come back. Doesn't Britt even see? I flung Mr. Scaly on the floor and now he's abandoned me, too.

"Don't worry sweetheart. Shush."

Why won't Britt help me find Mr. Scaly and Daddy? Hey, maybe Britt's getting ready to leave me, too. Oh, I'm sorry I was mean, Britt. Please don't leave me here all alone. I never want to be abandoned again.

"Waaa! Waaa!"

This is just like last time. I don't remember who was s'posed to be taking care of me, but I was left all alone. And it was so dark and so smoky and I was so scared....

Oh, I can't think about that awful time.

"Wa-a-a-a-a!"

Please, come back, Daddy.

I was so sure you liked me 'cause of all the new clothes and toys you got me, and when you smooched me, your green winkers got all sparkly. And 'member how you tossed me high in the air and caught me? Now, wasn't that fun, Daddy?

Guess not.

I knew I shoulda smiled more. Oh, Daddy, if you'll just give me one more chance, I know I can make you like me. If you're mad about that bow tie, I know where it is. And

*if we go to the elevator and get it, I'll put it on. Daddy, I'll
wear it every single day. . . .*

"Now, Romeo, you've got to be brave. Here, let's pick
out a nice new outfit for today. What about your sailor suit?
It's the kind big boys wear."

*Britt's bringing Mr. Scaly! Oh, Mr. Scaly, I promise I'll
never throw you on the floor again. And check out my
clothes drawer! Inside, it smells just like Daddy. Maybe he's
not gone after all. Aren't those his socks, Mr. Scaly?*

"That's right, Romeo, now just calm down."

*She's handing us one of Daddy's socks! It's clean but it
still smells like the big guy. How can I tell Britt I'm sorry for
screaming?*

"Goo-ga."

*Do you think she heard me? Oh, she's so patient and nice
and she rocks me when I cry and even gives me Daddy's
stuff to carry around. Britt understands everything. I sure
hope she's going to be my mommy now.*

*Especially since Daddy's coming back. Whew! I should
have known not to get overly excited. Some guys are just
built so you can rely on them. Like Mr. Scaly or my dad.
And now I know he'll never leave me. Not the big guy.*

"C'MON, BRITT." McSween sighed and seated himself on
the edge of the mattress. While he listened to the ringing
phone, his eyes panned the nondescript bungalow. White
walls, rust carpet, hurricane-proof slatted windows.

Two weeks had passed—and he was no closer to catching
the Swindler. Of course, Nate was having better luck. Judge
Elliot, the man who'd presided over Romeo's case, was on
a fishing trip somewhere in upstate New York, and Kay
Wilcox had left for Oregon three weeks ago.

But McSween's vacation time was nearly spent. And Duke
Perry was still free. Britt would have to return to New York

without her jewelry, which meant telling her father everything eventually. McSween winced. By now, the chief probably knew he and Britt had crossed paths in Hawaii.

"Britt?" he murmured again. Where was she? Every
evening, she picked up on the second or third ring. This was
the tenth or eleventh. His heart suddenly thudded against his
rib cage. Has something happened to her or Romeo?

"Hello?"

McSween sighed in relief. The low tone of Britt's voice
indicated she'd been napping. He imagined her stretching on
the unmade bed at the Aloha Oahu Hotel, her toes pointing and her sleep-tousled hair spreading over a pillow.

"Hmm—" McSween bunched one of his own pillows,
shoved it against the headboard and leaned back, getting
comfortable. "Someone else keeping you busy in my ab-
sence?"

"Yeah."

The husky smokiness of her voice made a warm tingle
spread through his limbs. "Is that right?" McSween
chuckled. "I'm not having much luck finding Duke
Perry...."

"What?" She laughed. "So, you think he came back
here?"

"Well, you said someone's keeping you company."

"Romeo, if you must know."

McSween wedged the receiver more tightly between his
shoulder and ear and smiled. "So how's the kid?"

"Quit calling him that!" she warned.

But this time, she didn't really mean it. *Do you miss me?*
he wanted to say. "C'mon," he said instead. "How's the
little guy?"

"You mean your archrival?" Britt asked.

"Yeah."

"I knew you weren't really calling just to talk to *me*."

"Oh, but I am," he returned.

Britt merely made a humming sound. A moment later, she said, "Say hello to your daddy." Romeo giggled. Against his will, McSween found himself grinning. What was Britt doing to make the poor kid laugh like that? Probably tickling the hell out of him.

After a long moment, Britt said, "Okay. So, can *I* talk now, McSween?"

"Sure." McSween shut his eyes, listening to her catalog her and Romeo's activities for the day. Romeo was still close enough that he could hear sighs and coos and giggles. When she paused, McSween opened his eyes. "Sounds like you've been having fun."

"Oh," Britt said breathlessly, "we have. A huge textiles convention has nearly taken over the hotel. We watched them check in. Then, before we went to the beach this afternoon, Romeo and I went to the Honolulu Zoo and..."

And all at once, as she talked about the zoo, McSween felt his heart wrench. He wasn't even sure exactly why. All he knew was that his throat felt dry and tight and that he was swallowing around a lump.

All the risks McSween had taken in his life flashed through his mind. He saw himself dismantling bombs and chasing men with weapons into abandoned warehouses. But the night he'd left Britt and Romeo, he'd almost wanted to deny the fool kid a kiss goodbye. The baby was just too delicate and fragile—and he posed a greater risk than men with guns ever could. So did Britt. Because both she and the baby threatened McSween's heart.

"McSween?" Britt said suddenly, as if sensing the shift in his attention.

"Hmm?"

"You okay?"

He stared down at where his oxfords were crossed at the ankles. *No, I'm not okay.* "Er...calling you every night reminds me—"

There was a long pause.

"Of married life?" she prompted.

He grimaced. "I really did work a lot, didn't I?"

"No offense," she said, "but yeah."

"Britt...I'm—"

"Don't be sorry, McSween. I never took it personally."

But he knew she had. Hell, she'd been right to. He could almost see himself—night after night, hunched over old files. Chinese takeout littered his desktop; cheap wooden chopsticks protruded from white cartons of half-eaten rice and foil containers of vegetables. He would always dim the lights so he could concentrate while he pored over the old unsolved cases. All the while, Britt had been right around the corner. At home. Where he should have been.

"It really is okay," Britt finally said.

Suddenly he wished they weren't on the phone. He wanted to see her and touch her and smell her. He wanted to hold her tight, wrap her in his arms and maybe even tell her he loved her. He blew out a breath. "So, is Romeo doing more of his pull-ups?"

Britt's laugh sounded a little forced. "Yeah, I hope he waits for you to get back before he takes his first real steps." Speaking to Romeo, she said, "You pulled your stroller right over, didn't you?" To McSween, she continued, "It barely missed his head, but it just scared him."

"Well, I can't wait to see him." *And you, Britt.* Did the woman guess that he would do just about anything for her— to protect her, provide for her? *Everything except love her enough to give her a family, McSween?*

"McSween?"

He cleared his throat. "Yeah, I'm still here."

"Nate found Kay."

It was the last thing he'd expected her to say. For a moment, he felt as if his heart had quit beating. "Where is she?"

"A place called the Visions Retreat in Oregon."

"The Visions Retreat?" he echoed, not liking the sound of it. Had Kay left Romeo to go off and join some kind of cult? If so, McSween would definitely have to take custody of the baby.

"Nate hasn't talked to her yet," Britt continued. "He just knows she's there."

McSween visualized a dark, enclosed compound. Maybe Kay had joined a back-to-the-earth organization that didn't believe in electricity. "Don't they believe in phones?"

"Of course they believe in phones." Britt sounded puzzled. "Kay works for MCI, and she's at a communications conference."

"Oh." Still, this meant Kay had willfully abandoned Romeo and that she didn't deserve to be his mother. *Or am I looking for reasons to prosecute her, so I can gain custody?*

"Nate's left some messages in Oregon," Britt went on, her voice sounding oddly unsteady. "But he didn't want to leave details about why he was calling."

"Well, thanks for letting me know," McSween managed, sounding more stiff than he'd intended.

"No problem."

"Look, Britt, I'll be back tomorrow."

And every night after.

Their very first night together suddenly rushed back to McSween. *I'll be back tomorrow and every night after,* he'd whispered. *I just bet you will,* she'd whispered back. That night, they'd both believed their love would last forever.

Now, Britt said, "Well, I'll see you."

And McSween slowly replaced the receiver in its cradle.

Chapter Eight

Britt felt guilty for having been so moody the previous day, so when the phone rang, she snatched it up, mustered her sexiest voice and said, "Hey there, McSweetheart."

When McSween said nothing, she glanced swiftly over her teddy and squinted at the clock. She and Romeo had napped until three! Surely McSween was calling from the airport, wanting her to come for him in the rental car. She decided she would dress Romeo in the cute new shorts outfit with the airplanes on it.

"Why the silent treatment, McSween?" she purred. "Did my ultrasexy voice render you speechless or what?"

"McSween!"

Britt gripped the phone tightly and bolted upright in bed. "Daddy?"

"Last week, yes," her father boomed. "This week, I've decided to disown you, Brittany."

Romeo chose that inopportune moment to start yawning and squiggling in his playpen. *Oh, Romeo, please, don't cry!* Britt sucked in such a quick, nervous breath that it sizzled between her teeth. "Uh—could you just—er—hold on, Daddy?"

Wedging the phone receiver under her chin, she leaned over the playpen and lifted both Romeo and his little green dragon into her arms. Romeo emitted one long yowl, as if to intentionally alert the chief to his presence, then he chortled softly. He felt a little damp, but there wasn't a darn thing she could do about it now.

"I'm back, Daddy." Feeling unnerved, Britt bunched a pillow against the headboard and leaned back, so both Romeo and the dragon were sprawled on her belly. "The—er—television..."

"Television?" her father echoed derisively. "That's no television. Nate already told me the case involved a baby."

"Case?" Britt queried innocently. Somehow, she had to keep her father talking, so she could find out if he knew about her marriage to Duke Perry. McSween just had to find Duke and her jewelry, she thought in panic.

"Now, about that baby," her father said short-temperedly.

His voice was just like McSween's. Rusty and gruff, it didn't contain a clue as to what he was really thinking. Romeo wailed again. "Please, sweetie," Britt whispered, wrestling both baby and dragon into submission. *Please, call as little attention to yourself as possible, for your daddy's and my sake.*

"Is that—or is that not—the baby in question, Brittany?"

The very one. "Well, Daddy..."

"Don't 'Well, daddy' me!"

As her father's thunderous voice rumbled across the phone line, Britt imagined heavy black cables vibrating overhead—all the way from New York to Hawaii.

"Everybody here is determined to cover for that darn McSween," her father stormed, "down to the very last man, woman and child in this precinct!"

"The Thirteenth Precinct doesn't employ children," Britt reminded weakly. "It's against the law."

"Harrumph."

Unable to decide on her best course of action, Britt nervously twirled the phone cord around her finger. It was hard to believe her father was a cool-headed cop. When matters involved her, he went right off his rocker.

"Now, would you please tell me about that child?"

"Daddy, of course, I'll tell you everything." She sat up, crooking her knees, and Romeo and his dragon slid inside the cradle formed by her legs. Romeo grasped the dragon's red cape and smiled contentedly. "McSween—"

"Went outside his jurisdiction, to track down Duke Perry!" her father barked. "I got that much out of Nate."

Relief washed over her. If her father knew she'd married Duke, he would have mentioned it by now. "Well, Daddy, I—"

"And McSween's making you baby-sit?"

McSween wasn't "making" her do anything. "Daddy," she said carefully, "could you please stay out of my love life?"

"Love life?" he exploded. "What love life?"

Good question.

Britt heard her father stomp across his office and slam his door. At the earsplitting thud, she imagined every single cop in the squad room jerking to full attention. The chief stalked back across the room. Then he flung himself into the ergonomic chair she'd bought him last Christmas. She recognized the squeak of the wheels.

"Love life!" he exclaimed. "You're..."

His shouting was making her nervous. She could probably have heard him across North America and the Pacific Ocean without the aid of a telephone. "Yes, Daddy?"

"Oh, honey—" His voice suddenly cracked. "You're *divorced.*"

She gasped. He didn't have to make her sound so pathetic. "I'm sure you didn't call to discuss my failed marriage!" In the long pause, she could almost hear her father wringing his hands.

"Oh, I just wish your mother was alive," he finally continued. "She'd understand this whole mess and know exactly what to do... what to say."

"My love life isn't your problem," Britt said, gentling her tone.

"Oh!" Her father drew in a sudden, sharp breath. "Now, I see!"

Britt tensed. "See what?" she asked warily.

"Nate really *was* covering for McSween. And McSween wasn't chasing Duke Perry at all. He—he followed you to Hawaii to patch things up."

Now that her father's mental wheels were spinning, his voice dropped to a resonant baritone. McSween would never believe it, but her father adored him. He'd put McSween on deadbeat-dad detail to make him want kids, not punish him. A grim smile flickered across her lips and her chest flooded with a sweet kind of pain. She was all her father had in the world.

"Don't worry, Daddy," she said. "McSween and I have spent a little time together. And McSween does have a baby—"

"Nate said that, but he wouldn't tell me anything else," her father said miserably. "Not even when I threatened to fire him."

Britt chuckled wryly. Everyone knew her father was all bark and no bite. He was cool under fire, but in times of crisis, he personally made sure that officers' families were cared for. Since the death of Britt's mother, he'd dedicated himself totally to his daughter and his job.

"Like I said," she continued, "McSween has a baby."

"I'll kill him, honey."

"You don't have to do that, Daddy."

"I don't?"

She shook her head. "No, he had the baby before we were even married."

The chief gasped. "It's a baby by another woman?"

"Daddy—" Her father was naturally suspicious of everything, but when it came to her, he possessed zero skills of detection. "We have dinner together all the time. If I'd gone through a pregnancy, don't you think you'd have noticed?"

"Well . . . I *suppose* so."

"I'd say that's a definite."

Her father's voice dropped another calming octave. "I had word that Duke Perry was spotted in Hawaii. I don't know if you remember, honey, but I told you about him. He's the Sutton Place Swindler."

Britt cleared her throat. "Uh-huh . . . I think I remember your mentioning him."

"Well, I just assumed McSween was chasing Perry. And then I realized you were in Hawaii." Her father's sigh of satisfaction said he'd just solved the case. "So, McSween brought his baby on vacation, so you two could get acquainted. . . ."

He was fishing. When she said nothing, he continued, "Is it a boy or a girl, Brittany?"

"A boy."

"Ah, a little boy," her father echoed. "And how old?"

Britt glanced down at Romeo and considered. "A year."

"Well, maybe that's why McSween didn't want to have children with you quite yet. Your mother always said babies should be *two* years apart. Of course, we never had—" Her father inhaled audibly. "Not that I'm not the happiest

man in the world having only one daughter. It's just…there
was a time when we thought . . .''

"I know, Daddy.'' He was making her feel guiltier by the
second. She wanted to tell him everything—that she'd married Duke Perry, that Duke had stolen all the jewelry her
father had given her mother, and that she and McSween
probably weren't getting back together. She heard rattling
behind her and squinted quickly over her shoulder. Hadn't
she hung the Do Not Disturb sign on the doorknob for
housekeeping?

"You're all I need in the world,'' her father was saying.

And sometimes the weight of responsibility was almost
more than she could bear, Britt thought, turning her attention to the phone again. "Daddy,'' she suddenly said, "why
don't you promote McSween to full detective? He's got the
highest solved-case record in the department. You *know* he
deserves it.''

Behind her, the door slammed hard.

Clutching Romeo, she whirled around. She hadn't even
heard the door open. And it wasn't housekeeping; it was
McSween. Beneath the dark shelf of his narrowed eyebrows, the slits of his green eyes looked murderous, too.
With calculated calm, he leaned against the door, hanging
his garment bag on the knob next to him.

Her eyes trailed over him and her heart fluttered. For
three weeks they'd been together again. For the past two
they'd flirted on the phone as if it were the old days. Right
now she wanted nothing more than to fly into his arms and
welcome him back.

She blew out a heartfelt sigh, thinking he looked awfully…virile. A loose tan sports coat hung open over a
V-necked knit shirt and olive slacks. He hadn't bothered to
cut his hair and the added length was slicked back, pushed
behind his ears. His strong jaw was shaded with a stubbly

five o'clock shadow. *Too bad he heard me ask Daddy about the promotion.*

"He's there," her father suddenly said.

Realizing she'd nearly dropped the receiver, Britt snapped it to her lips again. Her eyes remained riveted on McSween.

"Britt?" her father prompted.

"It's Daddy," she mouthed. McSween might be mad, but surely he wouldn't light into her until she got off the phone. "It's just housekeeping, Daddy, but I'd really better hop off," Britt said perkily.

"Put him on the line," her father growled.

She sighed. It was no use pretending McSween wasn't here. "There's no reason for you to talk to him."

Except that McSween was now crossing the room with a grim smile and his large hand outstretched. As she handed over the receiver, their fingers touched—and awareness shuddered through her body.

"McSween here."

His voice rippled through her like his touch, making her think it was no wonder she'd married him. She gulped as his eyes drifted over her flimsy pearl-colored teddy.

"Yes, sir," McSween said.

Britt searched his face for clues as to what her father was saying. Catching her gaze, McSween abruptly turned his back to her.

"McSween," she whispered urgently.

He didn't turn around, which tweaked her temper. Didn't common courtesy dictate that he should tilt the phone receiver in her direction so she could hear? After all, it was *her* father.

"Of course," McSween said curtly.

Britt snuggled Romeo and the dragon against her chest, got up and marched self-righteously toward the new port-

able change table. "C'mon, sweetie pie." As she wiped and
powdered, she glanced between Romeo and McSween.

"Yes, sir," McSween said. "You've received a lead that
Duke Perry is in this area."

Suddenly McSween glanced over his shoulder. Not that
his eyes revealed a thing. Except that he was getting angrier
by slow degrees.

"I'm well aware of your daughter's large inheritance,
sir," McSween continued curtly. "And yes, I understand
that she might be just the type of divorced woman usually
targeted and victimized by the perpetrator."

There was a long pause.

"Yes." McSween's voice now moved at a brisk staccato
clip. "I am most certainly aware that your only daughter is
now single again, so she's at much greater risk than if she
were married and protected by a loving husband."

Britt wished the floor would open and swallow her—and
that her father would give up these misguided attempts at
matchmaking. Did he really expect McSween to protect her
from Duke Perry? *If he only knew.*

Finally, McSween quietly replaced the receiver. Britt
trained her gaze on Romeo, affixed the sides of his fresh diaper, then placed him on the floor. He crawled away with
the speed and dexterity of a spindly insect. McSween stared
at her so long that she remembered her attire. Unfortunately, she didn't see her robe. Under his intense scrutiny,
her cheeks grew warm, but she stood her ground.

At least until he started walking toward her.

He came slowly and deliberately. But with him, he seemed
to bring a tidal wave or a great wind. She backed up, not
stopping until her legs hit one of the white leather armchairs. Her knees buckled and she plopped into the seat.

Just as she started to jump up again, McSween leaned
over, placing his hands on either armrest, trapping her. In

spite of his obvious fury, his proximity made her heart pound with longing. She wanted nothing more than to reach up, grab the lapels of his sports coat and pull him toward her for a kiss.

He glared down at her.

Chin up, girl. She smiled back innocently.

"Did I really hear you ask your father to promote me?"

The hem of her teddy was already grazing the tops of her thighs, and when she crossed her arms defensively, the movement only served to raise it another uncomfortable inch. She gulped. "Mind if I get dressed?"

McSween's eyes dipped downward, warming everywhere they touched. Otherwise, he didn't move a muscle. "As a matter of fact," he said, "I do."

"Feast your eyes," she said airily, "because the rest of you is surely going to starve."

A trace of a smile appeared and his tongue flicked at his upper lip. "Sure about that?"

Not very, she decided when he leaned a fraction closer. Her eyes darted past him. On the other side of the room, Romeo was pulling himself up on the playpen, practicing his fledgling steps.

Her eyes drifted to McSween's again. "C'mon," she said, "Quit trying to threaten me with your body language."

"My nearness didn't used to bother you."

"We used to be married."

He sighed. "I hate to tell you this, but—" He stopped in midsentence, surveyed her, then merely shook his head. When he pushed himself off her armchair and stood, she felt a little bereft. He seated himself in the chair opposite. "I can't believe you asked your father to promote me."

She sniffed. "I just asked why he hadn't. Besides, you deserve it."

"Yeah," he retorted, "I do."

"Everybody *knows* you do!" Only after the words were out did she realize they weren't actually arguing. Was his marriage to her really what was holding him back? She sat up straight in the chair and squared her shoulders. "I'm sorry you married me!"

"*You're* sorry?" His expression said no one could be sorrier than him. He rose from the chair, shrugged out of his jacket and tossed it onto her rumpled bed. Then he started to pace, looking like a caged tiger.

She followed him. "I don't think you should be penalized. Especially not now..." She hoped he never realized the fantasies she'd been spinning—where she was pregnant and he accepted it; where Kay begged her and McSween to raise Romeo; where she and McSween had never really divorced, somehow.

He whirled around so fast she nearly bumped into him. "Now?"

"Especially not now that we're divorced," she continued. "Daddy's just a bit jealous. He's old and all alone and I'm his—"

"I'm well aware you're his only daughter!" McSween exploded. "Do we really have to go into the saga of your poor old dad?"

That got her back up. "My dad—"

"Is as sharp as a tack. He runs one of the most powerful precincts in Manhattan. The only trouble with your dad is that he won't share you with anyone—including your husband."

"First," she returned icily, "you're not my husband. And second, if you'd given him a grandchild, maybe there'd be somebody else for him to focus on!"

McSween grabbed her wrist and brought his lips so close that she could feel his breath against her cheek. "Every single time, it comes back to this."

She shimmied backward. "To what?"

"To your infernal desperation to reproduce."

Desperation. The word made her furious. She tried to snatch away her wrist but he held it tightly. "Or to your fear," she said.

He raised an eyebrow as if to say she was out of her mind. "Fear?"

She nodded. "Fear."

He caught her other wrist, then leaned against the wall, pulling her with him. "Why can't I be enough for you?"

"Why don't you loosen your iron grip?" She struggled against him. When she couldn't evade him, she settled for stomping her foot. "My having a baby has nothing to do with you!"

He gasped. "It has *everything* to do with me." His eyes roved over her face and his voice dropped to a soft taunt. "Why can't I be enough for you, Britt? I mean, me. Just me. All by myself."

"Because you're just not!" Her voice rose. "I want a man who loves me enough to have a family with me!" And the trouble was, she wanted that man to be Sean McSween.

With a quick tug, he brought her right against his chest. His voice lowered, becoming deceptively gentle. "You sure know how to change the subject."

She glared at him. "How so?"

"You were discussing my career with my boss. An unethical boss, I might add, who keeps making me work with kids because he thinks that'll make me want one."

So, McSween *had* guessed her father's motives. "You have one," Britt reminded stoically. She started to glance toward Romeo, but McSween's arresting green-eyed gaze held her transfixed.

His eyes narrowed. "When I fault you for interfering in my career, you turn the tables and make it my problem. We're back to square one."

She wished with all her heart that he would let her go. Through the thin fabric of her teddy, she could feel the hard beating of his heart. "Square one?" Her mouth had gone dry and the words were a barely audible croak. She licked her lips and swallowed.

"Yeah, square one. Where I'm the Peter Pan who won't grow up and play stud."

Britt sent him a falsely bright smile. "Aren't you mixing metaphors?"

"Aren't you changing the subject again?"

"What exactly do you want me to do?"

"Stay out of my life."

The room went dead silent. And then Britt heard a cooing sound. Her head jerked toward the playpen. Romeo had let go of the side bars. With his dragon clutched in a tiny hand, he was walking toward his daddy.

McSween instantly dropped her wrists. "Where's the camera?" he asked urgently.

Britt flew toward the dresser and grabbed McSween's Nikon. "Are you sure it's loaded?" Before he could respond, she started snapping.

"It's loaded." McSween dropped to his knees and held out his arms for Romeo. "Are you getting this, Britt?"

Hearing his voice catch, she felt a lump lodge in her throat. *Darn it, McSween, this is why you need to be a full-time dad,* she thought. *Oh, Sean, can't you hear the hope and love and excitement in your own voice?*

"Are you, Britt?"

"I'm getting it."

The shots caught Romeo in a series of movements. Romeo's right foot raised, his left foot. The second he almost fell backward. How he leaned forward to correct his balance and then kept coming at a headlong run. Each second of each step was recorded, to be cherished forever.

"Isn't this amazing?" McSween said.

Britt continued to snap away. "It sure is."

Especially the final shots. Romeo and his dragon crashing into McSween's open arms...McSween grabbing his son in a tight bear hug...the dragon tumbling to the floor as McSween kissed Romeo and lifted him into the air, victorious.

"Did you see that, Britt?"

What she'd just seen was a whole other side of McSween. A side she'd always known was there—the hidden, secret side she loved most of all.

He whirled around with Romeo in his arms. "Did you?"

She blinked back sudden tears. "Yeah, McSween," she said softly. "I sure did."

HOW DO YOU LIKE THAT, Mr. Scaly? I took you all the way from our bed to Daddy! Daddy was so darned impressed that he forgot all about fighting with Britt. Now he keeps smooching and hugging me. Then he sweeps me right off my feet and zooms me through the air!

I guess the big folks really like it when a little guy like me takes an afternoon stroll. Well, I'll show off for them again after dinner. For now, whaddaya say we just rest on our laurels, Mr. Scaly?

"Next thing you know, he'll be wearing wing tips, Britt."

"C'mon, Romeo, let's see a big smile, sweetie pie."

A guy can't help but giggle. Britt's still got that camera snapping a mile a minute. Makes me feel first-class—like a real celebrity. Hey, maybe I'll be a movie star when I grow up. A whole bevy of beauties'll buzz around us, Mr. Scaly— and every single one'll be just as pretty as Britt. Lights will flash and drumrolls will announce our all-important approach.

Ah, my dear Mr. Scaly... aren't we the best?

BRITT SMILED. "THANKS for taking us out to celebrate."

McSween shrugged. "I figure first steps rate a decent dinner." He'd taken Britt and Romeo to a fancy restaurant that Lina's son had recommended. As McSween opened Britt's door, he found himself hoping that no new rooms would become available tonight. He was on a waiting list, but the textiles convention had booked most of the hotel.

As Britt grazed past him into the room, her long stocking-clad legs made whispering sounds. She lifted Romeo away from her chest, kissed his nose, then settled him against her again. She'd dressed the kid in a cute two-piece outfit made of sailboat-print cloth. Suddenly Britt's warm brown eyes narrowed seductively. "What in the world are you thinking about, McSween?"

About how we shared this space while we were getting ready for dinner. He arched an eyebrow. "Sure you want to know?"

Her lips twitched in a bewitching smile. "No."

He chuckled and started backing her toward the bed. Britt laughed and bounced onto the mattress with Romeo. Leaning over them, McSween tweaked Romeo's tummy, making the baby giggle. What exactly was coming over him? McSween wondered. All he knew was that he felt great. Exhilarated. A baby's first steps, he thought now. What could be more important? More new and fresh? Without thinking, McSween opened his arms wide, whirled around in a circle and fell onto his back next to Britt and Romeo.

Romeo stared at him in openmouthed awe.

"Has your daddy gone crazy?" McSween asked.

"Definitely," Britt replied with a soft chuckle.

McSween draped his arm around Britt's shoulders. She was wearing another simple sundress, this one brown. It enhanced the brown of her eyes and the honey color of her hair. "You look great," he said huskily.

She leaned on her elbow and scooted closer. Getting squinched between them, Romeo looked concerned. After a moment's reflection, he scrambled onto his daddy's chest.

Britt smiled. "You don't look so bad yourself, Mc-Sween."

"Sorry I blew up earlier," he murmured.

"I'm not." Britt nestled her chin on his chest, next to Romeo, then gazed into his eyes. "Sometimes when we fight, I think we might still be able to work things out."

McSween just wished their fights actually led to solutions. He drew in a deep breath of her perfume. The delicate scent infused his senses, and heat flooded his relaxed limbs. Impulsively, he ducked his head and kissed her forehead.

"So, what were you thinking a minute ago?" she asked.

He lightly blew a lock of hair from her forehead, while his hand slid down her side and settled on her waist. "I was thinking about how... nice it felt to get dressed in the same room with you."

She smiled and rolled her eyes. "You were in the other room," she reminded with a soft laugh.

He sucked in another deep, heavy breath. As he exhaled, his eyes drifted halfway closed. "But I was so aware of you...."

"You did zip me up." She chuckled throatily. Against his chest, she shook her head. "If zipping me up does it for you..."

"Implying I haven't seen much action lately?"

"McSween," she murmured in censure.

"Here, you little rug-rat." McSween lifted Romeo from his chest and set him on the floor. "Do me a favor and practice walking or something." The baby crawled off like a shot. McSween's eyes followed him until he stopped in front of his building blocks and started to play.

Britt's eyes narrowed. "Sending the baby away?"

"For a good cause," McSween assured as he swiftly rolled, drawing her on top of him. Both his hands glided downward, toward the hem of her dress. "You know..."

"Hmm?"

McSween slowly lifted her hem, his fingers luxuriating in the soft silk of her stockings. "Watching Romeo take those steps really did me in."

"Did you in?" Britt shifted her weight on top of him and put her arms around his neck. "Assistant Detective McSween, you make it sound like a murder."

In some strange way, he did feel as though some old part of him were dying. "I..." *Felt so alive seeing him walking for the first time.* He tried to find the right words. "It's like you're watching all the stupid, boring, mundane things you do every day, like walking and eating—"

"But it suddenly matters in a way it hasn't for years," Britt finished.

He nodded.

"That's why I want babies," she whispered.

"I know that now," he whispered back.

She kissed him then. Sliding her hands down his sides, she twined her fingers with his. When she rested her cheek against his chest again, McSween sighed.

"Zipping your dress was good," he murmured. "But unzipping it would be so much better." Was it his imagination or did Britt suddenly tense against him?

"I've got something to tell you," she whispered.

"No, I've got something to tell you." They were still married, and he wanted to tell her. But then he simply wanted her, too. Wanted her with a thirst that suddenly felt unquenchable.

Swiftly, he rolled so that she was beneath him. His mouth covered hers completely, drinking her in, slaking his thirst. Diving between her lips, his tongue explored her, then resurfaced only to dive once more. It was a kiss of ownership. A kiss that wasn't meant to end. A prelude to lovemaking.

"I want you," he murmured raggedly, running a languid trail of hot, wet kisses down the slender column of her neck.

Before she could answer, his lips claimed hers again. His hands roved over her back, then slid lower and lower. Finally, his fingers traced the silken strips of thigh between the tops of her stockings and her panties. Just as his thumb dipped beneath the rim of her hosiery, the phone rang. He groaned against her lips in protest.

"We'd better get it," Britt whispered breathlessly.

"It's probably the front desk calling to say they found me a room," McSween managed to say, feeling none too happy about it. He wanted to stay with Britt tonight. Needed to, even. He would, he decided, even if the entire textile convention vacated the hotel.

He stretched and lifted the phone. As he rolled away from Britt, his gaze swept down the length of her. She looked beautiful—disheveled and soft. That her dress was askew and her panties showed made him smile. With a start, he remembered he was clutching the phone. "Yeah?"

"McSween?"

Something in the voice commanded McSween's attention. He shot a concerned glance in Britt's direction, then rose to his feet. "Nate?" he said carefully.

"I've got some bad news, buddy."

As if sensing she might be needed, Britt scooted toward the edge of the bed. McSween lightly rested a hand on her shoulder. Had Nate had a conversation with Kay? Or found the judge who had presided over Romeo's case? "What kind of bad news?"

Nate cleared his throat. "Well..."

Why was Nate pussyfooting around? The lawyer usually came right to the point. Gazing down into Britt's helpful-looking eyes, McSween said, "Just spit it out, Nate."

"I'm sorry, McSween, but Romeo is *not* your biological child."

Part 2

New York City

Chapter Nine

McSween lifted Romeo's stroller across the threshold of his apartment. "I can't believe somebody willed me a baby."

"Me, neither." Britt shook her head. In shocked voices, she and McSween kept repeating the scant facts Nate had given them, as if by retelling the traumatic news they might convince themselves it was true. "Well," Britt said, as she had many times, "when we find Judge Elliot, he'll shed more light on this." *Or else John Sampson will,* Britt thought. He was the attorney who'd settled Romeo's mother's estate.

"But why would some woman I don't even know will me a baby?"

Britt shrugged, her eyes panning over Lina Itami's pastel portrait as McSween gently leaned it against the wall. In the picture, McSween was staring down at Romeo, his expression indulgently paternal. *Seeing the way you've bonded with Romeo, I think she made the right choice, McSween.* "I didn't even know you could leave babies in wills."

"I guess you can name anyone as a guardian."

Anyone? It sounded as if McSween didn't think he'd be much of a father. But that was crazy. Was her ex-husband so cut off from his emotions that he didn't realize how much this news had devastated him?

The past twenty-four hours had been a nightmare. After receiving Nate's call, they'd hurriedly packed, but there were no available New York-bound flights. Wordlessly, McSween had donned a pair of sweat pants and climbed into her bed, and she'd nestled against his chest, offering only her comfort. Clearly, he didn't want to talk about his emotional reaction to the news, so she didn't push him. At first light, the three of them had been in a taxi, speeding for the airport.

Now Romeo squawked, and McSween reached into the stroller, lifting him. "Can you take him, Britt?"

Her feet were killing her, so she quickly kicked off her high-heeled sandals. Smoothing the skirt of her floral-print sundress, she said, "Sure." As she accepted the wiggling child, McSween's hand settled briefly on her bare shoulder, resting there in a sweet caress meant to impart strength.

Just glancing from the baby to McSween, Britt felt her heart stretch to breaking. How could fate have been so cruel as to let McSween believe Romeo was his flesh and blood?

For the first time since Nate's call, McSween attempted a grin. "Too bad, hon," he said, looking at the baby, "but I'm pretty sure he's wet."

"He feels wet." The corners of Britt's mouth curled. "You know, diaper detail's not proving to be your strong suit, McSween."

His grin tempered to a wry smile as he switched on the air conditioner. "Sorry, but we'll probably be long gone by the time it cools down in here."

Britt glanced around. McSween's loft apartment was a rental on the seventeenth floor of a high-rise in Astoria, Queens. Through the wall-to-wall windows that comprised one side of the large main room, there was a perfect view of the East River and of the Manhattan skyline in the East Seventies. The apartment was all sharp lines and angles.

Cool masculine colors and empty spaces. All at once, Britt felt McSween's eyes on her face. "You're such a Spartan," she commented.

He chuckled softly. "Should I start ducking?"

She sent him another droll smile. Had they really had knock-down-drag-out fights about how neat he was? And about how messy she was? Of course, the real fight had always been about something more serious.

She glanced down at Romeo, sadness squeezing her heart. Why had the baby's mother named McSween as guardian? And where had his father gone? "Poor Kay. She must have been completely shocked when Nate asked her about Romeo."

"Nate said she was."

"And you swear you've never heard of Valerie Lopez?" That was Romeo's biological mother.

"I keep thinking and thinking…." McSween sighed. "But it rings absolutely no bells."

Britt stared down into Romeo's sparkling eyes as if they might hold a clue. "And you really think Romeo's father might be alive?"

"There's nothing to indicate otherwise."

Britt could read the hurt in McSween's expression, but his voice remained unnervingly calm and matter-of-fact. Romeo's missing biological father could have been the perpetrator in a case, or one of the deadbeat dads McSween often sought.

McSween shrugged. "Judge Elliot's assistant said there's no mention of the father on the paper he found in the office. The will naming me guardian belonged to Valerie Lopez and was handled by John Sampson."

Britt sighed and glanced around again. At one end of the large room was a futon covered with a black comforter. At the other end was a black-leather sectional sofa and a slate coffee table. The sofa faced a built-in entertainment center. Movable panels could apparently hide the television and CD player. Beyond that was a simple archway leading to the kitchen. It was all very self-contained; so neat and tidy. So "McSween."

Britt nodded toward the coffee table. "Mind if I change him there?"

"Not at all."

From the surface of the table, McSween casually lifted a paper and whisked it into his jacket pocket. With a flash of insight, Britt was sure he hadn't wanted her to see it. Her eyes narrowed. "What was that?"

McSween arched an eyebrow innocently. "What?"

It was hardly a time to joke, but Britt couldn't help but smirk. "The paper you just hid in your pocket," she said pointedly as she held Romeo in one hand and laid a plastic coverlet on the table.

"Being Spartan," McSween returned, "I'm merely putting away messy items. You never did trust me."

I always did. "Of course not."

"So, I guess I can't trust you, either."

"In here?" she asked with a smile. "Alone in your apartment?"

"Not quite alone."

Not by a long shot, she thought. All the empty space only increased her awareness of him. Her eyes drifted over his loose-fitting cream linen suit and the casual mint green T-shirt beneath it that enhanced his eyes. Then she zeroed in on his sports-coat pocket, as if the fabric had become invisible and she could see the paper inside. Well, maybe it was nothing. She rummaged in a tote for a fresh diaper. "Why don't you go ahead and get your stuff?"

McSween nodded, then headed for a walk-in closet near his front door. She frowned as she rummaged around for the wipes and powder. Had she really asked McSween to stay with her?

You sure did, Britt. She gulped, not particularly wanting to explore her own motives.

On further inspection of the room, she started noticing her influences. There were throws on McSween's simple sofa. One artsy lamp with a tall, hand-twisted metal base. In spite of how he'd teased her for being a coffee connoisseur, a Krups cappuccino maker was visible in the kitchen.

Somehow she felt as if she were snooping. "I just hope Judge Elliot turns up," she suddenly called out.

McSween's gruff voice rumbled from inside the closet. "I'll keep looking for both him and Romeo's father. I just can't believe the judge didn't even tell his assistant where he was going."

"You know, not everyone works on their vacation," Britt reminded, as she shimmied a fresh diaper under Romeo's behind. She could hear the hangers in McSween's closet rattle as he drew them back. "Well," she ventured, "whoever or wherever Romeo's father is, he obviously doesn't want anything to do with his son."

There was a long pause.

Britt waited, hoping McSween would say something definite about his plans. All along, when she'd thought Kay Wilcox was Romeo's mom, she had assumed McSween could work out some kind of joint-custody agreement. But now? She lifted Romeo from the coffee table. "Eskimo kisses," she whispered, as she rubbed her nose against Romeo's. When she set the baby on the floor, he merely giggled and snuggled next to her.

"I really appreciate your letting us stay at your place, Britt."

"No problem."

But glancing up, she knew it was a definite problem. *A man who looks that good should be outlawed,* she thought. It was his face she liked most. It was as tough as his eyes were kind. But if other women noticed him, she decided, it would be because sheer self-possession clung to him like a second skin.

Pinpricks of sudden awareness dotted her nape. She and McSween kept acting as if they were the one thing they could never really be—just friends. Within twenty-four hours of their first meeting, they'd been tangled in each other's arms, making love. Now their newfound friendliness was a thin veneer that barely covered the old heat that still coursed between them.

"Looks like you've packed quite a bit there," she managed to say unsteadily, looking at the carry-on slung over his shoulder and the garment bag draped over his arm.

He shrugged. "Who knows what I'll need?"

One look, and Britt knew exactly what *she* needed—him. How had she lived without him for a year? If he'd wanted to make love last night, she would have. All through the night he'd held her close. It was just how it used to be—and she'd felt so safe and at peace in his protective embrace.

Suddenly he frowned, set down his bags, and returned to the closet as if he'd forgotten something. Her eyes followed his broad back as he vanished inside. *However temporarily, he's really moving back into my apartment.* "This is crazy!" she whispered. Oh, it had seemed reasonable enough last night—and on the plane this morning.

In fact, most of the arguments for it had been hers. Because McSween had to return to work, he'd suggested that his mother could watch Romeo. Britt had countered by saying that Ellen McSween, who'd just turned sixty, might not be in the mood to house a near toddler, much as she loved kids. But then, driving Romeo into Manhattan from

Queens every morning seemed troublesome, so Britt had suggested McSween simply use her guest room. They could even set up a crib for Romeo in the living room.

It had all seemed so natural. Now, Britt stared at the open closet doorway feeling sure she'd lost her mind. They'd teamed up in Hawaii, but then McSween had been chasing Duke Perry. *Whom he didn't find,* she reflected, glancing down at her bare, usually beringed fingers. Next to her, Romeo pulled himself up using the edge of the coffee table. "Going to walk for me, sweetie pie?"

"Goo," Romeo said.

Britt laughed. "Goo?"

Romeo giggled.

In the closet, McSween chuckled. "I always knew you were capable of philosophical conversation, Britt."

"So you like that learned discourse of mine?" she teased. McSween didn't respond. But speaking of deep talks, there were so many questions she wanted answered. *Where is Romeo's father? What are McSween's plans for Romeo? Is there still a chance for me and McSween?*

"I'm almost ready," McSween called.

Romeo tilted his head toward the closet, then let go of the table and ran four steps. When he fell onto his freshly diapered behind, he chortled, then rapidly crawled in the direction of the open closet door.

The baby was as attached to McSween as McSween was to him, she thought. "What if you find Romeo's father?" Britt ventured, just as Romeo disappeared inside the closet.

"Depends," McSween replied cryptically, in a tone that didn't exactly invite further conversation. "I've definitely got to look for him. I want to make sure...nothing bad comes of all this later."

Britt willed herself not to react, but her heart swelled, feeling too big for her chest. McSween was going to take care of the baby. Talk-show segments she watched flashed through her mind. She remembered one case where a couple gave away a baby years earlier—and then demanded to have custody again. The adoptive parents were utterly destroyed.

That could never happen to McSween. He was a strong man, yes. But he couldn't come to love a child, only to have that child taken away from him. Oh, yes, they had to make sure absolutely everything was in perfect order. *But haven't you already gotten too attached to Romeo?* Even if McSween became the incontestable guardian of the baby, that didn't necessarily mean she and her ex had a future.

What had McSween said? *Why can't I be enough for you, Britt? Just me. All by myself.* He'd had a right to ask. After all, love in a marriage wasn't supposed to be conditional. It was "for richer, for poorer; in sickness and in health." With her own lips, she'd spoken those words. And she hadn't taken one single vow that said her husband should make a baby with her.

"Have you seen that dragon?"

Britt drew in a sharp breath, her hand shooting to her heart. "You scared me."

"Didn't mean to." McSween was standing near the closet door, his carry-on looped over his shoulder again, his garment bag draped over his forearm. Romeo was settled on his hip.

She glanced around. "The dragon's with the stroller."

McSween sighed in relief. "If we ever lose it, Romeo will have a fit." His eyes scanned the room. "Well, I guess that's about it. You ready?"

Britt blew out a long sigh. "Ready as I'll ever be."

"C'MON, ROMEO." Just as McSween resituated Romeo on his hip, Britt nodded him across the threshold of the apart-

ment they used to share. Glancing over his shoulder, Mc-
Sween watched her swish self-consciously inside, the flouncy
hem of her sundress swirling around her thighs.

He couldn't take his eyes off her. Since he'd found out
Romeo wasn't his biological child, McSween needed Britt
more than he ever had. She hadn't pushed him to talk about
his feelings—she knew he wasn't much of a talker—but he'd
needed her last night. Needed to hold her, to feel her heart
beating next to his.

McSween tried to ignore the lump that was lodging in his
throat. *How can this kid not be mine?* He set Romeo on the
floor, so that he could do some exploring.

Britt lightly kicked the front door shut with one of her
high heels and smiled. "Well, make yourself right at home."

This used to be my home. McSween slowly lifted his gaze
from her long, shapely legs. "I'll sure try."

When her face colored, he guessed she'd just realized
what she'd said. Looking for a diversion, he glanced
around—and realized she'd totally redecorated. Well, almost totally. The floral chintz was gone, replaced by cool
blue furniture. But Lina Itami's beautiful watercolor remained in its place above the mantel. Snapshots of his and
Britt's honeymoon were still displayed on the end table
nearest the fireplace, too.

I can't believe she never moved them. His gaze settled on
a shot of Britt feeding him an ice-cream cone. The picture
was so good that Britt had framed a duplicate for his
mother. He'd seen it not an hour ago, since they'd stopped
by his mother's house to say hello.

Britt cleared her throat loudly. "Can I get you anything?
Coffee, tea, soda?"

He shook his head, thinking about how much his mother
loved Britt. His four sisters always said she was the best
thing that had ever happened to him, too. They were prob-

ably right. "No, thanks." He grimaced at the rustiness of his own voice.

"Positive there isn't something you want?"

You. McSween shook his head. He started toward the long hallway that led from the central room, with Romeo following him at a brisk crawl. "I'll just put my stuff in the—" Last night, he'd shared Britt's bed, even though they hadn't made love. "The . . . uh . . ."

"Guest room," she said quickly.

The false perkiness in her voice grated on his nerves. Or maybe he just wished she'd said the master bedroom. "You redid the kitchen," he called from the hallway. When he paused on the threshold, Romeo crawled past, then seated himself in the middle of the kitchen floor with his dragon.

Britt came up behind McSween. "I needed a change."

And no doubt, he was the reason, he thought guiltily. The red-and-white country-style kitchen had been repainted a more subdued mustard yellow. The table was of blond wood, as were the new cabinets, and the moldings had been painted forest green. The only object he recognized was the wicker magazine rack beneath the window.

He squinted at the plants, which hung in every corner. "Who's been watering them?"

"Mr. Hornsby." Britt shrugged. "Daddy may have come by."

Gazing into her eyes, McSween fought the sudden urge to kiss her. But somehow, a hotel room in Hawaii seemed more neutral. Here, everything seemed too undefined. And McSween liked definitions. Wouldn't kissing her or making love with her here be tantamount to saying he wanted to start a family? He settled for trailing a finger down her cheek. "I like the kitchen better this color," he said.

"Really?"

There was no mistaking the skip in her voice. He nodded, feeling touched at how she still sought his approval. His chest constricted as he surveyed the new kitchen again. Yeah, divorce could do strange things to people. Women dyed their hair, went back to school, or completely redecorated their homes. Men...

Well, he had no idea what men did. *He'd* bought throw pillows, a nice lamp, and a Krups cappuccino maker.

Not that he was really divorced, of course. The unsigned papers, which he'd whisked off his coffee table, were still in his pocket.

He shot Britt a guilty look. She smiled back a little wanly. No doubt, she was long accustomed to the changes she'd made in the apartment; before she'd brought him here, she hadn't stopped to think about his reaction to all the redecorations. *She's really missed me.*

Messy throws and stacks of books had vanished. So had the bright prints and country-style knickknacks. Now everything looked cool and trim. Neat and tidy. It looked like... *My apartment. It's almost as if she's redecorated for my return. As if she fears I left because she didn't give me enough of my own space.*

"Well," she said with an embarrassed start, "I guess you remember where the guest room is."

"Maybe not—" He shot her a quick smile. "I didn't much stay in the guest room."

For a long moment, they simply gazed at each other. Then he must have made a barely perceptible movement toward her, because she tilted back her head, inviting a kiss. Was he really ready to give what she most wanted from him? Thinking better of it, but unable to stop himself, he angled his head downward, imparting a kiss that was quick and hot, deep and wet.

"Did I ever tell you you were beautiful?" he murmured.

"Countless times." Britt leaned against the doorjamb, her throaty laughter catching in the air. "I think you said it right here, in this very doorway, Christmas before last. Of course, that may have had less to do with my physical charms and more to do with the mistletoe."

He chuckled softly. He leaned to kiss her again, but she gently drew away. He wished she hadn't. But then every kiss brought them closer. And they couldn't be together if the problems between them weren't resolved.

"Why don't you go ahead and get settled?" she said huskily.

He shook his head ruefully, playfully. "A kiss like that—and I'm still staying in the doghouse?"

"It's a guest room, not a doghouse, McSween."

He smiled.

Suddenly she pointed. "Look."

McSween turned just in time to see Romeo walk unsteadily to the magazine rack and put his dragon to bed on top of *The New Yorker*. McSween guessed it was as good a place as any for Romeo's little friend to settle in, but watching the kid, McSween felt a hand reach inside his heart as if to rip it out.

He's not yours. McSween should have guessed. After all, he just wasn't cut out for fatherhood. In some deep part of himself he almost wished the kid would vanish now. But then he didn't; Romeo still *felt* like his own flesh and blood.

"I think I'll unpack," he said.

"Okay," Britt replied softly.

His jaw clenched at the sheer gentleness of her voice. No doubt, she was reading his mind. She always had. "Thanks," he said gruffly.

The guest room was the last door on the left. And the long hallway felt like a tunnel leading him right into the past. With every step, memories flooded back. He'd been a damn fool to come here. There wasn't an inch of horizontal space—not a floor or counter or bed—where he hadn't made love to Britt. Made love with reckless abandon—running naked through this hallway, washing her in that tub, wrapping her in blankets in these beds.

They'd done it all, he thought, as he entered the guest room. Except taken that next step—and started their family. Had he wanted them to live one long love affair, remaining honeymooners forever? Or was his real reason for not wanting children something deeper?

McSween laid his garment bag across the mattress, then he frowned. Something was out of place. But what? The room was comfortable, with cornflower-blue walls and soft lamps with yellow shades. Touches of pink in the throws on the bed were offset by chocolate brown. Neither masculine nor feminine, this was the perfect guest room.

And then it hit him with the power of a revelation.

The room was predominantly pink and blue and yellow. And he would bet his life that Britt had always intended for it to become a nursery.

A second later he realized what else was strange. This was the only room in the entire apartment that she had not redecorated.

BRITT PAUSED IN THE hallway and shot a meaningful glance toward the kitchen where her father sat. Casually flinging her arm around McSween's neck, she lowered her voice. "Just don't tell Daddy anything."

Her soft, pleading whisper made his ear tingle. "We can't let your father continue to think Romeo's my son," he returned in a hushed tone, hoping the chief couldn't hear them.

"If you tell him now—"

McSween slipped both his arms around her waist and brought her against him. "Then he'll know I disobeyed orders and went to Hawaii to chase Duke Perry."

"Right," she murmured throatily.

She had a point. Besides, the wrongful assumptions about Romeo's paternity were making the chief much nicer to be around. He would find out the truth soon enough. In the past week, McSween had been following some hot leads on Romeo's biological father. It was only a matter of time until he was found. McSween just wished he was having the same luck with the Swindler.

Britt lightly kissed McSween's lips. "You won't say anything?"

"Not yet." How could he deny her anything? She smelled tangy—of red-hot chili peppers and garlic—and her silk sundress teased his palms. He longed to keep holding her, but he forced himself to let her go. She hesitated as if she, too, would rather stay in the hallway wrapped in his embrace. He chuckled softly, leaned and nuzzled his face against hers.

"McSween," she whispered in censure.

"You'd better scoot or I'll get a lot worse," he promised. Just as he playfully pinched her waist, she laughed and spun away from him.

"Sure you won't have some carrot cake?" Britt said in a loud, perky voice as she reentered the kitchen and headed for the counter nearest the sink. "It's the kind you like. You know, from Balducci's."

As McSween seated himself at the table again, his eyes followed Britt. He loved watching her bustle around a kitchen, her hands a flurry of motion, her short skirts swirling about her thighs. When she cooked, she frowned in deep concentration and she pushed out her lower lip and blew, to lift wayward tendrils of hair from her forehead. In winter there were often dusty white dots of flour on her sweaters, from where she'd pushed up her sleeves.

"Daddy?" she repeated without turning around.

Chief Buchanan's dark, perceptive eyes pierced the air as he shifted Romeo from one knee to the other. "Well, like I said, I only dropped by to return your apartment keys...."

McSween rolled his eyes. On the pretense of just dropping by, the chief had now stayed two hours. The devious man hadn't bothered to actually turn over the spare keys, either, which he always kept. Since the chief had been in city-council meetings all week, McSween hadn't seen him at work, so he supposed they were due this visit. Chief Charles Buchanan wanted to know what exactly McSween was doing with his daughter.

"C'mon, Daddy," Britt crooned. "Since you're here, you might as well have some cake."

"Please, do," McSween forced himself to say.

"Well...I guess I will."

While Britt replaced her father's dinner plate with a dessert plate, McSween drew in a deep breath and glanced around the kitchen. The air still smelled of stir-fried vegetables and Parmesan. A colander of linguine was on the counter. Just as his eyes landed on the salad bowl, Britt whisked away the enticing concoction of artichoke and palm hearts and sun-dried tomatoes. McSween's gaze landed on the chief again. *So much for a romantic dinner with Britt.* McSween watched as Romeo reached up and tugged one of the few gray hairs that were raked over the chief's bald head.

In response, the chief emitted a rusty chuckle. Then he murmured, "Ah, your mother's dishes."

Britt glanced over her shoulder. "The dessert plates?"

The chief nodded. And then he frowned. "Where's your jewelry, Brittany?"

Britt cleared her throat. "I—er—took everything to be cleaned."

McSween sighed. He *had* to find Duke Perry—and fast. As Britt placed a slice of carrot cake in front of him, he noticed a smear of icing on her finger. On impulse, he lithely caught her hand, then licked away the smear.

"Aren't I sweet?" Britt whispered naughtily.

"When you want to be," McSween returned softly, just as she whirled from his grasp.

Fortunately the chief didn't even notice the flirtation, but merely stared down at Romeo who was wobbling on his knee. Britt returned with her own dessert, seated herself, then started teasing the edges of McSween's cuffed pant leg with her bare foot. He shot her a censuring glance. She smiled innocently at her father, then back at him.

"You are bad," McSween mouthed.

"You love it," she mouthed back.

"There's my boy," Chief Buchanan said gruffly. He shot McSween what might have passed for a smile, then bounced Romeo on his knee again. Abruptly, the chief nodded, as if he'd just won a long debate he'd been holding with himself. "He's a good kid."

McSween almost chuckled. Sometimes his father-in-law could be as endearing as he was annoying. "Yeah," McSween said simply. "He is." *But he's not mine.*

McSween took a bite of cake, but it turned to meal in his mouth. He could feel Britt's sympathetic gaze. And just looking at the chief with the baby, McSween knew he and Britt were digging themselves in deeper by the day. The chief suddenly stood, rounded the table and deposited Romeo into McSween's lap.

"I'll just be a minute," Britt's father said, by way of explanation.

McSween sighed again. Every time he so much as held the kid, he wound up feeling sad. His eyes followed the chief's back as he left the kitchen. The guy was so terse. Maybe Britt was right, he mused. Maybe he had more in common with her father than he would ever admit.

Romeo reached up and squeezed his cheek. "Gee-bah!"

Feeling as if his insides had been scooped out and hollowed, McSween smiled down at the baby. Then he tilted his head.

Britt's eyebrows knitted together. "What?"

McSween nodded toward the hallway, a wry smile stealing over his lips. Next to the bathroom door, the leather soles of the chief's regulation shoes seemed to come to a halt. But the man didn't really stop walking. The steps merely dropped in pitch, then the chief surreptitiously continued down the hallway. No doubt, the chief was checking to see if McSween and Britt were sharing the bedroom.

A full five minutes passed before the creeping footsteps came back down the hallway. Then the toilet flushed loudly. When it did, even Britt giggled.

"What was he doing?" McSween whispered. "Trying on all my suits?"

Britt's eyes narrowed meanly, but her lips twitched into a smile. "Now, you leave Daddy alone."

The chief stomped from the bathroom, sounding like an elephant. McSween nearly chuckled out loud as he handed Romeo to the older man again. And then he sobered. Whom would McSween hand Romeo to...when all was said and done?

Surely he couldn't keep him. Maybe the biological father would fight for custody. *The minute you heard he wasn't yours, you should have called Donya Barrakas and arranged for someone else to take him.*

"C'mon to Grandpa," the chief said, whisking Romeo back to the other end of the table.

Grandpa? McSween felt himself caving in. Was it because of the chief's matchmaking pressure? Or because he couldn't live without Britt any longer?

Feeling Britt's toe on his pant leg again, McSween glanced up—and right at the chief. There was no mistaking the glimmer of approval in the old man's eyes. Or how good it made McSween feel. After all, he was guilty of harboring a secret respect for his father-in-law.

Quickly, McSween glanced from Britt, to the chief and Romeo. Yeah, tomorrow he was going to have to decide what to do.

MOMMY AND DADDY, how could you forget my dear Mr. Scaly?

"Where's the dragon, Britt?"

"I think he put it in the magazine rack in the kitchen again."

"I'm back, kid. Here's your little green dragon."

Ah, good. They had me worried there for a sec, but now Mr. Scaly's in the brand-new crib that was delivered today. I can't believe we've finally got a bed to call our very own—and nobody can get in it 'cept me 'n Mr. Scaly.

And boy, do we need a bed! This week really wore us out. Only the most extreme powers of concentration and all my growing detection skills allowed me to figure out what all's been happening. A while back, we were on the other side of the world—and we flew over oceans and through clouds and then we came to this place, which must be our real home, with Mommy and Daddy.

To make sure Britt knows I want her for my mom, I've been trying to say both "Mama" and "Dada." I think I'm making progress, too.

The thing is, I really do need a mom. Much as it pains me to admit it, the big guy'll fork me over if he thinks any real work's involved. It's Britt who rubs me with lotion, changes my diapers and wipes the cracker crumbs off my smoochers. She'll even dab at my winkers if they get a bit crusty during my beauty sleeps. And well, as much as I love being dirty, I'm a bit vain, too. Let's face it, a guy's gotta have some pride.

Correct me if I'm wrong, my dear Mr. Scaly, but aren't the pieces of the proverbial puzzle starting to fit together nicely? All of a sudden my short little life seems to be falling into place. I can walk, and pretty soon I just know I'll talk in proper English.

Yep, next thing you know, I'll have the career and the little house with the picket fence. Not to mention the station wagon, the dog, and the 2.5 kids of my own...

What, Mr. Scaly? Oh, I do suppose I might be getting just a bit ahead of myself!

Well, there's nothing like the present! We even got ourselves a brand-new grandpa. He's big and old and wrinkly, just the way a grandpa's supposed to be. And he's got even less hair than I do!

Oh, Mr. Scaly, can this all really be true? The big guy's our daddy, and now we have a mommy and a grandpa, too. Not to mention our own bed in our own home...

Home.

Oh, my dear Mr. Scaly. We've finally come home.

Chapter Ten

Was giving Romeo up for adoption really the only option? McSween wondered. Just a few hours ago, McSween had found out what had happened to the Lopezes. And now, whether he liked it or not, he had to start making plans for Romeo's future. He rested his hands on his hips, stared over the squad room, and blew out a long sigh. Glancing downward, his eyes landed on his desk—and on the newly framed snapshot of Romeo that Britt had brought by this morning.

In the picture, Romeo was just inches from McSween's embrace. The grinning baby waved his toy dragon in the air and took one large, final, victorious step. *One small step for man,* McSween thought, his gaze lingering. The kid looked so proud that he really could have been Neil Armstrong putting the flag on the moon.

Don't let your emotions get in the way, McSween. A cop who does that might not survive. Yeah, as hard as it was, he had to do what was right for the kid. All morning, the pros and cons had been spinning around in his mind.

Sure, he felt responsible for the baby. Even more than that, he'd grown to care for him. But what kind of future could he offer? He had to work, which meant leaving Ro-

meo with someone else during the day—either with Mc-
Sween's mother or at a day-care center.

One thing was certain: Britt shouldn't figure into Mc-
Sween's decision. As much as she wanted to be a mother, it
was unfair for them to confuse their rekindled emotions
with their feelings about the baby. If he and Britt got back
together, it had to be solely because they loved each other.

Shaking his head, McSween reminded himself of his am-
bitions, of his long hours and the dangers inherent in his
job. He was single, too, separated from his wife and living
in an unsafe city on a cop's salary.

These were the facts.

This was the reality.

Abruptly, he forced himself to pick up the phone and call
Donya Barrakas. "So, can you start the adoption proceedings?" McSween found himself saying moments later. When
he realized his eyes had riveted on the picture of Romeo
again, he averted his gaze and wedged the receiver more
firmly between his jaw and shoulder.

"Sure . . ." Donya's lulling Jamaican accent rolled across
the line. "Judge Elliot's assistant found enough papers that
I can go ahead. But you know, now that the father's been
found . . ."

The way's free and clear for you to keep the baby.

"The father is *dead*," McSween reminded succinctly.
He'd phoned Donya earlier, when he'd located Alonzo Lopez. The man had died in the same apartment fire as his
wife, Valerie. The baby, Romeo, had been rescued by a
fireman. McSween had driven to the burned-out shell of the
East Village walk-up building, but he could swear he'd never
answered an emergency call there. No, the Lopezes were
complete strangers.

"McSween, are you sure you don't want to wait and hear
what John Sampson has to say?"

Since Sampson was the lawyer who had overseen Valerie Lopez's will, he remained the one man who could reveal the connection between McSween and the Lopezes, if there was one. McSween grimaced, then reached up and loosened his tie as if that was what was keeping him from breathing easily. "He's supposed to call me," he muttered, "but like everyone else, he's on vacation."

"Well," Donya said softly, "it *is* summer."

A gray diamond appeared on McSween's phone console and his second line beeped. *Fine time for someone else to try to reach me.* Had Judge Elliot been found upstate? Or was Sampson returning his call? Maybe someone had found Duke Perry. Surely, whoever was calling would leave a message. "Anyway, Donya," McSween continued, "Romeo's . . . not really mine."

In the pause that followed, he could almost hear Donya say, *Families are made, not born.*

Feeling uncomfortable, McSween glanced through the glassed-in wall of his office. Across the general squad room, he could see the opposite bank of windowed rooms. The chief was pacing inside his office as usual, barking commands into a telephone. *Come to Grandpa.* McSween's throat closed like a tight fist.

"Are you *positive* you want me to start proceedings so soon?" Donya asked.

"Absolutely." She had to. McSween ran down his list of reasons as if they were a checklist: long hours, dangerous job, separated from Britt. *Or are those convenient excuses, McSween, just as Britt says? Is there some deeper reason you don't think you'd make a decent daddy?*

"Absolutely," he repeated gruffly.

"McSween—"

"Look," he said swiftly. "This kid's got to get settled. Somewhere, with a married couple." Who knew what was happening with him and Britt? Even if they got back together, there was no guarantee it would last.

As if reading his mind, Donya said, "Does Britt know?"

"I'll tell her."

"So, she doesn't know?"

McSween felt as if he were about to blow a gasket. "It's been hard enough for me to make this decision."

"Well...this could be a long, drawn-out process." Donya began listing the upcoming steps she would take—retaining a lawyer and meeting with prospective couples.

McSween did his best to block out the details. When his phone beeped again, he wondered guiltily if the caller was Britt. But no, it was after noon. She and Romeo had gone to see *One Hundred and One Dalmations.* As far as McSween was concerned, such a movie seemed advanced for a one-year-old, but then he was sure that Britt knew best. The film was playing at one of the retro theaters—the Film Forum or Cinema Village; McSween couldn't remember which.

Donya wrapped up her monologue by saying, "Okay, McSween?"

"Everything sounds just fine, Donya." *And it's better this way.* He could almost see Romeo—the rosy chubby cheeks, the silly grin, the unruly spray of black hair. And he could see Lina's family portrait as surely as if it were hanging on his office wall.

But the images would fade soon enough.

Sure, he was falling in love with Britt again. Or, really, he'd never fallen out of love with her. But he couldn't let her raise Romeo and get pregnant herself.

He had no idea why, really. He just knew he couldn't.

He couldn't live in a world of lies, either—where his father-in-law was wrongfully informed about a baby's paternity; where his wife thought they were divorced; where she pretended she loved him just because the baby she'd always wanted was within her reach. Yes, the longer he drew this out, the more painful it would get for all of them.

"McSween?"

Donya's voice roused him from thought. "Yeah?"

"I just asked if you want to meet them."

"Who?"

Donya sighed. "Haven't you heard a word I said?"

McSween shook his head. "No," he admitted.

"I said if you're really serious about this, I might be able to speed up the adoption process. I know one couple who'd love to see that baby. The state's already approved them."

McSween's heart sank. "Great."

"Mind if I tell you about them?"

Yes. "No." He was just glad this was a phone conversation instead of a face-to-face. Otherwise Donya would realize how torn he was. In the background, he heard her riffling through file folders.

"Their names are Chris and Kathy Hayes," Donya continued. "And they live in San Diego. They're nice, affluent, cultured. He's a dentist, she's an interior decorator, and they've already got two boys—ages eight and ten. This time, they've decided to adopt rather than get pregnant because they feel it's the right thing to do. You know, since there are so many parentless children in the world . . ."

Yes, I know, dammit, McSween wanted to shout. Instead, he grunted noncommittally. His stomach felt positively hollow, as if he hadn't eaten for years.

Donya's voice was tinged with regret. "Well, Romeo would certainly want for nothing."

McSween swallowed hard. "And I really get a say in this?"

"Sure. You're currently the boy's legal guardian."

Legal guardian. That meant Romeo was his responsibility. Surely it was as wrong to give up the baby as it was to keep him. *Forget what you want. You've got to do what's right for the kid.*

"Set up the meeting, Donya. Anytime's good for me."

McSween's temper flared as he hung up the phone. Just who the hell was Valerie Lopez—and by what right had she done this to him? He'd never so much as heard her name. He had no idea how he was connected to her. And yet she'd named him legal guardian of her only child. She'd taken it upon herself to suddenly, irrevocably wrench McSween's life from his own control. Who was she to try to change his life forever?

And why would she expect him—a single male who was separated from his wife—to take in a complete stranger's baby and raise it as his own?

McSween shook his head. "Well, Valerie, you must have had a real faith in the human spirit," he muttered.

Lifting his gaze slowly from the cradled phone receiver, he realized Chief Buchanan was barreling toward him through the squad room, creating a commotion in his wake. A second later, McSween's office door swung open.

"Next time I call," the chief roared, "you'd better answer your phone!"

McSween had worked in an environment of crisis long enough to know when to ask questions—and when to act. Without a word, his hands slid over his suit, checking his holster and badge, and then he followed the chief toward the front door at a brisk clip. As he stepped from the air-conditioned precinct onto the concrete sidewalk, the humidity hit him. Twenty-third Street was lined with police vehicles—regular cars, two paddy wagons, a rescue unit. The chief slid into the driver's seat of a dark unmarked sedan, and McSween got in the passenger side and slammed the door.

"So, what's going on?" McSween asked.

"They found a live one at that movie theater over on Eleventh and Third, and I want you to dismantle it." The chief turned the key in the ignition, tossed a flashing light onto the dashboard, then squealed away from the curb. "It's under a front-row seat."

Well, it wouldn't be the first time the bomb squad had called Chief Buchanan. The device was probably very sophisticated. Either that or the bomb squad was understaffed today. McSween sent the chief a quick glance. There was one thing he could say about his father-in-law: the man could drive. He yelled a lot, but he always stayed calm under pressure. Technically, the chief wasn't required to leave the office in cases such as this, but he loved street work. As he zipped into and around the Manhattan traffic, he continued filling in McSween.

"The perp meant to put the bomb under a seat in that other movie. You know, the controversial one."

McSween nodded. A recently released thriller had prompted a few phone calls, although all had been hoaxes. "You're sure it's a live device, not just a threat?"

"It's ticking," the chief assured.

"So, the guy called because he put the thing in the wrong theater?" McSween sighed and shook his head. "It's that multiplex place, right?"

Chief Buchanan nodded curtly. "Yeah," he said grimly. "In a theater where they're playing a Disney movie."

The blood rushed from McSween's body. Was that the movie Britt and Romeo went to see?

"McSween?"

He turned slowly from the windshield. "Britt may have taken Romeo there."

"She definitely did," the chief said coolly. "My daughter informed me of her plans for the day."

McSween merely gaped at the man. How could he be so disconnected from his own emotions? Hearing sirens just around the corner, McSween prayed Britt had changed her mind and stayed home. When it came to dismantling explosives, McSween had always been successful, of course. But now his wife and child might be in danger.

My wife and child. God help him, but that was how he thought of them.

"Get ahold of yourself," the chief growled as he rounded the corner and squealed to a stop behind another unmarked car. Already, the bomb squad and fire trucks were on the scene.

McSween leapt from the car and ran toward the front doors of the theater, the chief close on his heels. At the door, he laid an iron grip on his father-in-law's arm. "Didn't you hear what I just said?" *Britt and Romeo could be in there!*

The chief brought his face so close that their noses nearly touched. "Why do you think I told the squad you'd dismantle the device and took the time to bring you here personally? You're my best man, McSween. So, get in there and get to work."

Already, a member of the bomb squad was helping McSween out of his sports coat—and slipping on protective clothing. McSween's eyes darted over the crowd. With relief, he realized people had been evacuated. He glared at the chief. "I take it you'll be out here."

Chief Buchanan had the audacity to smile. "Well, that is one of the perks of being the boss."

"I wouldn't know."

"You will someday."

"Lately, your 'best man' has been spending a lot of time doing work better suited to rookies. Mind telling me why?"

Chief Buchanan put his hands on his hips, giving McSween the once-over with his piercing dark eyes. "This is a fine time to be asking about your promotion, isn't it? But don't worry, you'll get it.''

"When?"

"When you've had a good dose of humility!" the chief snarled. "And when you learn to give of yourself. And when that self-centered hard head of yours cracks a little. And when—"

"I think I get the point," McSween said tightly.

The chief merely glared at him, as if to say he didn't get the point at all. "Everything comes too easily to you."

McSween glanced pointedly down at his leaded vest. "Oh, yeah, my life's a real bowl of cherries."

The chief's eyes narrowed. "Just get in there!"

McSween sighed. "While you're standing out here, maybe you can ascertain if your daughter and the baby are safe."

At that, the chief nodded amiably. "Be glad to."

Without another word, McSween entered the building. It was quiet. In fact, by the time he got to the second floor, there wasn't a single sound. He squinted at a brave, lone uniformed officer who was standing guard next to the double doors. The man was wearing a leaded vest and a hard hat.

In the eerie silence, McSween's voice sounded loud. "McNutt?"

The eager red-haired rookie came forward and slapped a small flashlight into McSween's palm. "It's in there. Front row, first seat on the left."

A moment later, McSween was shining the flash under the seat. The house lights had been raised, but nearer the floor it was still dark. Very carefully, McSween dislodged the device and pulled it from under the seat, his eyes roving over the tangled wires. They were blue, green and yellow. Digging into his pocket, he found his wire clippers and brought them out.

And then suddenly, for the very first time in his career, panic seized him.

He couldn't breathe, couldn't move. He couldn't cut off his emotions. A whole lifetime—the lifetime he could miss if he died—flashed before his eyes: helping Britt settle Romeo onto the seat of a bright red bike; tossing Romeo the football he'd carried to victory in the Fordham University homecoming game; taking Romeo to his first Giants game and buying hot dogs smothered in chili and coleslaw.

But a cop's got no right to be a father.

No right, he thought now, because his own father had had no right. Because one snowy January day, his daddy—whom he'd loved more than anyone in the world—had gone to work the way he always had, and then he'd never come home.

McSween's eyes stung. His father had left him. Died. But McSween, a ten-year-old kid then, had been so damn brave. No, he hadn't cried twenty-six years ago and he sure wasn't going to start crying now.

"How's it look?" McNutt yelled.

It looks like I made the right choice. Romeo deserved a father who was going to stick around. A guy who, unlike McSween's own father, wasn't likely to get caught in somebody else's crossfire.

Or in a blaze caused by faulty wiring in an old East Village walk-up.

Or blown to bits.

McSween stared down at the mess of wires. Exhaling slowly, he brought the clippers downward, wishing, as he always did, that he was just a little more certain about which one he was supposed to cut.

"Anything I can do, McSween?" McNutt yelled.

"Yeah," McSween muttered, forcing himself not to think about Britt and Romeo. "Duck down and hold your breath."

"EXCUSE ME! PLEASE, excuse me!" Heart pounding, Britt tried to wrestle the stroller through the crowd. Giving up, she unstrapped Romeo, lifted him and his stuffed dragon, then folded the stroller and carried it toward the long blue sawhorses that served as NYPD police barriers.

"Quit shoving!" someone exclaimed.

"Get out of my way and I won't shove," Britt returned. She wasn't proud of it, but she could be as rude as the next guy when circumstances warranted.

With a final push, she found her belly flush against a blue barrier. "You okay, sweetie pie?" she murmured in Romeo's ear. The baby giggled agreeably, his bright, long-lashed eyes taking in the profusion of people. Holding him close and supporting his head with her palm, she scanned the crowd. Where was her father? Was McSween here?

Britt hoped they were both safe at the precinct. Right after the movie previews had begun, the lights had snapped on and ushers had urged people through an emergency exit. Britt had been half sure she and Romeo would be trampled. Instead, carried on the wave of the swelling crowd, they'd landed safely outside. Only when she'd reached the sidewalk did Britt realize she'd been carrying Romeo's stroller. For the past few minutes, rumors about a possible bomb threat had been circulating.

"There's Daddy," Britt murmured to Romeo in relief. Near the theater's front doors, her father was talking to a member of the bomb squad. He didn't look particularly worried, but then her father never did. Neither did Mc-Sween in such situations. The whole world could go up in smoke, and the two men would simply put their hands on their hips and grimly survey the action.

"Please back away, ma'am."

Britt lifted her chin a notch and found herself face-to-face with a guy who had to be a rookie. He couldn't have been more than twenty-five and the nameplate on his pocket said, Nelson. "I'm Britt Buchanan and—"

"The chief's daughter?" Nelson's blue eyes widened. "That means you're—er—McSween's wife?"

Hearing the respect in the man's voice made Britt's heart swell with pride. She nodded.

Nelson ran a hand through his short dark hair and squinted at Romeo. "I didn't know you two had a baby. I thought..." His voice trailed off as if he were confused about Britt's relationship with McSween.

You're not nearly as confused as I am, she wanted to say. "Do you know if McSween's in there?" she managed to ask. *Please, let them have sent someone else in.*

"I'm afraid he is," Nelson said gravely. "Look, I'm not supposed to let people through, Ms. Buchan—er, Mrs. McSween. But if I look the other way, I think you can probably slip right under the—"

Before he could finish, Britt made sure Romeo's dragon was safely wedged against her chest, then she clutched Romeo and the stroller more tightly and ducked beneath the sawhorse. "Thank you so much," she said. Just as she started squeezing between officers and members of the press, the electronic double doors of the movie house whooshed open and McSween appeared.

He had a flashlight in one hand and a heavy leaded vest in the other. Lifting a hand, he waved in victory. Scattered applause and whistles sounded from the crowd—and Britt's stomach muscles clenched. No doubt, there really had been a bomb, and McSween had deactivated it. She bolted toward the doors—and him.

"Brittany!" she heard her father bellow from the curb. "Those sawhorses are there for a reason! Jane Q. Public—which means you, young lady—is supposed to stand behind them. They are there for your protection and..."

She didn't hear the rest. She reached McSween and flung herself into his arms. With Romeo and the dragon snuggled between them, McSween caught her lips in a fiery, explosive kiss.

When she drew away, she realized he was grinning down at her. "Worried about me?"

She shot him a long, sideways glance. "A little."

He licked his lips and smiled, as if tasting her kiss. "Felt like more than a little."

"Okay." A grin tugged at the corners of her mouth. "Maybe a little more than a little."

He squinted at her, his luscious green eyes twinkling. "Doesn't that mean a lot?"

She chuckled shakily. "Oh, McSween, I was worried sick." As she shifted Romeo on her hip, McSween took the folded stroller from her. A siren whooped once and fell silent. The officials—pressmen, police officers and rescue workers—were all starting to drift apart. "They evacuated us," Britt said. "And I couldn't see you or Daddy."

"We came. Your dad knew you were at the movie."

"I know." She suddenly gasped. "And he sent you in?"

McSween's smile held a touch of grimness. "He said he wanted his best man to save you."

"Did he really call you that?"

McSween's smile deepened. "Yeah."

"He likes you, you know." Britt reached up and pressed her hand against McSween's cheek. "That's why he's so hard on you. He's afraid he'll slip and show favoritism."

"Could have fooled me." But the sparkle in McSween's eyes said he believed her. "Hey, can kids that age really appreciate a movie?"

Britt shrugged. "He likes TV."

McSween didn't respond. By degrees, she watched his eyes turn flatter, more watchful. With bone-deep surety, she knew he was going to tell her something terrible. "What?" she suddenly said.

He drew a deep breath. Then he merely kept watching her as if he had something truly horrible to tell her—something he didn't quite know how to say.

Well, she wanted to talk, too. Should she tell him she might be pregnant? She was so tired of keeping that lie between them. *No, wait until after your blood test.* As much as she wanted to gauge his reaction, there was no use telling him something that might not be true.

Except that she was sure they were going to have a baby. And she knew the real reason she didn't want to tell him, too: because he might reject both her and their child. And then he might take Romeo away. Her grip tightened on the baby. McSween was still watching her thoughtfully.

"What?" she said again.

"Do you see why..." He tilted his head and leaned closer. Then his voice lowered, becoming gently urgent. "Why I've worried about us having kids?"

It was the last thing she'd expected him to say. Britt tried to tamp down her temper, but failed. Clutching Romeo and his little stuffed dragon as if they were anchoring her to the pavement, she stared up at McSween. "Why? Because it's such a tough world out here?"

McSween glanced away pointedly, as if asking her to look around. She took in the policemen and sawhorses as if they didn't concern her in the least. Then she shot her ex-husband a purse-lipped stare.

"Britt—"

"In terms of violent crime," she snapped, "New York City is rated lower than most other major cities—and you know it. Even if that weren't true, which it is, the solution to the problem is hardly for the human race to quit reproducing!"

He sighed. "I didn't say it was."

"But it might be?" she retorted.

"Maybe."

Color flooded her cheeks. *Did I really marry this man?* she suddenly wondered. And yet the day was fresh in her mind. The white lace dress, the small bouquet of summer flowers, the trip to the Honolulu courthouse. That day, she'd known with absolute certainty that their love would last. But how could it with a man this dense?

"Maybe," she repeated derisively. "Spoken like a world-weary cop."

"I *am* a world-weary cop."

The words affected her like a shot of adrenaline. She wished with all her heart that there was something within arm's reach that she could throw. "Are you really going to resign yourself to that lousy attitude at the ripe old age of thirty-six?" she demanded. "Why not just fling yourself into a grave? I mean, why solve crimes if they just happen again? Why make beds? Why have children? Why—"

"Thirty-six is old, Britt."

"Old is relative, McSween."

He sighed. "Do we have to fight?"

She scowled at him. How could he be the legal guardian of the sweet baby in her arms—and then imply that people shouldn't have children? She backed up a pace, thinking the man was too close for comfort. She could still feel his lips on hers, and in spite of the circumstances, she found herself wishing they'd never divorced.

"I'm sorry, Britt," he began.

The persuasive gentleness of his voice infuriated her. She could only hope he felt every bit as guilty as he looked. "About what?"

"Just sorry," he nearly whispered.

For long moments, they simply stared at each other. Maybe it was because there wasn't much left to be said. All the feelings, emotions and arguments had long since been on the table.

Finally she said, "When I look around at a place like this..."

"At the scene of a crime?"

She nodded. "I see all the more reason to bond together, to connect and have a family." She glanced at the thinning crowd again, at the men and women who were talking to each other about being evacuated. "People have to support each other."

"You just see the family you never had, Britt," McSween said softly.

"And you see the father who left you," she retorted, thinking he surely knew how to cut her to the core. She raised her chin a haughty notch. "But you're absolutely right, McSween," she continued coolly. She had always dreamed of being surrounded by kids...of being the mother she'd never had. "I need to be needed, McSween—and not just by one man."

"There were two, if we include your father."

She tossed her hair back with two quick jerks of her head. "Well, there's more love in my heart than that!"

Lithely, McSween leaned over and caught her forearm, drawing her closer. "You make me sound like an ogre."

"You are an ogre." She busied herself with resituating Romeo's legs around her waist.

"All right, Britt." McSween's voice turned rusty. "I'll think about it."

Her eyes narrowed. "About what?"

McSween glanced around the crowd. His gaze seemed to land on her father who was now leaning in the window of a marked cruiser. After a moment, the chief stood and patted the car door, then the cruiser pulled away from the curb.

"I'll think about starting a family," McSween said.

Britt's heart skipped a beat. Something in his eyes said he wasn't as sure as he sounded, but she desperately wanted to believe him. "Oh, McSween," she whispered breathlessly. A second later, all her anger vanished and she was wrapped tightly in his arms again.

Chapter Eleven

"Hey there, stranger!" As Britt gave Donya an impulsive hug, then ushered her inside the apartment, her eyes roved over the other woman's loose, cream-colored maternity dress. Matching beads peeked from Donya's French braid and she wore cream-colored flats. Britt smiled. "Well, you're as perfectly put-together as ever."

Donya chuckled. "Glad to see you, too."

"C'mon in the kitchen and have some coffee." Britt's gaze flickered over Donya's swollen belly. "It's decaf," she assured.

"Ah—" Donya flashed her a quick smile "—that sounds like pure heaven."

"McSween's still dressing." He'd said he was helping Donya with one of her knotty cases today, and he'd offered to take Romeo along so Britt could shop. Holding up a spoon and a plastic cup, Britt now slung a messy white towel over her shoulders. Then she glanced down in feigned apology. "Feeding time," she explained.

Donya merely nodded.

Was it her imagination or did the other woman's dark eyes linger on her, looking inquisitive and sad? The impression was so intense that Britt actually felt panicky. She squinted at Donya. "Is there egg on my face or something?"

"Not at all. I think I just need that cup of coffee." Donya nodded toward the hallway and inhaled a deep, exaggerated breath. "Chocolate-raspberry?"

Britt recovered her equilibrium and smiled. "McSween always laughs at my eclectic taste in coffees. But then he's the first in line with a cup."

Donya glanced around the living room. "You've made this place so nice for the baby," she said with soft approval.

Britt followed her gaze. Romeo's crib was in one corner, a playpen in the other. Trucks and building blocks were arranged neatly in an open toy chest. Britt fought the urge to offer to show Donya the guest room. It would make such a perfect nursery and Donya—since she was pregnant—would surely appreciate that.

But when Britt's eyes landed on the mother-to-be again, Donya smiled too quickly and glanced away. Another wave of indefinable uneasiness washed over Britt. It was as if Donya were hiding something. *You're just being paranoid. No doubt, it's your overactive hormones again. You shouldn't have eaten all that chocolate last night.*

Shrugging off the odd feelings, Britt said, "C'mon. Just follow me." Glancing over her shoulder as she led the way to the kitchen, she asked about Tony and the coming baby. It felt so good to visit with the wife of another cop. Last year, while she'd been avoiding McSween, she'd felt so cut off from precinct life.

In the kitchen, Britt nodded toward the high chair. "Go ahead and sit next to Romeo while I get the coffees."

"Coochie-coo," Donya said in baby talk. In her adult voice, she continued, "Well, I— What have we here, hiding on my chair?"

Romeo squealed and clapped his hands.

As she took two mugs from a cabinet, Britt glanced at Donya and her shoulders began shaking with merriment.

"No, we really don't make guests sit on the dragon—do we, Romeo? Donya, you can just move the toy anywhere. Romeo hides it in the strangest places." A moment later, Britt placed two steaming cups of coffee on the table and seated herself. "So, your baby's due in just another month."

Donya added cream to her coffee, took a sip, then emitted a mock groan. "Yes—and thank heavens!"

"Do you know if it's a boy or a girl?"

"A girl." Donya shook her head ruefully. "At least I hope they're right. Everything I've bought is pink."

"A girl . . ." Britt's gaze flickered over Donya's maternity outfit again. Would she, herself, have a girl? Oh, she hoped so. After all, if things worked out with McSween, she would already have Romeo.

Donya leaned nearer to the high chair and offered Romeo a rattle.

"He's walking now," Britt couldn't help but say.

"Really?"

Britt nodded. Even though she knew better, she felt a twinge of maternal pride. Sitting here with Donya, another expectant mother, she felt so connected. *Don't jump the gun. You haven't seen the doctor yet.* Pushing aside the thought, Britt got up and returned with a photo album. In the inside cover, she'd inserted a blank sheet on which she'd written, "Romeo's first steps."

Donya chuckled as she leafed through the album. "These are priceless."

Britt grinned. After a moment she said, "So, Tony finally got his desk job?"

"Thanks to your dad." Donya set aside the album and sipped her coffee. "Tony loves it. We were both scared to death when he was on the street."

Britt shook her head in understanding. "I was actually at the movie theater the other day, during the bomb scare."

Donya's eyebrows knitted together with concern and she pressed a hand against her heart. "You're kidding."

Britt nodded grimly. "No."

Somehow, the dangers inherent in a cop's life seemed to warrant a moment's silence. Britt sighed, gave up on being good, and dusted just a few sprinkles of sugar into her coffee.

Suddenly her eyes caught Romeo's. "You're going somewhere," she said, "aren't you, big boy?" Romeo grinned as her eyes roved over his outfit. Since the baby was going with McSween this morning, Britt had taken extra care dressing him. He was wearing his trim gray shorts suit with a crisp white shirt.

McSween. Down the hallway, in the guest room, she heard him pacing. Without so much as seeing him, she knew he was choosing a tie. That was what a year of living with a man could do to a woman. Once again, she wondered if they might really have another chance. But yesterday, when he'd said he was thinking about starting a family, strange feelings of discomfort had stolen over her in spite of her happiness. Surely, she was wrong . . . but McSween's eyes had looked so guarded that it almost seemed as if he were lying. *Lord, Britt, you really are getting paranoid.*

"You know," Donya said, "once McSween makes detective, he'll be away from the immediate dangers on the job. He'll be using his head mostly."

"Hmm." Britt hoped so. In spite of her bravado outside the movie theater, the incident had scared her. Her father was a cop, but now he served primarily as an administrator, overseeing intellectual, behind-the-scenes work on tough cases.

"I'd love to see McSween make chief one day," Britt said.

Donya laughed. "Lord knows, the man wants it bad enough."

Britt smiled in agreement. "And what he wants, he usually gets." Romeo was wiggling impatiently in the high chair, so Britt removed his bib, lifted him out and set him in her lap.

"I really do think McSween's got a shot at the job," Donya went on. "And everybody agrees. He's a natural-born leader. Even though he's only an assistant detective, all the guys turn to him when your father's gone."

McSween no longer belonged to her. No more than Romeo did. Yet Britt felt as responsible for his good work record as she did for Romeo's first steps. She frowned as her eyes traced over her fingers. She just wished McSween would find Duke Perry—and her jewelry—soon. She realized Donya had been scrutinizing her and arched an eyebrow in inquiry.

"McSween may be a natural-born leader," Donya said, "but you're a meant-to-be mom. That child's definitely taken to you."

Before she thought it through, Britt leaned across the table and squeezed Donya's forearm. "Oh, Donya, lately... well, I keep hoping McSween and I will get back together. For one, I really miss being involved with things at the department."

Donya smiled and patted her hand. "We wives have missed your company," she assured.

"And... I've missed McSween so much," Britt said in a rush. How had she made it during the past year without cops' wives to talk to? When she and McSween separated, she'd cut herself off from the precinct entirely. Now that seemed almost impossible.

"I don't know exactly what we're doing here together," Britt continued. "For now, he's in the guest room, and I'm just going with the flow. I mean, he kisses me and we hold hands—" She glanced quickly down at Romeo. "Well, I love this baby so much. And...next week I have an appointment for a blood test because I think I might be..."

Donya's eyes widened, and she chuckled softly. "Guess you *have* been going with the flow, so to speak."

Britt laughed. "Well, we've only made love once since we ran into each other again." She lowered her voice to a whisper. "But I *am* pretty sure I'm pregnant. And I've been dying to tell someone. But please don't say anything to McSween. I can't tell him until I know for sure."

Once again, the vague discomfort Britt associated with bad premonitions washed over her. "I didn't mean to put you in the middle," Britt said quickly.

"No problem." Donya's smile didn't quite reach her eyes. "I live in the middle. It's my job."

"McSween always says you're the last of the true diplomats," Britt replied sympathetically. Donya had to please so many people—adoptive parents, parents who were giving up children, the children themselves. Suddenly, Romeo tugged Britt's ear. Pulling back, Britt crooned, "Watch it, kiddo!" With a smile, she removed one of her dangling earrings. "I don't know what made me think I could wear them."

As if glad for the distraction, Donya said, "You like those earrings, don't you, cute fellow?"

Romeo merely grinned lopsidedly.

"He really is adorable," Donya continued, her voice almost wistful. She leaned toward Britt quickly, conspiratorially. "Britt, from a professional standpoint, I probably shouldn't...but I want to tell you, I..."

Britt felt it again—that instant, sure sense that something was wrong. "What, Donya?"

"Well— Oh, McSween!"

McSween breezed across the threshold. "Sorry, ladies."

Britt frowned. Whatever Donya had been about to say was now lost. *Surely, it had nothing to do with you and*

McSween. She forced herself to smile. "Hey, Mc-
Sweetheart."

He laughed. "McSweetheart?"

Britt smiled back, her eyes drifting over him. He looked
deliciously cavalier, with a starched white shirt accentuating his tan and a summer sports coat draped casually over
his shoulder. But her eyes narrowed when she saw his expression. Surely she was wrong, but she could swear Mc-
Sween shot Donya a warning glance. Why would he do such
a thing?

"Here—" When Britt stood and handed over the baby,
McSween planted a soft kiss on her nose. "Are you sure you
don't mind taking him this morning?" she asked.

McSween shook his head. "No."

In spite of her uncomfortable feelings, Britt forced herself to smile at Donya again. "I've found it's so much easier to do the weekly shopping without the baby in tow," she
explained.

Donya's smile looked positively plastered on her face.
Even worse, she said absolutely nothing.

"Well, let me just walk you guys to the door," Britt
managed. As she headed in that direction, she tilted her
head as if listening for Donya's inner thoughts. What in the
world had just transpired? At the door, McSween gave Britt
a quick kiss goodbye.

A moment later, right before Britt shut the door, Donya
urgently said, "Well...*please* do call me if you need anything."

Britt leaned against the closed door and exhaled shakily.
Everything seemed so ordinary. McSween had kissed her
goodbye and taken the baby off her hands, and Donya was
pleased to visit after so long.

And yet, Britt was sure that something terrible was about
to happen.

SHIFTING HER WEIGHT on a beige sofa, Kathy Hayes glanced critically around the lobby of the airport hotel as if she were considering redecorating the place. When her eyes met McSween's, she smiled tentatively, then nodded at the floor next to McSween's armchair.

"May I pick him up, just one more time?" she asked softly.

Get your hands off my baby. "Sure," McSween managed to say.

Just pretend you're working, he thought, as Kathy lifted Romeo from the stroller. *Just pretend this is a particularly grisly case, and you have to divorce yourself from your emotions.* The trouble was that this nondescript hotel lobby next to LaGuardia Airport really did feel like the scene of a crime.

And McSween himself was the perpetrator. Outside the apartment, Donya had railed at him for not telling Britt about the meeting with the Hayeses. Even worse, outside the movie theater, the other day, he'd spoken his innermost thoughts and told Britt he might want to start a family. Hell, he didn't know what he wanted anymore. He definitely didn't want to upset Britt unnecessarily. For all he'd known, the Hayeses might not be interested in Romeo.

But of course, they were.

"You're so adorable," Kathy said.

Her quiet, breathless voice made McSween cringe. So did the sheer crispness of her suit. Nevertheless, the couple was perfect. They were kind and responsible. Preapproved by adoption officials. And their two boys, who were playing on the other side of the lobby, were obviously well-raised.

He would tell Britt later today. And surely she would understand. After all, he *was* doing what was right for the baby. He and Britt would be wrong to let their romantic feelings become confused with what they felt for Romeo. The poor kid had already lost one set of parents. He deserved a safe, stable home. McSween suddenly realized that the Hayeses were beaming hundred-watt smiles his way. He forced himself to smile back.

"He's such a happy baby," Chris Hayes commented.

"And our boys just love him." Kathy cradled Romeo against her chest and nodded toward her sons.

McSween just wished the Hayeses weren't quite so post-card perfect. Kathy was young, bright and talented. Pretty, too, with short curly dark hair and sparkling brown eyes. Her husband was as quick to smile as she, and they clearly had a strong relationship.

"Do you really feel you're going to be able to do this?" Chris asked.

There was no doubt what he meant. Could McSween really give up Romeo? "I want him to be well taken care of," McSween said rustily.

He looked at Donya, but she glanced away. Although she was sorely disappointed that he hadn't told Britt, she was maintaining her professionalism and moderating the meeting between McSween and the Hayeses.

"Well, then, that about covers it," Donya said with a smile. "McSween?"

McSween forced himself not to look at Romeo. But just out of the periphery of his vision, he could sense the baby grinning at him. "Well...I'll have to get all his things together." *And break the news to Britt.*

"Can we just stay in the city this week, honey?" Kathy said.

Chris picked up her train of thought. "And head back to San Diego next Saturday, on the noon flight?"

Kathy nodded. "That's what I was thinking."

McSween stared at Chris. The man had a deep tan, perfect teeth and the kind of build that said he played golf. Yes, he was definitely a guy who didn't live in the line of fire. *Yeah, he's the kind of guy who'll definitely stick around.*

McSween cleared his throat. "I can bring him out here next Saturday." Maybe that would be the least painful thing. He would quickly put the kid on the plane, then he would leave.

"So, let's meet here next Saturday at, say, eleven o'clock." Donya glanced at her own watch, as if she were starting to count the minutes. "I can have all the papers in order by then."

Maybe by then there would be some word from John Sampson, too. And an explanation of why Romeo had been left in McSween's hands in the first place. "Saturday," McSween murmured.

It seemed a very long time away, McSween thought, as Kathy Hayes stood and deposited Romeo in his arms again. And none of it seemed quite real.

THANK HEAVENS, MY DEAR Mr. Scaly. We're back in our own personal bed!

Frankly, that scare we got today plumb wore me out. I thought the big guy was going to put us on one of those airplanes again. It would have been awful, too, especially now that we've finally got our home fixed up how we want it— with a mom, a dad, and a grandpa and this bed that's all ours.

Why, just watching those planes zoom past the hotel made my ears pop and my head spin and my tummy feel queasy. 'Course, it turned out that we were just there to show me off to Daddy's friends. Personally, I didn't like them all that much. The lady was too quiet and the man laughed too loud. Still, I tried to impress them for the big guy's sake. Especially since Mommy took the trouble to dress me up special in my gray suit. Did you notice I didn't even cry once, Mr. Scaly? Well, anyway, it was awful good to see that other lady, the nice one who gave us to Daddy in the first place.

Ah, but we're back at home now. Safe and sound. Snug as bugs in a rug.

"Britt, let's have coffee on the balcony."

"Sure, but let's check on Romeo again first."

"I'm pretty sure he fell asleep while I was reading him *Hansel and Gretel.*"

Don't Mommy and Daddy have the nicest voices, Mr. Scaly? Hers is like bubbles in the bathtub. And his is like rumbles in thunderstorms. One of these days, I'll be able to say their names in English. And I'll understand every single word they're saying, too.

"Night Romeo."

That's me! That's me! Oh, good night, Daddy!

"McSween, isn't he the sweetest little thing in the whole world?"

Look, Mr. Scaly, they're so tall! They're leaning over us and peering right into our faces. We'd better shut our winkers and pretend to be asleep, the way we're supposed to be.

Ah... good night, Mommy and Daddy.

And thank you for loving me and giving me and Mr. Scaly a perfect home.

"I'M OUT ON THE BALCONY, Britt." McSween set two steaming coffee cups on a narrow table, then he slipped off his sports coat and draped it over the back of a wicker settee. Just as he seated himself, he heard Britt behind him. Stretching an arm across the sofa back, he glanced over his shoulder toward the screen door. "Thanks for dinner."

She merely smiled at him.

"C'mon out," he said.

"Why?" She arched an eyebrow and playfully grated a fingernail across the screen. "So you can have your wicked way with me?"

No, so I can break your heart, honey. McSween drew in a sharp breath. Somehow, he managed to shrug casually. "I just want to talk."

She blew him a flirtatious kiss. "I'll bet."

Damn—but he felt guilty. *Why did you tell her you were thinking of starting a family with her?* He blew out a sigh. *Because I am.* His meeting with the Hayeses felt almost like nothing more than a bad dream. He didn't want to tell Britt about it because there was still a chance he would change his mind. And yet, he knew he had to go through with his plans. Romeo deserved a good life—the best. Certainly more than a single father with a dangerous job would offer. Or a busy cop, who was only recently reunited with his wife.

Britt suddenly chuckled. She poked at the screen door and it began to open slowly. "If you aren't going to try to have your wicked way with me, then I'm not coming out."

McSween tilted back his head. "Is that a threat or a promise?"

She laughed again. "A little of both."

In spite of the circumstances, he couldn't help but smile. "Well, the longer you wait, the wickeder I'm going to get. And that's a promise."

Britt shimmied her shoulders in a mock shudder. "Oh, you scare me, McSween."

I should. Oh, Britt, I can't believe I haven't talked to you about Romeo yet. Somehow, he wiggled his eyebrows playfully. "If you want a real case of the shivers, you'll just come outside." As soon as the words were out, the double meaning made him cringe. *You're a terrible man, McSween.*

Britt's eyes narrowed. "No man makes me shiver in July."

He forced himself to smile. "Just try me."

For a long while, they smiled at each other through the screen. There was no doubt he could make her shiver and more, he thought. Some strange miracle happened every time they touched. The spark they generated was so electric and undeniable that it made their relationship feel predestined. The second their eyes had met they'd known they belonged together. And tonight, in spite of the lies between them, that spark still flared bright.

"Come out—" he sighed as if he were bored "—or else I'll have to come in there and get you."

Britt's bubbling laughter filled the air. She made a great show of opening the door and stepping across the threshold. The short hem of her navy skirt brushed her thighs, and her white tank top hugged her breasts. Through the shirt, he could see the lace of her bra. When he glanced down, he realized she was barefoot. Giving her a quick once-over, he let out a long, soft wolf whistle.

"No need to whistle, McSween."

"No?"

She grinned. "The way you looked at me during dinner convinced me you like the outfit."

"Hate the outfit," he retorted. "But I'm desperate for what's in it."

"What's in it is all yours," she said, sliding onto the settee next to him. His arms dropped from the back of the sofa to her shoulders and she snuggled against him. The warm bare skin of her arms circled his waist and she gazed up at him with those dark, doe eyes.

"Kiss me," she said.

"That's what I like," he murmured. "A woman who knows what she wants."

She leaned her head farther back. "Or are you scared this wildcat won't stop at a kiss?" she purred.

"I'm quaking in my boots," McSween returned huskily.

"Maybe I'll stop, maybe I won't," she singsonged.

He drew his eyebrows upward in mock horror. "How will I find out?"

"Like I said." Britt hooked her index finger in between the buttons of his shirt and pulled him close. "Kiss me."

"Sure." His palm glided over the silken softness of her arm, until his fingers twined through hers. And then he dipped his head, his lips slowly parting hers, drinking in the honied warmth of her mouth.

After a long moment, she drew away. "Hmm." She leaned forward, took a sip of coffee, then snuggled against him again. "You looked so cute when you were reading *Hansel and Gretel* to Romeo."

McSween winced. "Cute?"

She nodded. "And you know what else?"

"Hmm?"

"Your kisses sure taste great with orange-flavored decaf."

He frowned. "It's decaf?"

"What?" She grinned up at him. "Am I putting you to sleep?"

He chuckled. "Hardly."

He felt wide-awake and ravenous for the taste of her. His gaze drifted from her eyes to the rail of the balcony. Below, the early-evening sun dappled the sidewalk. No one was on the street, and the trees in Gramercy Park were so thick with foliage that the tall black wrought-iron park gates were barely visible.

"It's strange when quiet descends on the city like this," Britt said as if she were reading his mind. She sighed contentedly. "This always has been my favorite spot in the apartment."

"You never told me that." Somehow it seemed significant. He knew her so well, and yet he could still discover small simple facts about her tastes.

Britt smiled up at him. "I never told you?"

"Not that I remember." He tried not to think of the things he wasn't telling her now. "When I first saw you, I knew I wanted to learn everything about you,'' he found himself saying.

She trailed a finger down his chest. ''Well, you know an awful lot.''

''I sure do,'' he said huskily. ''But I bet I could discover a few more things.''

The longing in Britt's eyes made clear what she was thinking—that McSween knew the secrets of her body as only a husband could. But even before he'd first made love to her, he'd known how to touch her. It was as if some voice had whispered her secrets into his ear, so that he could anticipate her—sensing where to caress her and for how long, and how to tease and arouse her until she cried out, hovering torturously on the brink of sheer ecstasy.

Before McSween thought it through, he turned to her and grasped her hands. ''Britt, I've missed you....'' He gazed deeply into her eyes, then lifted a hand and cupped her chin. ''Oh, God, I've missed you.''

In the next instant, her arms were around him. Holding him tight. Pressing him close. Filling him with need. Against the solid wall of his chest, he felt the tips of her breasts harden and pebble. Heat pooled in his groin until his lower half felt thick and heavy, like a tree branch after a quick summer shower, bending under the weight of rain-drenched leaves.

''Ah, Britt,'' he whispered on the soft moan that escaped his lips. He drew in a deep breath of her. And then another. Her delicate floral perfume was mixing with the musk of her skin. That scent and one quick, hot, yearning brush of her lips against his own fed his desire, the way oxygen might feed a fire. Her impulsive embrace said he was becoming the man she'd dreamed of, the man she would grow old with, the man who would father her children. It said she wanted him, too, with a raw, unbridled need. How could he disappoint her now?

His mouth covered hers like a lock for which there was no key. And as surely as a vaulted door, that kiss shut out the rest of the world. Alone, with his eyes shut tight, McSween gave himself over to pure desire. Time and time again, his tongue delved between the heavenly velvet softness of her lips in a kiss that became ever deeper, softer and wetter. With each new assault, McSween became more relentless, more demanding, until finally Britt arched against him, her voice catching in a strangled, whimpering cry.

"You still want me, don't you, Sean?" she whispered tremulously against his lips.

"Always," he said simply. As his tongue plunged between her lips again, he captured her hand in his own and guided it along his thigh. Drawing it into his lap, he pressed her fingers against him. His voice was low and throaty, almost a growl. "I want you," he said, willing her to feel the truth of it. "I want you now."

Her hand closed over him then, touching his erection through the blousy fabric of his summer slacks. While his lips sought hers again, his fingers glided over the smooth skin of her bare legs, edged beneath the hem of her trim navy skirt, then sought the juncture of her thighs. His splayed hand rested on the silk of her panties, his palm pressing against her mound. At the soft steady pressure, she gasped again and he captured the sound with another kiss.

"Please, take me inside," she said on a choked sigh.

"I want to be inside," he whispered raggedly against her lips. "Inside you, Britt."

Without another word, he rose and extended his hand. She twined her fingers through his and they walked into the apartment, past Romeo's crib and down the hallway.

"Britt..." he began hoarsely once they were in the master bedroom. *I have something to tell you.*

She pressed a finger to his lips. "It doesn't matter why we're doing this now, or what it means." She rose on her tiptoes and kissed him hard. "I just want you." Unabashedly she lifted her tank top over her head and tossed it aside.

His breath caught. Her bra was revealing—nothing more than wisps of transparent pink attached to underwires. Against the fabric, her nipples were hard and taut. Whatever protest he'd been about to voice died on his lips. To hell with the truth. He wanted her now. And he would have her.

"Sean..."

He sucked in a quick breath. "Oh, Britt." Just looking at her made his heart wrench. He could still remember how shy she'd been when they'd first made love. He'd taken her against her front door—in a quick erotic frenzy. For days afterward, she'd assured him she'd never behaved so brazenly, as if he actually might have thought she could be loose or easy.

"You've changed so much," he whispered.

"Since a year ago?"

He shook his head. "Since we first made love."

"Is it a good kind of change?"

His eyes roved over her face, then dipped to her full, rounded breasts. "It's just a change." He would like her—love her—no matter what.

Brushing a lock of hair from her forehead, he let his eyes slowly pan the room, to commit the day to memory. Early-evening sunlight peeked in slivers through the louvered wooden shutters. In the slats of light, small specks of dust whirled. Overhead, the ceiling fan circled lazily. When he looked at Britt again, he said, "You're so incredibly beautiful."

"Really?" she asked raspily.

His mouth had gone bone-dry. He licked at his lips and nodded. Reaching forward, he released the center catch of the bra, then he felt her breasts spill into his waiting palms. One by one, he took them into his mouth—licking, suckling, nibbling. It seemed as if a thousand long years had passed since he'd made love to her.

"You taste so good," he murmured.

Her throaty whisper was barely audible. "Do I?"

He half carried, half walked her to the bed. And once she was lying down with his body covering hers, he continued to merely kiss the taut, pert tips of her breasts, until she writhed beneath him. He wanted her so much. And now she was offering herself in a way he'd imagined countless times in the past year. For weeks, he'd imagined this...longed for it. He meant to draw it out, to make her climax again and again.

"Sean," she suddenly gasped, twisting beneath him. "I'm ready...."

And he was on fire with wanting her. She was his wife, after all. The one woman to whom he'd pledged his soul. Sliding his hands under her behind, he drew her against him as she tried to unbutton his shirt.

"I..." she began just as he reached beneath her skirt, deftly found the waistband of her panties and eased them down her legs.

"You?"

There was no response—only gentle cries that rained down around his ears. Her fingers were trembling with such need that they fumbled over his shirt buttons, and her breaths started coming in pants. He unbuttoned his own shirt, shrugged out of it, then unzipped her skirt and slid it down her thighs.

Britt drew in an audible, quavering breath. "Oh, maybe I should tell you—"

His mouth covered hers again, capturing her soft moan. "You can tell me anything, love."

But whatever she'd been about to say was forgotten. "Love..." she murmured raggedly. "Oh, do you still love me, Sean?"

"Yeah," he whispered brokenly. "Oh yeah, I do."

She lost herself then, gliding her hands over the muscles of his bare back. As he rid himself of his slacks and briefs, she buried her face in his shoulder, twined her fingers through the hairs of his chest, and pressed sweet cries against his skin.

He decided he would make love to her gently, the way he used to on long, lost rainy Saturdays. Deeply thrusting inside her, he would withdraw ever so slowly.

Kneeling between her legs, he drank in the sight of her naked body. In the soft early-evening light, her skin glowed a flushed rose color. When he touched her belly, her skin felt hot to the point of blistering. And her face... It was so open and vulnerable. Staring into his eyes, she shifted on the mattress, her quivering thighs parting just another fraction.

He told himself he would love her slowly, but he hadn't counted on how much he'd missed her, how much he'd craved her. And the moment he lowered himself on top of her and sank into her enveloping softness, he was gone.

This time, it was he who gasped. "How could we have forgotten this?"

"Oh, Sean, I never forgot."

He barely heard her. With each deep thrust, his movements became more frenzied. The room seemed to recede into darkness—until he was left with nothing more than a series of vague impressions—wild tongues missing mouths and landing on scalding skin, Britt's fingernails digging into his back, her legs squeezing around his waist in what was sheer silken torture. When he could no longer hold back, he whispered, "C'mon, Britt."

It was as if she'd been waiting for his voice alone. With damp hands, she grasped him tighter, clutching him in such a heartfelt embrace that he was sure she would never let him go.

"Sean!" she cried out. "Oh, Sean."

And then he lifted her clear off the mattress, thrusting deep within her, and they came together—their bodies one, their spirits joined.

For a long time afterward, McSween could still feel those shocks and tremors. He didn't move, but remained buried inside her, listening to her pants and whimpers die out against his shoulder. And then there was nothing but her steadying breaths against his skin and the feeling of her lips as they curled into a smile.

Peace and quiet enveloped him. Then, suddenly, he realized he hadn't used protection—not tonight or the night they'd made love in the hotel. That was strange, especially since he'd been so careful during their marriage. He tried telling himself he'd merely gotten careless in the heat of the moment.

But it was more than that.

He couldn't live without Britt. Making love like this— unexpectedly in the early evening, not even at night—made him realize it. He hadn't used protection because he wanted babies. He wanted their marriage again...a family. He opened his eyes and drank in her face.

"Now can I tell you something?" he whispered.

She smiled at him, her eyes full of acceptance. "Sounds like I'm not going to like it much."

"You're not."

"What is it?"

He rolled onto his side, leaned up on an elbow and gazed down at her. "I was going to give Romeo up," he said softly.

Her eyes widened slowly and she looked confused. "What?"

McSween's heart fluttered. By degrees, her face was turning dead white. He couldn't help but wish he'd never opened his mouth. *Well, it's too late now.* "I was going to give him up for adoption."

Britt struggled to sit up, but he placed his hand gently on her belly. "Please, hear me out." He strained to keep his voice even. "I went today... to meet some prospective people who Donya's been talking to for a while."

"Donya..." Britt murmured. She stared at him as if he were a complete stranger.

He took a deep breath. "I don't blame you for being mad."

"Mad?" she whispered. Abruptly she rolled away from him and rose to her feet. A second later, she'd slipped into a robe. Her voice rising, she said, "That doesn't even begin to cover it, McSween."

"Britt—"

"Get out!"

"Britt, I'm saying this now because I think maybe we can work things out." He hardly wanted to have an argument in the buff, so he reached for his slacks.

Her voice trembled with barely contained emotion. "While you dress, I'll get the baby ready."

Without another word, she turned on her heel and marched for the living room. What did she mean by saying she would get the baby ready? His lips parted in astonishment. After the way they'd just made love, wasn't she even going to hear him out? He blew out a long sigh and shrugged into his shirt. When he was fully dressed, he strode down the hallway.

Reaching the living room, he stopped in his tracks and merely stared.

The front door of the apartment was open. Romeo was outside, awake and in his stroller. Beside him were his packed tote bags. The playpen and crib had been dismantled and shoved into the hallway, and McSween's own garment bag was draped over Romeo's new toy chest. McSween felt as if he'd entered a time warp. How had Britt packed the bags so quickly?

She was standing next to the fireplace. She pointed at the door. "I said, get out."

Her voice was as rigid as steel. This was no quick explosion that would blow over like a tropical storm. Everything in her face said that she'd already done all her yelling. Her heart had been broken. And Sean Michael McSween had just blown his very last chance.

"You were making arrangements for people to adopt this baby, to take him from behind my back—" Her voice snapped like a taut wire.

At least she was talking. If he remained calm, maybe they *could* work this out. "I wasn't going to upset you unnecessarily."

She gasped. "You weren't going to upset me?"

"That's right."

She shook her head as if he were simply beyond her comprehension. "Take Romeo and just get out."

He swallowed hard. Outside in the hallway, Romeo smiled from his stroller, completely unaware that his future hung in the balance of this argument. *Tell her the rest of it now.* "I've got something else to say, Britt."

She stared at him with utter calm. "What?"

"I never signed our divorce papers."

For a moment, Britt offered no reaction at all. Then her eyes widened and her knees buckled. Flinging out a hand, she caught the mantel and supported herself. Then she said, "Well, I suggest you find a pen and do so."

His temper flared. "I couldn't bear to sign them."

"I'm not wasting one more day of my life with you." Britt's jaw set stoically. Then her gaze darted to the hallway, and tears welled in her eyes. "Bye-bye, baby," she said, her voice cracking. "Oh, sweetie pie—oh, baby—I'm so, so sorry."

McSween was hardly one to beg. His chest squeezing tight, he forced himself to say, "Please, Britt..." The rest of the words came in a rush. "I still don't even know how Valerie Lopez knew my name. Or her husband. I've no idea why I was chosen...." Britt's shoulders suddenly straightened, as if someone had run a rod right down her spine, and she shot him a look of judgment that chilled him to the bone. "You *were* chosen and that should have been enough," she stated with finality.

"Britt, please try to understand—"

"I could live a thousand years and never understand you."

With that, she withdrew her trembling hand from the mantel, then strode across the room with measured steps. Brushing past him, she started down the hallway.

Please, Britt, look back at me. Look back at the baby. Give me some sign you can forgive me. McSween thought the words over and over, like a mantra. *Please, look back.*

Her footsteps halted and her head turned slightly to the side.

"Britt?" he called out.

"Please, shut the door when you go," she said simply. And then she continued on down the hallway.

Chapter Twelve

The minutes were ticking by so slowly. The wall clock was simple and old-fashioned, with a large, round white face and big, black, easy-to-read numbers; it was the kind of clock that had hung on the walls of classrooms where Britt had gone to grade school.

Oh, c'mon. Please, hurry.

A half hour ago, Britt had taken the blood test that would determine whether or not she was pregnant. Now, as the excruciating minutes passed, she toyed nervously with her sunglasses—lifting them from her chest, bringing them upward until the leash that held them around her neck pulled taut, then replacing them against her chest.

Why haven't they called my name? Are they ever going to call it?

Britt glanced around the bright, sunny doctor's office—it was decorated in green, yellow and blue—and her gaze rested on a dark-haired, dark-eyed baby in a stroller. When her lips began to tremble, she worried the lower one between her teeth and blinked back tears. There *would* be a baby in here who was the spitting image of Romeo.

Just ignore him.

But Britt couldn't. As her eyes roved over the little Romeo look-alike, her nose burned and her eyes stung. Even though she was inside, she rationalized that she was in direct sunlight and quickly slid on her sunglasses, willing herself not to cry or to think of McSween's betrayal.

How she'd managed not to break down in front of the man, she would never know. Not that one more crying jag would matter now. Ever since she'd heard McSween shut her front door last week, she'd been weeping. She felt weak from it. Half the time she couldn't even see because her darn eyes were so red and puffy.

For so long, she'd wished her divorce wasn't really final. And at the very moment when she'd realized she had to leave McSween forever, she'd found out he was still her husband. It was more than her soul could bear.

Read your magazine.

She stared into her lap and forced herself to thumb through a copy of *Movie* magazine—until her gaze landed on a group photograph of hot male film stars. The mostly dark-haired men all made her think of McSween.

Britt heard a rustling nearby and lifted her gaze. Was it her imagination or was the receptionist behind the window really moving in slow motion? It seemed to take the woman forever to turn the next page in the large green appointment ledger. Britt's grip on the magazine tightened and her thigh muscles tensed.

Get ready to get up. She's going to call you now.

"Amy Anderson," the receptionist said. "If there's an Amy Anderson, you need to fill out some papers before the doctor sees you."

Why isn't she calling me? Doesn't she know I can't wait any longer? I simply can't stand this.

Next to Britt, a very pregnant twenty-something woman with short blond hair hoisted herself to her feet.

"Need a hand?" Britt offered, thinking the woman must be Amy Anderson.

"No, but thanks. I can use the exercise."

Britt's eyes followed the young woman as she waddled over the bright emerald carpeting, past the yellow walls and a bank of connecting, blue upholstered chairs. At the front desk, Amy took a clipboard and a pen from the receptionist and then, just as slowly and laboriously, she came all the way back to her chair.

Maybe pregnancy wouldn't be all that wonderful, Britt told herself nervously as she watched Amy squeeze into her seat again. And yet it would be. Soon enough, Amy Anderson's weight gain and other complications would all be forgotten, and she would join the ranks of motherhood.

But would Britt? The anxiety was killing her. At least her doctor, who was on vacation, had given this place a high recommendation. They promised immediate on-the-premises results, too. Not that a half-hour wait exactly constituted "immediate." Or that Britt had any real doubts about her condition.

She had to be pregnant. Already, she was feeling nauseated. Suddenly, unexpectedly, the strangest things would turn her stomach. The smell of this morning's eggs, for instance. Even though she was now following her doctor's prescription for PMS—no sugar, salt or caffeine—she felt moodier than usual.

Of course, McSween's lies might have everything to do with that. And yet, surely the bloatedness, achiness and lethargy meant something more....

It had to.

Only the thought that she was pregnant had gotten her through the past few days. She'd kept it firmly in sight, the way the captain of a wind-tossed ship might focus on a lighthouse. She still couldn't believe her relationship with her husband was over.

But it was. *And you've got to be a big girl. Accept it and move on, just as a million other women have.* She slid an index finger beneath the rim of her sunglasses, swiping away a tear before it could fall.

"Afraid you're pregnant?" Amy Anderson whispered compassionately.

Britt turned her head and stared at the young stranger. "Oh, no," she returned quickly. "I want to be pregnant." *With all my heart.*

Amy smiled and squeezed her arm. "I know how happy this has made me, so I'll be wishing the best for you."

Somehow, Britt managed to return the smile. *Don't worry, Britt. There's a part of McSween still with you, growing inside you. Very quietly, you're going to have his baby. He'll never know. But you'll make a life together, just the two of you.*

Oh, sometimes she wanted to track down McSween and yell and scream and tell him all the many things she'd left untold. She would say, "You never really loved me, at least not enough. And I wasted myself on you, McSween, giving you the deepest, most precious part of myself I had to give— my love."

Maybe she would even go on and say, "McSween, you're never going to die the way your father did, because you're too mean and stubborn and selfish. Oh, yes," she might continue, "I should have listened when my father told me no man was good enough for me. Especially not you, Sean Michael McSween. Because this time, Daddy was right."

But then McSween's face would float before her eyes. And Britt knew she could never truly regret one hour or one minute or one second of their time together.

Sometimes she found herself longing for all the joy and wonder that could have been theirs to share, too. Other times, she would find herself imagining the awful moment, which Donya had told her was a mere hour from now. Britt could almost see McSween in midstride, holding out Romeo to a stranger. To Kathy Hayes from San Diego.

You have to quit thinking this way, quit remembering that name.

She felt Amy gently elbow her side.

"They called a Brittany Buchanan. Is that you?"

Britt gulped. "Yeah."

"Good luck," Amy said.

Britt managed to nod. When she stood, she became conscious of her heart's loud pounding.

The receptionist pointed. "Right through the door."

The words played over and over in Britt's mind, sounding nonsensical. *Right through the door. Right through the door.* She sighed shakily. *Door number one,* she thought illogically as she entered the private area. *Or is it door number two, or door number three? Which has the baby behind it?*

She headed toward the correct office, thinking about how much she needed this baby. She so needed something smaller than herself to care for and hold and protect. And she needed to be loved back—totally, unconditionally.

Inside the office, a young man rose from a chair behind an expansive desk, smiled and indicated that she could take a seat.

"You look too young to be a doctor," she said, trying to be conversational. Her voice came out strangled. When she glanced nervously around the office, her eyes landed on a family snapshot. It looked as if the man had four young daughters.

"I'm thirty-four," the doctor offered with a pleasant smile.

He's my age and he already has four little girls. Yes, she was running out of time. If only she could be pregnant now, surely love might come along someday—with another man, at another time. Not that she could imagine wanting a man other than McSween.

Please, give me this tiny part of him. Our baby to raise, especially since it's not going to work out between us.

''Well, I know you want to hear the news.''

She swallowed hard. Then she wondered if she'd said ''Yes'' aloud. She was so nervous, she wasn't even sure.

''I know you want to have a baby,'' he said, ''so I'm very sorry to have to say that you're not pregnant at this time.''

She'd simply heard wrong. She was sure of it. She'd felt the nausea and tiredness—or had they been wishful symptoms? *Impossible.* ''No...'' she said in a strangled voice. ''I...''

''You're not pregnant.''

Britt stared into the man's kind eyes. Of its own accord, her hand rose and she covered her mouth. So, this was the final betrayal. She was facing the darkest moment in her life without McSween.

And oh, she'd never felt more empty than now...without any life inside her, without a baby of her own.

WELL, *THIS IS GOODBYE.*

Cradling Romeo against his chest, McSween glanced around the roof of the crowded parking garage. Then he lifted the empty stroller into the elevator, punched the Down button and wondered why babies had to be so darn tiny. Tilting back his head, he glanced down at Romeo. He'd dressed the kid in the Hawaiian-print shirt he'd bought him in Hawaii, and the baby's chin was resting on McSween's shoulder. Romeo was just so...delicate, so fragile. So, well, needy.

And it's you he needs, McSween. You and Britt.

The elevator doors opened.

McSween stared across the cars on the lower-level parking lot, and at La Guardia Airport's ground-transportation areas across the street. Then he started walking slowly toward the terminal. This was the fourth trip he'd made between his car and Gate 21, which was the Hayeses' boarding gate. McSween had declined Chris Hayes's offer to help—and he'd carried Romeo with him on every trip.

But now, nothing was left except the stroller. And the baby.

Every single, last thing was inside the airport. The playpen and crib had been packaged and shipped. Near the gate were Romeo's tote bags and car seat. Inside a plain brown bag were Romeo's rattles and teething ring and favorite plastic cup.

Absolutely everything was neatly arranged at Kathy Hayes's feet, including her two boys. They were respectfully, almost reverently quiet, awaiting the arrival of their new baby brother.

And McSween was starting to feel downright panicky.

Why didn't Donya come to help? McSween wondered as he finished making his way through the parking building. Standing on the street curb, he watched the cars whiz past and swallowed hard. *Maybe the cars'll keep coming and I won't be able to cross the street.*

But they stopped. McSween shifted Romeo against his chest again, then headed across the street. He'd been so sure Donya would mediate today's exchange. But Donya had wordlessly processed all the necessary papers. As legal counsel, she'd involved Nate Simon, meaning to make this as difficult as possible for McSween.

Well, the Hayeses would be good parents. As a boy who'd grown up with sisters, McSween had always wanted brothers. Surely, Romeo would be happy with two of them. At the thought, something resembling a lump lodged in his throat. Instinctively McSween stopped, set the stroller beside his knee and reached to loosen his tie. Then he realized he was wearing a crewneck T-shirt beneath his sports coat.

Be strong, McSween. Do the right thing. This kid deserves a good life.

Overhead, a plane zoomed past. McSween raised his chin, his eyes following it. And suddenly, his palm splayed wide over Romeo's back and he pressed the baby just a little harder against his shirtfront. *Oh, kid, I wish it was you and me on that plane.* McSween pushed aside the thought and stepped onto the mat that activated the glass double doors.

A businesswoman brushed past McSween, her high heels clicking. "Your son's adorable!" She smiled, raised her briefcase in a wave, and blew Romeo a quick air kiss over her shoulder.

He could have been your son, McSween thought as he headed for the metal detector. Was he really going to hand Romeo over—and let him call Chris Hayes "Dada"?

Of course, he was. He and Britt were finished. Even if they started a family with Romeo, they'd had a rocky marriage. And a baby needed a stable home life.

Well, I'm gonna miss you, kid.

A woman at the metal detector giggled and tweaked Romeo's nose. "I bet you'd like to go through the X ray, wouldn't you? Now, that would be an adventure!"

McSween tried to smile at the woman, but he simply couldn't.

"Ready, kid?" he asked, once he and Romeo were through the detector.

Romeo grinned.

Maybe that was the worst thing. Here he was, holding Romeo and the stroller and heading down the concourse, over countless moving walkways, all so that he could say goodbye to Romeo for good. And Romeo didn't have a clue.

I should have taken him to Britt's, just so she could say goodbye one last time, when she wasn't mad at me, when she could say a real goodbye, just for Romeo.

"Over here!"

McSween glanced up. Chris was waving at him, his airplane ticket flapping in his hand. He approached Mc-

Sween, with Kathy on his heels. McSween blew out a sigh and inadvertently tightened his grip on the baby.

"We'd like to begin preboarding now for Flight 2467," a flight attendant said through a microphone. "Anyone who needs extra time in boarding, families with small children..."

Small children. McSween's heart dropped to his feet. That meant Romeo. His eyes trailed over the passengers who were forming a queue. He realized that Chris had moved Romeo's totes next to the final boarding gate, and that the Hayeses' two boys were standing guard over them. Something didn't seem right, but McSween was sure he'd remembered everything. *You just feel strange because you're leaving Romeo.*

"I guess we can preboard," Kathy said softly.

McSween managed to nod. Quickly, he pulled Romeo against his chest and squeezed him tight. With the baby's cheek right next to his, he drew in a deep sharp breath of pure baby; the sweet scent of powder and soap suddenly seemed to make his eyes and nose sting.

"Nice knowin' ya, kid," McSween whispered.

And then somehow, Romeo left his arms. Either he forced himself to hand the baby to Kathy, or else the woman peeled him from his chest—McSween wasn't sure which.

"It was nice to meet you," Chris said solemnly.

McSween shook the man's hand.

"We'll send pictures if you like," Kathy nearly whispered.

McSween sounded as if he'd been chewing gravel. "I'd like that."

Romeo wrenched around in Kathy's arms and grinned. It was that special Romeo grin—a little lopsided, showing a lot of gum. *Look, the kid's grinning. He won't even miss you. He's going to be happy with this couple. Brothers. Money. Good schools.*

"Well," McSween forced himself to say.

"I will send pictures," Kathy told him.

From the ticket podium, the two boys waved. "Goodbye, Mr. McSween," they called out in unison.

And then Chris and Kathy slowly turned their backs and started walking toward the gate. At the podium, Romeo started squirming in Kathy's arms. His chubby little legs gripped Kathy's waist, his chin rested on her shoulder and he stared at McSween.

Oh, Romeo, please, don't cry.

The baby didn't. The corners of his mouth merely turned down in a deep frown.

"You're such a brave baby," McSween murmured, raising his hand in a final wave. "Bye-bye."

A second later, Kathy Hayes entered the boarding tunnel—and Romeo was gone forever.

"WAAA! DAAAA!"

Where are you, Mr. Scaly? Oh, my dear friend, I'm truly all alone. Wherever you have gone, can you still hear me?

Our daddy looks so sad and lonely. But it doesn't matter because he's lifting his hand and waving and saying, "Byebye, baby."

And now he's gone! Can't somebody please stop this lady? If I could just say Daddy's name ... and tell these people I'm his baby. But they're strapping me in a seat, and the lady's calling someone on the phone.

Outside, the plane propellers are turning and the engines roar. No, this time, they're taking me through the sky and clouds, so far away that I can never find my way back home again.

Oh, Mr. Scaly, my dearest friend ... goodbye. And goodbye, Mommy. Goodbye, Grandpa.

Oh, Daddy, how could you do this to me?

Oh, Daddy... I loved you so much, Daddy.... Good-bye.

WELL, IT WAS DONE. McSween shoved the key in the ignition. As he turned it, he stepped on the gas pedal with far more force than was necessary, making the engine of the tan sedan roar to life.

Just quit thinking and keep moving. The words went through his mind as he shifted gears into Reverse. Behind him, he heard a horn—and he slammed on his brakes. Somehow, the merry-sounding toot didn't belong in this world—in the world without Romeo. McSween told himself he'd done the right thing, but it didn't make him feel any better. Not even his years of training could help him ignore his emotions now.

McSween glanced in the rearview mirror, then through the windshield. He was stuck on the roof of the parking garage, hemmed in by cars on three sides and by a concrete barrier on the fourth. Through his slacks, he could feel the boiling hot vinyl of the car seat.

He rolled down the window, then watched the string of cars behind him file past his bumper. Not a soul looked particularly inclined to let him out. He noticed a string of bright neon orange cones that dotted the way to the elevators. They followed each other in a snaking line. Looking at them made McSween think of the night he'd read *Hansel and Gretel* to Romeo.

Not that the trail of winding cones had anything in common with the trail of bread crumbs in the story—the ones Hansel and Gretel had used to find their way home.

How's Romeo going to find his way back home?

McSween sighed. *He's not. That's the point. Romeo's going to the West Coast to live with the Hayeses.*

Suddenly, something else caught his eye—and his gaze darted from the rearview mirror to the windshield. Another plane. His eyes followed it as it darted upward at a forty-five-degree angle, then soared through the clouds.

Was it Romeo's plane?

Somehow, his eyes stinging, McSween was sure it was. Glancing into the back seat, his heart suddenly wrenched. Damn. He knew he'd forgotten something.

"The dragon." He reached back and grabbed the toy, his long, tanned fingers falling between the scales. Hell, there was a stray bottle in the back seat, too. And McSween remembered Britt showing him how to hold and feed the baby; how she'd said Romeo was bonding with him while he fed.

Had he really let the baby bond with him—only to turn around and give him away? *Lord, McSween,* he thought, *how did a woman as wonderful as Britt ever fall in love with you?*

There aren't any guarantees in this world, McSween, he suddenly thought, gazing down at the little stuffed toy. *So, maybe it's time you give up and start joining the living.*

His grip tightened on the dragon. He swiftly turned off the car, got out and slammed the door. And then Sean McSween—usually so calm, cool and collected—wedged the dragon beneath his arm like a football and began to run. He ran hard. Harder than he had for years. Maybe he'd never run so hard, not even in that long-ago Fordham University homecoming game where he'd brought the team to victory.

"This is La Guardia, not Giants' stadium," yelled one man as he passed.

Damn. The line at the metal detector stretched for a city block.

"Hey, wait your turn!" someone else protested.

McSween didn't slow his steps. Whipping out his badge, he shouted, "McSween. NYPD. Let me through. This is police business."

The woman at the X-ray machine looked terrified. "Oh, no, is there a problem with one of the planes?"

McSween speeded his steps. "Call ahead and stop Flight 2467!"

He felt breathless, his lungs were burning and aching, but he kept moving—his feet pounding on the carpet, then on the long, moving walkways.

But the door to Gate 21 was shut!

Gasping, McSween pressed the dragon to his heart, grabbed the back of a chair and stared at the door. The plane was gone. Romeo was gone. And Britt was just as good as gone.

But then suddenly, with no prompting, the door slowly opened again. And there, framed in the open doorway, was Kathy Hayes. She was holding Romeo. Over the distance, their eyes met. Hers were soft and brown and tender, reminding McSween of Britt's. His tried to apologize.

"When they stopped the plane, I knew it had to be you," she said, walking toward him. "I knew you could never do it."

"I didn't know it," he nearly whispered. He'd held his feelings at bay for so long, kept himself so distant, that maybe he'd never learned who he really was.

And right now, he was starting to think Sean McSween might be a man well worth liking.

Maybe even loving—if Britt would give him just one more chance. He gazed at Romeo, who was choking on sobs and wiggling in Kathy's arms. When McSween held up the dragon, Romeo calmed and started to smile.

"We've got two fine boys—" Kathy hugged Romeo a final time "—and we want to adopt, to give another child opportunities...but Romeo's yours."

Mine. The baby held out his arms as if asking for his daddy. McSween was barely aware that an airline steward was setting Romeo's belongings on the floor or that Chris

Hayes was writing down important information pertaining to McSween's reclaiming the baby. McSween wasn't aware of anyone except Romeo, whom Kathy transferred gently into his embrace.

When the baby's chubby arms circled his neck, McSween felt a rush of pure relief. He handed the dragon to Romeo, then pressed his son against his chest and brushed his lips over the fine hairs of his scalp. Leaning back, he gazed into Romeo's eyes.

"Da-deee!" Romeo squealed.

McSween's heart thudded against his ribs, and he held Romeo farther away, to survey him at a distance. Had his baby really said "Daddy"?

"Da-dee. Da-dee!"

"Oh, that's right, son," McSween whispered, drawing Romeo close again. "I'll always be your daddy." *With or without Britt in our lives.*

"Da-dee!" Romeo squealed again, his tiny fist squeezing around the dragon's red cape. "Da-dee! Da-dee! Da-dee!"

The urgency in Romeo's voice made McSween glance up. And he found himself staring at a sign that said Cape May.

"All passengers boarding the Cape May flight," the stewardess urged, "please, have your tickets ready."

Cape May? McSween thought. *No, this is just too easy.* But sure enough, midway down the line of passengers, Duke Perry was glancing around anxiously. The Sutton Place Swindler had been heading for Cape May, not Cape Hala-waka. And it was no wonder he looked nervous. McSween had created a stir, and now airport security officials were jogging down the concourse. McSween couldn't help but chuckle. "Ah, Romeo," he said proudly, "I think you just solved your first case."

Not that Romeo was going to make his first collar.

No, at the moment, McSween couldn't care less about his promotion or his solved-case record. Everything he cared about was right in his arms. Well, almost everything. Which was why he couldn't stop to make an arrest.

"McSween?"

McSween whirled around and found himself staring at a red-haired rookie. "McNutt?"

"I was passing by," McNutt said breathlessly. "It's my day off, but I heard on my radio there was big trouble out here. Some cop just asked security to stop one of the flights!"

McSween grinned as he shouldered Romeo's totes, then grabbed the car seat and stroller. "Well, McNutt, welcome to the biggest break of your career." He nodded at the Swindler and lowered his voice. "See that guy in the Cape May line? The one with the cream-colored suit?"

McNutt gasped. "That's—"

"Duke Perry."

And without another word, McSween turned on his heel and strolled down the concourse. Let the other guys handcuff the Swindler, find the jewelry, and track down Perry's female accomplice. Because it was a Saturday. And McSween wasn't working. Instead, he was picking up his son—and heading toward the one woman in the world he loved.

BRITT TOOK A QUAVERING breath and glanced around. Most of the tissues from the empty box beside her were wet, wadded up and strewn across the leather sofa cushions. She felt utterly empty. Hopelessly alone. And too wrung out to cry anymore.

The worst thing, she decided, was that she had bought the sofa on which she was seated because—like everything in the room—it looked so masculine. A year ago, she'd kept thinking that if she made the place more suitable for Mc-

Sween, he might come back to her—and want to raise a family.

It wasn't logical. But nothing about broken hearts ever was. And without McSween, everything in Britt's life was round holes and square pegs. Nothing made any sense.

Unseeing, she stared down at the letter in her lap from Valerie Lopez to McSween. Why did it have to come on the same day she found out she wasn't pregnant? But John Sampson had returned from vacation and, thinking Mc-Sween and Romeo were here, he'd promptly sent over the Lopez papers, via courier. Britt guessed things could have been worse; she could also have received McSween's signed divorce papers.

Still, things were pretty bad. As soon as she'd gotten home, she'd ransacked the apartment and found the pills she'd hidden from McSween. Now she realized she hadn't even taken the fertility drug, and that Duke Perry had slipped her a Mickey.

When the doctor had told Britt she wasn't pregnant, she was sure her emotions couldn't sink any lower.

But they had. Again and again. Not only had she read Valerie Lopez's letter when she got home, but an hour later, Donya Barrakas had phoned. Donya said Kathy Hayes had called her from an air phone as soon as she and Romeo were seated on the plane.

So, McSween had really given up the baby.

Britt groaned and shook her head. She'd cried so hard that her whole body ached, and now her heart was beating slowly, as if she might never again rally the energy to rise from the sofa.

Why couldn't this letter have come a week ago? Or never? What am I supposed to do with it now? Or with the other documents—such as Romeo's birth certificate and Valerie Lopez's will.

Britt stared down at the letter again. It was written on cream-colored stationery bordered with twined violets, and the paper was damp from Britt's tears and handling. She'd read it so many times she'd memorized it. Each time, it had made her cry all over again. Oh, she supposed she had no real right to read it, but then McSween was her husband.

Or at least he used to be.

Suddenly, she sat up straight. As washed-out as she felt, all her senses went on alert. Her mind raced. Had she heard a key in the lock? *Is someone breaking in?* Staring at the door, she soundlessly reached for the phone on the table next to her and lifted the receiver.

There was a quick knock as the door swung open. "Britt?"

"McSween?"

And then he was there. Right in front of her. Standing in the doorway, with Romeo cradled in his arms. Her breath caught. Very carefully, she replaced the phone receiver, and she clutched the letter in her lap, as if the tiny sheet of paper could keep her from running into his arms.

She was so shocked, her voice sounded as if it came from someone else. "You have the baby."

McSween shot her a quick smile. "Oh, ye of little faith."

Her heart leapt in her chest, but she was afraid to believe her eyes. "The Hayeses aren't taking him?"

McSween merely shook his head.

Britt's throat closed like a trap. "You're really keeping him?"

"Yeah." McSween resituated the baby on his hip.

She gulped. *Don't jump the gun. Don't assume anything, Britt.* "And why did you come back here?"

"Because you're my wife and I love you."

With that, McSween smiled again. And it was the most wonderful, sexiest, heartwarming smile she'd ever seen. McSween had come back because he loved her. Bending over agilely, he plopped Romeo on the floor. And still clutching Valerie Lopez's letter, Britt ran for her husband's arms. "McSween," she said simply, as he caught her in an all-encompassing embrace.

Britt gazed deeply into his green eyes, reveling in the strength of his arms around her. "This feels so good," she whispered.

His lips brushed hers. "Bet I can make you feel even better."

"I bet you can, too—" Her voice suddenly caught. "I really didn't think you'd ever come back. I thought—"

"How could I not come back?" McSween pressed his forehead to hers. "Honey, I could never love anybody else but you."

Tears suddenly stung her eyes. "Only me?" she whispered.

"Only you, Britt." His voice turned gruffer. "Always you."

Britt's hand tightened on Valerie Lopez's letter and she pressed her cheek against McSween's shirtfront. She felt she could stand there forever, just breathing in his scent.

"I want to be a family," McSween continued. "I want..."

Britt sniffed, fighting back tears, and she lifted her gaze to his eyes. "Hmm?"

McSween sighed. "To make sure we're never separated again."

"We won't be," she vowed solemnly.

"No, we won't." And then his lips captured hers in a kiss so steady and sure that it could have been an oath. It was a kiss meant to forge the deepest of bonds between them— ones that could never be torn asunder.

"Da-dee!" Romeo squealed a moment later.

McSween chuckled softly and relinquished Britt, draping his arm around her shoulder.

"I can't believe Romeo said that," she said breathlessly.

"All the way from the airport, I was trying to teach him to say 'Mama.'" McSween grinned down at the baby. "Mama?"

Romeo clapped his hands. "Mee, mee, mee."

McSween shrugged. "Close."

Romeo crawled nearer and tugged on McSween's pant leg in an effort to pull himself up. McSween lifted the baby into his arms again.

Britt found herself smiling at Romeo. "And you really want me to be a mother to him?" Even though she knew the answer, she wanted to hear McSween say it a thousand times.

"I sure do." McSween nodded. Then he tilted his head and angled it downward. His lips brushed hers and his tongue flickered inside her mouth. "Like I said," he murmured against her lips, "I want to have a family with you."

Britt's throat got tight again and ached with unshed tears. She raised Valerie Lopez's letter between them. "This came."

McSween glanced down, his eyes narrowing in concern when he saw the signature.

Britt cleared her throat and began to read.

"June 1, 1994

My dear Mr. McSween,

If you are reading this, my husband and myself have passed on.

Just two hours ago, here in Saint Vincent's Hospital in your precinct, I gave birth to my lovely son, a healthy baby boy, whom we have chosen to call Romeo.

This is the happiest moment of my life. I simply cannot describe the feeling of peace and joy and love I have when I hold my baby. I'm sure you'll think it's strange that at such a moment, I would be thinking of naming a guardian for my son.

But, Mr. McSween, I am from another country and lost my family to war. And in my country, there was a simple saying: Whoever saves a life will find one. That's how I know you are meant to be named the legal custodian of my baby, should anything happen to me and my husband.

I was in the delivery room, in my sixth hour of labor, when the lights went out. The power in the hospital was switched to the auxiliary mode. I experienced complications. And while they were minor, they would not have been if the regular source of power had not been regained. Only now am I hearing the rumors and stories—and watching your brave efforts on the television newscast.

They say that you single-handedly caught the four armed men who entered Saint Vincent's Hospital tonight. And in doing so, though you may never know it, you have saved my baby boy.

My dearest Mr. McSween, you saved so many lives today. And you are exactly the kind of man I most want my baby to become someday: a hero.

God keep,
Valerie Lopez''

Tears rolled freely down Britt's cheeks. Her gaze drifted from the letter, over the top of Romeo's head, then roved over McSween's face. His green eyes had turned a shade deeper, more somber and reflective. They said the puzzle of his connection to the Lopezes had been solved, and that he would do his best to live up to the responsibility of raising Romeo. Beyond that, McSween looked moved.

So was Britt. Apparently Romeo had been born on her and McSween's first wedding anniversary. And today her husband had gone to the airport, claimed Romeo, and then come back to her. Yes, McSween had saved her life, too, just as surely as he'd saved Romeo's—by keeping her heart from breaking.

Their eyes met and held. "Oh, McSween, you really are my hero," she whispered.

"Oh, no," he murmured gently, even though everything in his eyes said he would always try to be. He angled his head downward again and his lips gently grazed hers.

"But you are," she insisted, wishing that, for once, he would claim the title.

"I may be a hero," McSween replied, right before his lips claimed hers again, "but, Britt, without you, I'm nothing at all."

HOW'RE YOU HOLDING UP, my dear Mr. Scaly? Yeah, I'm a bit squished, myself. And boy, are these two sure going at it with their smoochers! Not that I'm complaining, of course. Isn't it amazing what a little guy like me can accomplish when he starts getting a handle on the English language?

Well, I don't know what made me think the big guy was leaving me. Over and over again, he's proved he's the kind of guy who'll stick around. Through thick and thin. Up hills and down. That's my Dad for you.

What?

Oh, you'd better believe it, Mr. Scaly. We're a family now. With a mom and a dad. Pretty soon, I bet even Grandpa'll visit. Ah…we've found our way back home again. And oh, my dear, dear Mr. Scaly, it feels so very, very good to be here.

Epilogue

Britt glanced around the candlelit tables at the summer awards banquet. "C'mon, sweetie pie, try to be quiet for another minute," she murmured to Romeo. With one hand, she quickly readjusted the baby in her lap. When Mc-Sween's fingers twined more tightly through those of her free hand, her rings—engagement and wedding rings included—sparkled in the candlelight. The jewelry had been found in Duke Perry's pockets mere moments after his capture. And within the hour, the Sutton Place Swindler had named his female accomplice.

"Tonight," the mayor intoned from a podium on a raised platform, "I am proud to say that New York City is a much safer place to live. While every officer here is responsible, I feel I must praise the efforts of one man in particular...."

"Donya and Tony asked us to go for coffee later," Britt whispered as she glanced around the banquet hall again. Up on the platform was a long white table, behind which a number of uniformed officers were seated. Her father, who had been introducing various speakers, most recently the mayor, was now slowly returning to his seat. Britt glanced at McSween. "Do you want to go with them?"

"Not really." McSween scooted his gray metal chair closer and nuzzled her neck.

Britt chuckled softly. "No?"

McSween shot her a long, sideways glance—and a smile that instantly warmed her heart. "Maybe we should just go home."

"Oh, but why?" she whispered with mock innocence.

"So that you can call me Sean in that husky voice of yours," he suggested.

"Somehow, I knew you were going to say that . . . Sean." Smiling, Britt gazed deeply into her husband's green eyes, thinking she could do so forever. *Will do so forever,* she mentally amended. "You know, McSweetheart, you've turned out to be quite the family man."

McSween sighed contentedly. "Only because I now have quite the family."

And it had changed him, Britt thought. These days, McSween seemed quicker to smile and, more often than not, those luscious Irish eyes twinkled with good humor. Her husband, she decided, had to be the handsomest, most desirable man in the world.

She bounced Romeo on her knee. "I just wish Romeo would tell me where he put Mr. Scaly," she said in a hushed tone. And that he didn't have that look of pure mischief in his eyes that usually spelled pure trouble, she thought. "You know, McSween," she continued, "he's getting downright heavy."

McSween's wry chuckle teased her ear. "How heavy can a little guy with a twenty-word vocabulary get?"

Britt arched an eyebrow. "Is that a trick question?"

McSween shot her a lopsided grin, then he leaned forward and took Romeo off her hands. "C'mere, son."

"Thanks," Britt whispered. Then she realized her husband's shoulders had started shaking with laughter. "What?"

McSween nodded toward the stage. "I think Mr. Scaly just surfaced."

"Sca-leeee!"

Romeo's squeal was lost in a round of thunderous applause, caused by something the mayor had said. Britt's attention turned to the stage again—and landed on her father, who had just seated himself. Looking mortified, the chief sent Britt a wan smile. Then he gingerly shifted his weight, extracted Mr. Scaly from beneath his behind and gently set the dragon on the table.

Britt's own shoulders shook with giggles. She tried to sound stern, but it was difficult. "Romeo, did you hide Mr. Scaly on Grandpa's seat onstage?"

Romeo's dark eyes lit with amusement. Then he nodded, looking incredibly proud of himself.

"Britt, you're not supposed to laugh when you scold him," McSween reminded with a wink.

Her lips still twitching, Britt glanced at McSween. She shrugged. On impulse, she mouthed, "Love you, Mc-Sweetheart."

He squinted at her, as if wondering what had prompted her to say it. "Nice non sequitur," he whispered. "And guess what?"

"What?"

"I love you, too."

Onstage, the mayor was now pumping Marshall Mc-Nutt's hand. "If this man wasn't a rookie, I'd make him a full detective tonight!" the mayor declared into the microphone. "Yes, let's have another big round of applause for the man who single-handedly collared the Sutton Place Swindler."

A very red-faced McNutt accepted an awards plaque from the mayor.

McSween's chuckle sounded against Britt's earlobe again. "Can you believe I've been upstaged by a rookie?"

She squinted at her husband. "Well, even though you won't admit it, I know you're the one who gave McNutt the collar."

McSween merely smiled. "Well, someone had to give that poor overeager kid a chance."

Britt sighed, thinking of the many chances that lay before her and McSween. They were raising Romeo and starting the large family they both wanted. Still, she wished McSween had made the arrest. If he'd done so, the mayor surely would have promoted him this evening. And it was beginning to look as if her father never would. She watched the chief rise and return to the podium again.

"I'd like to take a moment to acknowledge a man who's been with us for some time," her father said into the microphone. "A man who—" The chief's mouth quirked as if he was trying not to smile. "Who *does* know how to share credit. Although he may not have caught the Sutton Place Swindler, this man still has the highest solved-case rate in our department."

Britt sat up straighter. "Honey, that's you!"

"Oh…" McSween smiled against her neck. "What in the world's your father up to?"

"But more than possessing an unblemished record, this man has proved that he has what it really takes." The chief paused and cleared his throat. "Honesty. Integrity. A sense of team spirit. Ladies and gentlemen, in a word, this officer has heart. So, tonight, it's my pleasure to present a full detective's shield to…"

Heads turned in their direction.

The room became so quiet you could hear a pin drop.

The chief chuckled. "To Sean McSween," he finished.

McSween continued staring at Britt. Then his eyes narrowed, as if he was sure he hadn't heard correctly.

"Your promotion came through," Britt whispered excitedly.

"Good going, McSween!" someone yelled.

McSween suddenly flashed Britt a grin. "For a second, I thought I was dreaming."

But he wasn't. As he stood, Britt felt his body brush hers, leaving her awash with tingles. Then, as he leaned over and kissed her, the whole room broke into applause. Taking Romeo again, Britt watched her husband stride toward the stage, his confident gait that of a man who felt right in his own skin. When he stepped onto the stage and turned so that she could see his face again, his smile said life had delivered all he needed and more.

At the podium, McSween shook her father's hand. And then her father very solemnly handed McSween the shield.

The room became dead silent again.

"Thank you, Chief," McSween said gruffly.

"You're welcome, son," her father replied just as gruffly.

Son? The word reverberated in Britt's mind. McSween looked a little surprised. And then a long silence fell. Britt realized she was holding her breath, and exhaled shakily.

"Oh, hell," the chief suddenly said. Quickly, he stepped forward and slung an arm around McSween. The next thing Britt knew, her husband and father were clapping each other on the back like the oldest of friends.

How I love all my men, she thought, her gaze panning over her father, her son and her husband. Her eyes remained fixed on McSween for a long time. And when he looked at her, she realized she'd never seen him so happy. It was clear that whatever he'd given of his heart, he'd received back tenfold.

When he returned to their table, he showed her the shield with a quiet look of pride. The medal was shiny and new and nestled in maroon velvet. All around them, the crowd was breaking up. People clapped McSween on the shoulder and murmured goodbyes into Britt's ear. Some mentioned the upcoming Labor Day cookout she was busy organizing, making her realize yet again how much she'd missed her involvement in precinct life.

Romeo squirmed off Britt's lap and ran the few steps to Mr. Scaly and his grandpa. As her father lifted Romeo into his arms, his eyes met Britt's over the heads of the crowd. That one glance seemed to say what the chief had been saying aloud for the past few weeks: that he only wished Britt's mother was alive, to see how well things had turned out.

Britt's gaze landed on McSween's detective shield again. "I'm so proud of you," she said softly.

"Okay," McSween said, "I admit it. I'm proud of me, too."

She thought of how she'd waited for him to make a stronger, more lasting commitment to her. "It just goes to show that if you wait long enough, good things will come your way."

McSween smiled. "They sure do."

He draped his arm across her shoulders and drew her close. Leaning against him, she felt the heat of his chest sweeping through his clothes. Running a hand beneath her hair, he raked his fingers through the strands.

"We're in public," she reminded throatily.

The devilish sparkle in McSween's eyes said he didn't care. "But I thought you said you wanted to make some new additions to our family."

"I do," she assured him. And nowadays, because she knew McSween did, too, it was only a matter of time until another baby was on the way.

"Maybe tonight's our lucky night," he said softly.

Her voice caught. "I got the new prescription for the fertility pills and all day, my temperature's been just right."

His gentle chuckle floated to her ears. "Well, we've definitely got everything else we need."

"Everything else?"

"A whole lot of desire."

McSween's finger trailed lazily down her cheek and the gentleness of his touch said he wanted her tonight. When he tilted his head and ducked down to capture her mouth, his lips said he wanted her forever. And Britt savored that sweet, warm kiss. Because even more than words, it said that McSween would remain her husband, just as she would remain his wife—to have and to hold through all the ups and downs; to honor and cherish through all the good days and the bad.

"We really are in public," she whispered again.

"Well, then—" McSween tilted his head, ready to claim her lips once more "—I guess we'd better start heading home."

BRIDE'S BAY RESORT

UNLOCK THE DOOR TO GREAT ROMANCE AT BRIDE'S BAY RESORT

Join Harlequin's new across-the-lines series, set in an exclusive hotel on an island off the coast of South Carolina.

Seven of your favorite authors will bring you exciting stories about fascinating heroes and heroines discovering love at Bride's Bay Resort.

Look for these fabulous stories coming to a store near you beginning in January 1996.

Harlequin American Romance #613 in January
Matchmaking Baby by Cathy Gillen Thacker

Harlequin Presents #1794 in February
Indiscretions by Robyn Donald

Harlequin Intrigue #362 in March
Love and Lies by Dawn Stewardson

Harlequin Romance #3404 in April
Make Believe Engagement by Day Leclaire

Harlequin Temptation #588 in May
Stranger in the Night by Roseanne Williams

Harlequin Superromance #695 in June
Married to a Stranger by Connie Bennett

Harlequin Historicals #324 in July
Dulcie's Gift by Ruth Langan

Visit Bride's Bay Resort each month wherever Harlequin books are sold.

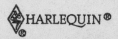

HARLEQUIN ®

BBAYG

HARLEQUIN®

A M E R I C A N ✦ R O M A N C E®

®

He's at home in denim; she's bathed in diamonds...
Her tastes run to peanut butter; his to pâté...
They're bound to be together

for Richer, for Poorer

We're delighted to bring you more of the kinds of stories
you love in FOR RICHER, FOR POORER—where lovers
are drawn by passion...but separated by price!

Next month, look for:

#640 BLUE-JEANED PRINCE

By Vivian Leiber

Don't miss any of the
FOR RICHER, FOR POORER
books—only from American Romance!

FRFP-2

A NEW STAR COMES OUT TO SHINE....

American Romance continues to search
the heavens for the best new talent...
the best new stories.

Join us next month when a new star
appears in the American Romance
constellation:

Liz Ireland
#639 HEAVEN-SENT HUSBAND
July 1996

Ellen couldn't believe her former husband
placed a personal ad for her—her *dead*
former husband! Well, at least that
explained the strange men showering
her with calls and gifts, including
Simon Miller. Ellen was attracted to
Simon—but how was a girl supposed to
start a relationship when her dead
husband kept lurking over her shoulder?

Be sure to Catch a "Rising Star"!

AMERICAN ◆ ROMANCE®

American Romance is about to ask that most important question:

Where were you when the lights went out?

When a torrid heat wave sparks a five-state blackout on the Fourth of July, three women get caught in unusual places with three men whose sexiness alone could light up a room! What these women do in the dark, they sure wouldn't do with the lights on!

Don't miss any of the excitement in:

#637 NINE MONTHS LATER...
By Mary Anne Wilson
July 1996

#641 DO YOU TAKE THIS MAN...
By Linda Randall Wisdom
August 1996

#645 DEAR LONELY IN L.A....
By Jacqueline Diamond
September 1996

Don't be in the dark—read
WHERE WERE YOU WHEN THE LIGHTS WENT OUT?—
only from American Romance!